WITHDRAWN

D0960266

DEC 2 9 2006

蛇警探

THE DEMON
AND THE CITY

Other books by Liz Williams include:

The Ghost Sister
Empire of Bones
The Poison Master
Nine Layers of Sky
Banner of Souls
The Banquet of the Lords of Night
Darkland
The Demon and the City: A Detective Inspector Chen Novel
Precious Dragon: A Detecive Inspector Chen Novel (Forthcoming)

SCIENCE
FICTION

蛇警探

THE DEMON
AND THE CITY

A Detective Inspector Chen Novel

Liz Williams

NIGHT SHADE BOOKS

SAN FRANCISCO & PORTLAND

The Demon and the City © 2006 by Liz Williams
This edition of *The Demon and the City* © 2006 by Night Shade Books

"No Logo" © 2006 by Liz Williams
(included in the limited edition of *The Demon and the City*)

Jacket art © 2006 by Jon Foster
Jacket design by Claudia Noble
Interior layout and design by Jeremy Lassen

Edited by Marty Halpern

All rights reserved.

First Edition

ISBN-10 1-59780-045-7 (Trade Hardcover)
ISBN-10 1-59780-046-5 (Limited Hardcover)

Night Shade Books
Please visit us on the web at
http://www.nightshadebooks.com

To the Witchcraft Shop Owner

Acknowledgements:

With thanks...

...to everyone at Night Shade Books for being such a pleasure to deal with.

...to Marty Halpern for his help and (considerable) patience.

...as ever, to Shawna McCarthy for all her hard work, encouragement and help.

...to everyone in the Montpellier Writing Group.

...to David Pringle, for accepting the first Chen story for *Interzone*.

...to everyone at Milford, who kept asking when the Chinese detective story was going to be published. (And now it is!)

...to everyone in the Cantonese group for their help and support, particularly Chris Priest and Leigh Kennedy, and also to Tanith Lee for her unfailing kindness.

...to my parents.

...and last but not least, to Trevor Jones, witchcraft shop owner, historian and best friend.

PROLOGUE

The Chinese inhabitants of Singapore Three say that August is an unlucky month. They say that it is called the month of the dead, for it is always during the endless burning days that the dead return, looking for the living, drawn by blood and breath. They tell their children: *You do not know how it was when we lived in the suburbs of Beijing and Guangzhou, or the willow villages of Szechuan, in the ancient cities where people understand how to keep the dead at bay. But in this great new city of Singapore Three, where the entrances to the Hell are closer and the veils between them are fractured, we no longer live in a place when a story is only a story, told to frighten a child in the darkness. Nor do you remember when the demons and the hungry ghosts were only dreaming shadows in an ordinary life, until we left the old cities and came to the new, and found that during certain months and certain times, when the eternal Wheel of Life and Death grates on its spokes, the world changes.*

At such times, one can only prepare for the possibility of death as best one can.

Deveth Sardai, stepping from a downtown tram, was not thinking of death. She was, instead, wondering how to extricate herself from the latest disastrous relationship. The policy of ignoring the girl was clearly not working: Sardai had not phoned her since the previous Monday, but a litany of messages, of increasing desperation, had been left on her answerphone.

Sardai smiled thinly as she walked down to the retailers' market, to wander, anonymous, beneath the girdered roofs of the warehouse shelter. The market was crowded with people on their way home from the production lines of Haitan. In fruitsellers' quarter Sardai nearly tripped on the vegetables that spilled out over the floor, squashed into mush across the dank concrete. She kicked aside a burst cucumber, turned the corner and found herself out of the fruitsellers' street and into the meat market. The *butcherei*, mostly women, glanced at her incuriously as she passed. The mild-eyed heads of the black cattle, swinging on their racks, held more expression. Sardai stepped queasily between the remnants which littered the floor; the concrete was washed with a faint pink gloss. Nothing was wasted, Sardai knew. The cattle were reared in the derelict lots between the apartment buildings of Bharulay and Saro Town; genes acquired on the black market and manipulated to produce Indian cows, of a sort. The *butcherei* slaughtered them illegally, bleeding them dry in hidden locations among the back streets in a literal moveable feast. The traders brought the bodies here before sunrise. The horns and hooves would be the first to go, sold off to the herbalists to be ground into powder and marketed as fraudulent aphrodisiacs.

At the end of butchers' street, a shrunken, cheerful woman was washing out a cloth in a bloodstained bucket. She beamed up at Sardai, who had paused.

"What you want?"

"I'm looking for the remedy market," Sardai said. It seemed to have moved since her last visit; they rearranged the market frequently, to baffle the inspectors. No one was fooled, except the hapless customers.

"Oh, sure." The woman wrung out the cloth a last time and heaved herself to her feet. "I'll show you."

She walked with Sardai to the end of the meat market. Beyond, in front of the pilings that raised the market from the water, the butchered cattle lay in heaps of unidentifiable flesh. From the corner of her eye, Sardai saw a lean, dark shape slink behind the piles.

"There!" the woman said, pointing. At the end of the meat racks, a helpful yellow line led along the warehouse floor. Obediently, Sardai followed it and came round to the familiar red-canopied corridor, the scarlet awnings incongruous beneath the rusted ironwork roof of the remedy market. The stalls were fringed with amulets: the almond-eyed shepherd god; My Lady simpering in a violet mantle with a sheaf of corn in her tiny arms; the little fox-faced demon of the mines. They shimmered before Sardai's gaze. Maybe she should buy her girlfriend a present, make it clear that it was a parting gift. She didn't dislike the girl, after all, it was just that once the first rush of intoxicated desire had passed, Sardai had started to feel suffocated. It was the same old story; it had happened before, it would happen again. Sardai gave a mental shrug. That was just the way she was. She did not intend to give way to guilt. She did not believe in it, and it solved nothing. Almost involuntarily, however, her hand reached out and unhooked the icon of a girl, an inch long, with the crescent moon on her brow. It was the sort of thing you hung in the kitchen window, or saw swinging on the dashboard of taxis. Sardai asked, "How much is this one? Can I have her?"

A swift hand, its owner unseen, wrapped the icon in red tissue paper to keep her safe on her journey, and Sardai dropped the little package into her bag. Our Lady of Storms, the woman from the sea, reposed amidst Sardai's pens, card wallet, keys and the rest of the junk in her bag. Her girlfriend would like the little icon since she lit candles to the goddess at festival time. Sardai herself followed a different path. Thinking of this, she smiled again. All magic is art, she thought, and she considered herself to be an artist in the truest sense of the word: one who is not afraid, one who dares to gamble for great stakes. She walked on to the herbalist's. Dried carcasses of snakes rustled in their pannier with the semblance of life. Someone was having a little joke, but Sardai wasn't going to gratify them by being startled. She leaned over the dry, writhing bodies and purchased a pinch of bitter mint and then a tiny bag of lobelia, imported from the West. The herbs were horribly expensive, but Sardai didn't care. They were useful, if one practiced a particular kind of art.

Her purchases completed, Sardai wandered to the end of remedy street and came out opposite the yawning exit. Beyond, the slick waters of the harbor were apricot in the falling light. It was time to go home. Sardai walked along the slippery platform that led from the market entrance and out into the southern end of Siling Street, a meandering labyrinth of iron shelters and cookhouses. The smell of frying meat and peppers filled the evening air. Chickens were rotating on a spit in the nominal gutter, where a shadowy man was blowing a fire into life. Sardai walked quickly; it was growing dark. She slipped into her usual routine, imagining herself ten feet tall and looking down on the people she passed, with her square shoulders back and her hand on the mace canister. Guns were banned; they were common enough on the black market but the penalty for shooting your assailant was death, anyway, so why bother? Sardai was always careful; there were very few nice parts of town.

At the end of the street a humpbacked bridge led over a narrow arm of the main canal, a winding stretch of water called the Taitai: the little wrist. Sardai crossed into a wilderness of apartment blocks separated by vacant lots where sparrow vine covered the fallen masonry. Something was always being built up or torn down. The exception was the Waste, the stretch of land which crossed Jhenrai southeast to northwest, a ragged scar created when an old mine had caved in and taken the apartment homes with it. The fires still burned, fueled by some persistent gas seepage beneath the soil. People lived on the Waste: the rootless, the insane. Sardai avoided it in daylight and at night took detours out of its way, but she was well past the Waste by now and nearly home to the row of old rickety houses in the eastern part of the quarter.

Turning back, she saw a last strip of pale green sky over the harbor. The tower of the Paugeng Corporation snaked up in absurd modernist spirals above the docks; the red bird logo catching the dead sun and glowing against the rearing wall. That was a weird setup, Sardai thought, with grim amusement. She had known the Paugeng heiress, mad Jhai Tserai, from their debutante days. And now, they had an even stronger connection. Smiling, she turned back and continued walking.

Something came fast out of the shelter of the darkness. Sardai had a brief glimpse of a lean shape moving too quickly to see, and then it was gone. She'd seen something in the retail market, her bewildered mind told her, sneaking among the bones, but that had been a dog, a little thing. This was a person. She swung the mace canister out of her pocket, looked about her warily. She could see nothing. She backed off, starting to run down Mherei Street, but it was right behind her, alongside her. She could see it out of the corner of her eye, pacing beside her, silent. She stopped, nearly stumbling, and turned but there was nothing there. Her breath whimpered in her throat. There was a great wave of soundless motion behind her, the smell of the sea, hot salt washed over her, roaring in her ears, bearing her down into the well of the apricot sky. She saw the crescent moon swing round, and then she was out into the gentle shallows, leaving it all behind.

Neatly, quickly, she was dragged into the silence behind the dark streets. No one had seen, animal-sense said, no one was watching.

HSIAO KUO:
THE SMALL GET BY

ONE

"Do we know who she is?" Seneschal Zhu Irzh asked, idly flicking the ash from his opium cigarette. The body sprawled at his feet, outlined by a faint nimbus glow. The girl had not long been dead, though there was no trace of her dismayed spirit in the immediate neighborhood and surprisingly little blood, given the state she was in.

Sergeant Ma eyed him askance and said, "No, not yet. Forensics is trying to get a positive ID on her now. And you shouldn't be smoking those. They're bad for your health."

"My dear sergeant, in case it had escaped your attention, I *am* already dead. In a manner of speaking, of course, seeing that I am a demon." Ma merely grunted. Zhu Irzh smiled to himself. Ma's attitude toward him was a combination of the disapproving and the protective, which was a long way from the sergeant's earlier attitude of insensate fear. Zhu Irzh had only been attached to the Singapore Three police department for a few months, but had already managed to provoke strong reactions in his colleagues, both positive and negative, yin and yang. Zhu Irzh liked to think that it was the hallmark of a masterful personality, but Detective Inspector Chen, his immediate superior, witheringly attributed the phenomenon to Zhu Irzh's otherworldly origins. Zhu Irzh reflected on this as he stood over the mutilated remains of what had, after some initial investigation, proved to be a young woman.

He found himself frowning. He missed Chen, and the Detective Inspector had only been gone for a week. If anyone deserved a holiday, Zhu Irzh thought, it was Chen, but still, Singapore Three's temporary loss was Hawaii's impermanent gain. He hoped, not without a trace of bitterness, that Chen and his wife were having a nice time. Meanwhile, he was still stuck here in the city, dealing with humans who had been foolish enough to get themselves mangled by unknown persons.

6

"If forensics doesn't turn anything up, we could go to the Night Harbor, couldn't we? Interview the victim directly," Ma remarked.

"I suppose so. Though I don't fancy shoving my way through that throng on a Saturday night trying to work out which spirit is minus her face. Or other bits. And I'm still having problems with my visa." Zhu Irzh gave a martyred sigh. Initially, he had been excited about his reassignment from Hell's Vice Division; the result of a political embroilment which only now was beginning to subside. The human world was novel enough to be interesting at first, but now it slightly depressed him. The colors seemed so insipid, the air so bland. It wasn't as bad as Heaven, which he'd visited only fleetingly, but it was getting close. The food was like the sort of thing you fed to cats: it smelled all right, but it didn't taste of anything. Besides, he'd had little to properly occupy him since he got here: a few routine gang killings, and a long and indescribably tedious investigation into the Feng Shui Practitioners' Guild, resulting in several boring visits to renegade dowsers. Zhu Irzh had done his best to get out of this last task, but had been thwarted by Chen. The latter seemed to be enjoying the novelty of having an underling, and had disturbingly little compunction in handing the most banal tasks over to Zhu Irzh. If one was of a flamboyant personality, the demon felt, one might as well make the most of it. He had not been allowed near the work of the Vice Division, where his experience lay. It was nothing but a waste. An earlier, oft repeated conversation, replayed itself in his mind.

"Your experience," Chen had said firmly, "has been in the *promotion* of vice, not its suppression. You surely can't seriously think they'll let you anywhere near drugs or prostitution, given that Hell's vice squad is responsible for most of it?"

The demon had bridled. "I'm not unremittingly evil—and me saying that just goes to show that I'm not a typical demon. I have feelings, too. I have a conscience. I helped you save the world, didn't I?"

Chen, though conceding that there was a measure of truth in this, had remained resolute. "I don't think you're unremittingly evil," he said. "I just think you're…slightly dodgy." Zhu Irzh had pretended to be annoyed, but admitted to himself that Chen might have a point. Vice was pretty much a consuming interest with him, and why not? It was fun, after all. It was a *vocation*.

However, human women tended to give Zhu Irzh a wide berth, thus negating another of the demon's consuming interests. This was perhaps understandable, but also cause for some lament. Back home in Hell, he had barely been able to turn round without falling over one or another girlfriend; here, it was a different story. And it was *cold:* even in this summer that humans described as sweltering. Morosely, Zhu Irzh poked the limp corpse with the toe of his boot, revealing the shattered pelvis and ribcage. Ma gazed at him in reproach.

"Don't do that. It's disturbing the crime scene. Forensics won't like it."

"Oh, don't worry," Zhu Irzh said. "She's probably swanning around the Night Harbor as we speak, awaiting her departure to the peach orchards of Heaven and unutterably grateful to be temporarily relieved of the shackles of her mortal flesh."

"Suppose she's destined for Hell?"

"I hope you're not implying that this unfortunate young lady deserved to die?" Zhu Irzh remarked satirically, adding under his breath, "And if she did, then lucky her."

"It's always a shock," Ma said defensively. "I don't suppose she thought that this would be the day of her death, poor girl."

Zhu Irzh laughed. "Few people ever do."

TWO

Dowser Paravang Roche, kneeling before the statue of the goddess Senditreya, was not thinking of death—at least, not of his own. Senditreya's temple was dark, shrouded in shadow and wreaths of incense. A complex sequence of patterns was outlined in silver on the floor, showing the energy lines which lay beneath the city; the energy wells of *ch'i* and *sha*. Among the hazy coils of smoke sat the statue, holding out her divining rods and her compass, and smiling down at her supplicants.

Bitch, thought Paravang Roche. He had an ambivalent relationship with his deity. He looked sourly up at the statue; studying the gilded loops of hair, the three bands tied around each wrist to signify the founding member of the dowsers' guild, elevated into goddess-hood seven hundred and twenty years ago.

To the left of Paravang, a man swayed forward on his mat, moaning and muttering. Paravang regarded him with distaste. Surely it wasn't necessary to make so much noise about one's worship. His neighbor rattled a hollow canister and shook out the yarrow sticks. Hastily arranging them into a pattern on the woven mats, he stared for a moment and then began to chuckle.

Well, good for you, Paravang thought sourly. *I'm glad someone is having good fortune, because I'm not.* He glared at his hilarious companion, who caught the enraged look on Paravang's face and subsided. Paravang arranged himself into a more decorous position and stared up at Senditreya. Sometimes he thought she winked at him. Sometimes he was right.

Underneath the carpet, and the stone floor, and the earth itself, Paravang could feel the energy line of the Great Meridian, running to the confluence of energy, the lake of *ch'i* which lays beneath Senditreya's temple. With such *ch'i,* how could there fail to be good fortune? Paravang asked himself. One would have thought that some of it, at least, might have rubbed off on a poor *feng shui* dowser. Paravang's lips pursed in resentment. He had worked hard all his life to win first this coveted place here in the temple, and then his contract with Paugeng Mining, and now it was all going to be taken away.

Above him, Senditreya's cow-eyed gaze blurred and faded, to be replaced by another face: the color of a shadow, golden-eyed. It was the face of a demon, named Seneschal Zhu Irzh. It was the face of his most recent enemy, and to Paravang's feverish gaze it seemed quite real, as though the demon himself were standing before him. As, indeed, Zhu Irzh had been, a week ago today.

Paravang had opened the door to find him standing on the step, a most unwelcome visitor. The scene replayed itself through Paravang's mind, as it had done so many times over the past few days.

蛇警探

"Who are you?" Paravang had quavered. "What do you want?" He'd always taken care to limit his dealings with Hell, but it seemed he hadn't been careful enough.

"I'm here about an irregularity in your *feng shui* dowsing license," the demon said. "My name's Seneschal Zhu Irzh. Want to see my badge?" At this point he had produced a piece of paper which, to Paravang's horrified gaze, had proclaimed him to be not only a citizen of Hell, but also a member of Singapore Three's police department. To Paravang's mind, this was a truly nightmarish combination. "Mind if I come in?" the demon asked, and without waiting for a reply, had brushed past Paravang into the narrow apartment and taken a seat on the sofa. It had all gone downhill from there.

It seemed that Paravang had actually forfeited his dowsing license some time before, the result of a small matter of unpaid taxes and undelivered bribes. Unlicensed, he was therefore practicing *feng shui* illegally, and must apply for a new license as well as pay the requisite fine to the authorities.

"Never mind," Zhu Irzh had remarked cheerfully. "I'm sure you'll get it all straightened out. Shouldn't take more than a few months." With this less than reassuring remark, he had left Paravang Roche to grind his teeth with helpless fury and hurl curses at the demon's unresponsive back. He had contacted the authorities, hoping that this might merely be some malignant joke on the part of Hell, only to find that Zhu Irzh was a fully paid-up member of the police department, assisting a Detective Inspector Chen, and completely entitled to act as he had done. Given the city's formidably ponderous bureaucracy, it would indeed take months for Paravang to retrieve his license, and a correspondingly huge drop in revenue.

蛇警探

Why do you despise me, Goddess? Paravang thought now, helplessly. The endless perfidy of the divine never ceased to amaze him. You gave your all, you turned up four times a year for the festivals and twice every week for your devotions; spent your hard-earned capital on presents and offerings; wasted nine minutes morning, noon and night in the requisite prayers, and for what? Only to be scorned. Rising abruptly, Paravang threw a handful of rice at the feet of his capricious deity and walked out into the evening dusk.

THREE

The city was baking in the morning heat, and Robin Yuan was late for work. The downtown tram rattled by her, dangling like a child's toy from its pylons, as she turned the corner of the block. She started to run, but it was too late. The downtown slowed for the next stop, saw no one waiting and picked up speed, vanishing around the curve of Shaopeng Street as Robin reached the platform. She swore. An ochre-clad nun swung around to stare at her reprovingly.

Screw you, Robin thought. *I'm late*. She was already sweating in the morning heat. Here at the junction of Shaopeng and Jhara, the restaurant backs emitted clouds of fragrant steam: *ghambang* and chowder for breakfast today. Robin had eaten prawn crackers, left over from the night before, stiff and cold in their greasy folds of paper. She watched the high-collared, shawl-suited men and women vanishing into the dark interior of the Pellucid Island Hotel and envied them.

The hot rails sang and the next downtown hurtled out of the Jhara embankment tunnel. *It's not going to stop! Too many people!* Robin thought, panicking, but the tram slowed to a halt and she squashed herself inside; leaning back from the bulging doorway and forward again as the doors closed. The downtown took off, lurching. The woman beside her directed a venomous glance at Robin.

"Can't you move?" she snapped. "I can't stand up properly."

"I don't think I can," Robin said. This was true; there was no room at all in the carriage and Robin couldn't reach the strap. It wouldn't matter if the downtown suddenly had to stop: she was too tightly constrained to fall.

"But I'm standing on my toes!" her neighbor wailed.

Grumbling faintly, the carriage rearranged itself in some minute fashion. Robin's neighbor lost height, sighing in relief. Robin stifled a yawn. Trying to keep her balance on the swaying, roaring tram, she wondered whether Deveth would call today. She had wondered the same thing for the last week, her spirits rising every morning, then sinking toward midnight as the day grew old, and still Dev did not call or come by. *Where are you, Deveth Sardai? Was I just your bit of rough trade?* If she'd had the nerve, Robin reflected, she would have called Deveth's parents, but the thought of contacting the aristocratic Sardais and interrogating them as to the whereabouts of their daughter made Robin's mouth go dry. She was fairly sure that this was one relationship which Dev would have taken care to keep quiet.

The downtown ground to a halt at Phikhat Square, spilling its cargo onto the crowded street. Wearing dark blue, ochre and gold, the money-workers made for the temples and Robin was able to sit down at last. She collapsed onto a slatted bench and watched the tops of the city whirl by in the steaming air. There were seven more stops to Semmerang and the laboratories. At last the downtown rang in triumph for the final stop, ready now to turn around and go back. Robin got out, her rubber-soled slippers padding on the platform, and headed for Paugeng Corporation and another day at work.

Inside the labs surrounding the Paugeng tower, there was a stirring atmosphere of activity and anticipation. People gathered in little knots, chattering. Robin was not part of the elite team, the chosen core, but the excitement infected her like a contagion as she hastened through the double doors of Y Lab. She passed her flustered colleagues and went straight through to the lift, heading for the basements. There, in the warren of rooms and corridors, the experiment was waiting for her, sitting up in his cot, arms around his knees, blinking blue eyes.

"How did you sleep?" Robin asked, a little anxious. "I'm sorry I'm so late."

The experiment smiled at her, vaguely. "It doesn't matter. I slept well, thank you. I dreamed."

Robin and her experiment had a number of choices about the playing of their particular game. So often it could take the form of doctor and patient, like the games you play in childhood, with the *frisson* of the forbidden. Sometimes, Robin was well aware, it could degenerate into torturer and tortured, if the controller had insufficient authority elsewhere. People take power where they can get it. Without really thinking about it, Robin knew exactly to which of her colleagues this description applied, but she did not find that axis seductive. She sympathized too much with her experiment, though she was well aware that she was not supposed to think of him as a person. He had no name, only a number. Robin, in a brief flouting of regulations, had asked him what he was called, but the experiment had only smiled and uttered a long string of syllables in a language like water. Robin, after some effort, had managed to break them down into something vaguely recognizable, and now she called him Mhara, but only under her breath, or in the privacy of her own head.

The experiment seemed too gentle to be demonkind, which made Robin's job even more difficult. But if he was a demon, then experimenting on him was necessary, wasn't it? Last year, the denizens of Hell had almost succeeded in vanquishing the city with a terrible engineered plague, and after that a number of research programs had been started up to combat the menace via scientific means. Paugeng had been given an enormous grant and the city's blessing; shortly after this, the experiment had appeared.

Robin had asked Mhara which level of Hell he came from, of course, but he had merely given her a vague smile. Robin was desperate to find out more, but the experiment was classified and she was unwilling to risk her good job by asking awkward questions. Yet despite their situation, Robin still got the feeling that Mhara trusted her, and at a time when she had little enough satisfaction, this was a source of comfort. He *needs* me, she thought now, vaguely aware of the abyss that was opening beneath her feet. Now, Mhara sat up straighter, and Robin plumped the pillows.

"Could I get up today?" he asked.

"I'm sorry," Robin said again. "Not today. One more day, and then we'll see how you're doing."

Mhara said nothing. Robin hated herself. She looked at the downcast experiment and the blue gaze turned to her as he smiled. They were marvelous eyes, and the contrast with his pale face and crow-blue hair was strikingly attractive. He looked nothing like the demons she had seen in the research files.

"It's not your fault, Robin. I know that."

It didn't make Robin feel any better. Stifling guilt, she went through the various tasks of her day in peace, until late afternoon when there was a sudden hubbub in the lift landing.

"Excuse me," Robin said. "I've got to go. I'll be back in a moment."

The experiment nodded. Robin went out and found her employer striding down the corridor. Jhai Tserai, wreathed in an amethyst silk sari, was surrounded by an adoring crowd, the young turks of Y Lab. Tserai's trademark cascade of dark hair was drawn back from the elegant curves of her face. She appeared delighted to see Robin standing drably in the office doorway.

"Robin!" She kissed Robin's cheek. "What a week, eh?" She gave Robin that eye-to-eye look which meant: *We've really been through it, haven't we? But we're still one hell of a team.*

She really isn't much taller than me, Robin thought, and yet somehow Jhai always seemed to be looking down on her. Robin deeply distrusted Jhai's attempts at friendliness, but when bathed in Jhai's famous charm, she couldn't help but respond. How did Jhai always manage to catch you off your guard? Robin wondered. She supposed it was some kind of charisma, but whatever it was, Jhai had it in spades. The subtle, provocative smell of Jhai's perfume followed her into the lab.

The morning medication had taken effect. Mhara was sleeping, lying curled on his side and breathing peacefully. He always slept neatly, like a cat: no drooling or snoring.

Jhai peered at the winking lights on the monitor. "Seems fine to me. Good work, Robin. It's never easy." She gave Robin a dark, concerned glance.

"He's so—accepting," Robin said guiltily.

Jhai reached down and turned the experiment's shoulder gently. The blue eyes were a dark well, open yet dreaming. The oval face was shadowed beneath a fall of hair.

"Where do we go from here?" Robin asked. Her boss shook her head.

"We just keep going until we figure out whatever neurological configuration it is that gives him his predictive abilities." Catching sight of Robin's unhappy expression, she added, "We need him, Robin. He can glimpse the future and we need to make sure that we're one step ahead of Hell."

Regular scientists were horrified by Jhai, Robin reflected. She was unmethodical, subjective, running on half-expressed intuitions, heretical and unrepentant. But because she was running the show she could work any way she pleased, and in the past the results had been impressive. Her disciple technicians trusted her, even when she outraged them. She rode the dragon and they ran along behind, imploring hands outstretched, pleading for her to slow down. She rewarded people who enjoyed being outraged: Robin was not one of them. Jhai, so forceful and vivid a presence in the dingy little lab, made her uneasy.

The experiment stirred and whimpered. Robin started fiddling with the hookups on the monitor. Another few minutes and then she would go home, and maybe Deveth would have rung. Better yet, perhaps she would find Deveth waiting on the step, her arms full of groceries, smiling up at Robin. *Dream on,* Robin thought. She glanced up to find that Jhai was staring at her, the gaze full of that assumed concern.

"Are you okay, Robin? You look a little tired."

"I'm fine," Robin lied.

"Good. Well, let me know if anything happens."

Robin nodded, willing Jhai to leave, and at last, after a final data inspection, Jhai did so. Robin turned back to the bed. The experiment was awake. The blue eyes burned into her own.

"Mhara? What's wrong?"

"The world," the experiment said, almost conversationally, "is going to end. Very soon."

"What?" Robin faltered. The experiment's gaze blurred; his voice murmured in the vaults of her skull.

"I can see everything," the experiment whispered. "Everything that will happen: blood and darkness and fire, demons devouring the city, ghosts running hungry through the streets. The end of *everything*."—and suddenly Robin could see it too, a vision of apocalypse conferred without grace. A tower crumbled and fell, crashing down into the street. The ground split and splintered under her feet and above her, the sky, too, cracked like a fractured eggshell. Robin's vision receded into a tunnel of night. She reeled back, her hand painfully striking the metal edge of the couch, and the lab was as before.

"What's going to cause the end of the world?" The question was no more than a thought, but the answer hissed in her head.

Jhai Tserai…

Robin blinked, and the vision was suddenly gone. The experiment sank back against the pillows.

"Mhara?" Robin whispered. She sat down heavily on the edge of the bed and gripped his shoulders. "Mhara? *What was that?* What did we see?" but he was already back in the tranquilized trance that passed for sleep.

Her mind racing, Robin tidied up the desk in the lab, made a final check of the monitor and settled the experiment down for the night, attaching the linkmote that would alert her if anything went wrong. She smoothed the dark hair over the experiment's brow. He smiled vaguely in his sleep. He looked so innocent, but the memories of what she had glimpsed were still vivid as nightmare.

"Goodnight," Robin whispered. She locked the door and took the lift up to the atrium. She walked through it in a daze, automatically checking her employee card at the door, barely hearing the doorman's farewell. Above her, the tower hummed with life; Paugeng worked round the clock. Robin stared numbly up at it as though she had never seen it before, and finally got herself sufficiently together to head for the tram. There was some hitch in the Shaopeng service, announced on the departure board, and the downtown was late, eventually arriving after seven. Robin's journey passed swiftly, lost in a haze of speculation.

She had been instructed to report anything Mhara said, directly to Jhai, but she did not want to anger her employer, and informing Jhai that she was apparently the cause of wholesale destruction seemed a good way to go about this. Robin herself was not even sure that she believed in Mhara's predictive abilities, but Jhai believed, and that was the important thing. Robin tossed questions to and fro in her head until she was too tired to think.

By the time she got home, the sky had darkened to rose. Deveth was not waiting on the doorstep. Robin tried to stifle the hope as she stepped into the hallway, but found to her own disgust that she was holding her breath. No one was waiting for her. *I told you so*, Robin said to herself. She climbed the interminable flight of stairs and opened the front door.

The apartment was minute: a box, a coffin. Inside the box, the heat was unbearable. Robin threw open the windows and a suffocating smell of garbage entered. The only choice was to stifle or gag. Robin compromised, shutting the little window in the bedroom and turning on the kitchen fan, which after a minute started to limp around its central spoke. A single step took her back into the main room. She took off her overall tunic and bundled it into a ball so that the Paugeng logo was no longer visible, then stuffed it under the pillow of her futon. The last thing she wanted to think about was work, and if she glimpsed it out of the corner of her eye, the logo looked like a bloodstain. If she looked crumpled next morning, then so be it. She turned on the television, hoping for the news, but no sooner had she sat down than there was a bang at the door. Robin bounced up and flung it open.

"Deveth—" she began, but there was only the empty air. Robin looked down. A small, resentful face was turned upward in reproach.

"I got your noodles," it said sourly. "And your pak choi."

"Good!" Robin said. She had forgotten that she had hired next-door's child to bring her a takeout. She forced money, evidently not as much as the child was expecting, into its grimy hand.

"Is that all?" it said.

"That's all you get," Robin told it, and shut the door.

She carried the oily paper packet back to the television, eating absently with one hand. On the viewer, Malaysian screen idol Inditraya Samay held up a rosy pomegranate and moved her winsome head to one side. *Revolting*, Robin thought. What had happened to the news? She reached for the remote and Samay's pretty pout was ruthlessly intercepted. A long shot of bodies on stretchers was more promising: the news on Channel 8. Robin settled down grimly to watch. Tremors in Sengeng had collapsed a road, compressing its four parallel lanes into a grisly sandwich. The cause—either a grumbling fault line or excessive open-cast mining in Sengeng Paray—depended on political affiliation. No mention was made of the Feng Shui Practitioners' Guild who had, it seemed, failed to predict the disaster. One of the senior dowsers was featured, loudly protesting their blamelessness.

Finishing her noodles, Robin took the greasy packet out to the kitchen. It was a mess. Normally, an old lady named Mrs Pa came in to do the cleaning, but poor Mrs Pa had been sick over the last few days, and the general chaos natural to Robin's apartment had mounted. A tower of takeout packets spilled over the sink and a stack of dirty plates sat precariously on the little work surface. Robin could barely see the floor of the main room for the clothes that were scattered over it. She piled them in a heap on the floor of the cupboard, then furiously attacked the kitchen, piling the rubbish into a bag and sealing it shut with a snap. She stacked the plates in the sink and hauled the garbage bag out through the small rectangle of the kitchen hatch onto the fire escape, which rose up from the side alley like an ironwork plant from its composting bed.

It was still hot, a humid, reeking heat. The neighboring buildings were squat shadows against the taller buildings of Shaopeng, and the sky was a deep, clear crimson, unusual for the polluted port. As Robin stepped out onto the fire escape, the evening heat wrapped around her like polythene: a moist embrace of carbon dioxide, drains and the oily reek of the river. Another, more organic, odor insinuated itself into the air. Looking down from the top of the fire escape, Robin saw that the black garbage bags had accumulated at the bottom until they burst, spilling a mélange of rotten vegetables around the iron feet of the staircase. Through this bath of odors wound a thread of incense from the apartment below, a spicy breath out of the squalor.

A rattling, scuffling sound arrested Robin's attention halfway down the fire escape. She stopped and peered into the dim alleyway. The sound was purposeful, determined, and came from the bottom of the fire escape. She leaned over the railing, and saw that the black back of the uppermost garbage bag was heaving. From her position at the fourth floor, and directly above, it resembled a seal; it rolled and wallowed in the filth that littered the alleyway. The bag spat tins, and a sheaf of old papers. Two floors down, a door was flung open and the voice of the occupant roared, "What's all that fucking racket? Get out of there! Bloody dogs!"

The animal backed out of its larder and bolted down the alley. Robin caught a glimpse of an ungainly gait and a fat, spotted spine; it did indeed look like a dog of some sort, but much larger. She descended the fire escape and picked her way warily through the litter. The animal was nowhere to be seen. Robin dumped her bag and pushed the rest of the mess around with her foot, until it lay in a heap. Let the collectors sort it out. By morning, half of it would be gone, sneaked away to sell to the recyclers. There was a pungent, animal smell around the alley, unfamiliar, but redolent of earth and meat. Uneasily, Robin climbed back up the rickety escape and shut the kitchen hatch. She spent the evening in front of the television, pondering her problem of Mhara's horrible prophecy until her head pounded.

Deveth did not call.

FOUR

Until this week, Zhu Irzh had been residing in a somewhat seedy boarding-house in Lower Murray Street, but Chen's trip to Hawaii had brought an unexpected offer.

"You can look after the houseboat for me, if you like," Chen had said, glancing amiably upward at the demon standing by his desk. "We'll be gone for three weeks; I'd like someone to water the plants and look after the badger."

"You're not taking the badger with you?"

"No, it might cause problems taking him on the plane even in his inanimate form and, anyway, he says he's happy to stay at home. I don't suppose he'll be much trouble. He'll probably be in teakettle mode most of the time. So. What shall I do, drop off the keys on our way to the airport?"

Thus, in the space of a morning, Zhu Irzh had acquired a new home and a familiar. He was becoming almost domesticated, he thought. He had always wanted to live on a boat, that traditional last resort of the poor. It was a long way from that pagoda fortress of his home in Hell, the balconies and verandahs of the Irzh clan, but Zhu Irzh didn't miss the luxury all that much. At least he didn't have to put up with his mother, and that was worth a bit of poverty.

The boat was moored some distance from the waterfront which, a short distance later, led round to Ghenret harbor. Chen had moved the boat closer to shore before a recent typhoon, and it was now reached via a few short hops over a series of pontoons. It looked out over the polluted waters of the Shendei, which, despite their filth, was why Zhu Irzh liked it. He supposed that Chen felt the same way. He could sit on the windowsill in the evening and watch the freighters plough across the harbor, until the swift night fell out of the sky and they became only moving lights.

It was a long way down the wharf. Zhu Irzh passed one of his neighbors on the way; an elderly lady who seemed faintly familiar, though all these people looked alike to him. She did not seem to see him, which was probably just as well. It would have been easier in ways if he had been equally invisible to his human colleagues, but the police station was covered with revealing spells, just in case something nasty decided to slip in and wreak havoc, and so Zhu Irzh stood out like a sore thumb once inside the walls of the precinct. The spells made him sneeze, to add insult to injury. Zhu Irzh tended to unnerve those folk who could actually see him, though the people who lived around the harbor seemed a fair old mix themselves. Sometimes fights broke out on the wharf; mostly, it was quiet. The whole community, with the exception of Zhu Irzh and a few other reclusive souls, decamped to the bars down the road during the evenings and lived out their dramas in more congenial surroundings.

Zhu Irzh unlocked the door and shut it behind him. The room was stuffy, so he opened the windows and let in a faint breath of air from the sea. At one end of the cubicle was a tiny shower, which generally worked. He stripped and stood, resigned, under the trickle of water. At least it was cold. Stepping from under the shower, he rummaged for fresh clothes, glancing at himself in the reflected mirror door of the closet as he did so. The reflection smiled back at him, turning and posing. Zhu Irzh frowned. He didn't feel much like the glittering image in the mirror. Any longer, and he might—terrible thought—start losing his looks. The human world was taking it out of him, depleting his energies. He needed a diversion. He needed a *girlfriend*.

FIVE

The heat grew as the night wore on. Robin slept badly, tossing the damp sheet off the futon and onto the floor, and toward dawn she got up and opened the kitchen hatch. She stood for a moment on the parapet of the fire escape, looking first up at the pearly sky and then down into the shadows of the alleyway. The animal had come back; Robin could see it scuffling among the garbage. It was even larger than she remembered. As she watched, the creature raised its blunt, dark muzzle and laughed at her as she stood half-naked on the fire escape. Its laughter was earthy, unlike the chilly mewing of the seabirds scavenging over the port. Bemused and scared, Robin stepped back into the kitchen and brewed green tea to clear her head. Her dreams had been filled with images of the city, burning.

The world is going to end.

Now, the thought seemed uncomfortably close to madness. She was imagining things, Robin thought. But surely she couldn't have imagined the whole thing? Mhara had definitely made the prophecy. She couldn't have dreamed it.

Behind her, something gave a hoarse, rattling laugh. She spun round. The brindled beast was sitting on the kitchen floor. Robin yelled. Unhurriedly it rose to its feet and shook itself. Loose hair flew around the kitchen. It was, she realized, nothing like a dog. It had *tusks*. There were only a few feet between the creature and Robin, and the gap was lessened when the beast stepped forward. She heard a small sound break the silence: her own voice raised in squeaky panic. The animal stopped and glanced at her in mild curiosity. Then, ignoring her, it snuffled around the kitchen bin, and Robin was overwhelmingly relieved that she had tied up the full bag of garbage and taken it out earlier. Finding nothing, the animal trotted through the doorway; squeezing past Robin, who backed up against the wall. She felt its heavy, greasy coat brush against her shins and the contact made her shudder. She felt, nauseatingly, as though she'd been molested.

The animal conducted a thorough investigation of the apartment, peering beneath the desk and the sofa and looking into the ashtrays. It paid no attention to the frozen Robin. Eventually, its path returned it to the back door, and now, for the first time, it turned and looked her in the face. Its eyes were neither animal nor human; they held her gaze for a long moment and then the beast raised its head again and laughed. It laughed like a fool, a child, a woman and then it laughed like death. It bunched its squat hindquarters together and sprang through the kitchen hatch. Robin heard its clumsy descent as it bolted down the fire escape. She slammed the hatch closed and sank down on the kitchen floor. She wrapped her arms around her body and clamped her betraying teeth tight and quiet. The kitchen reeked of the uninvited guest, a pungent odor with a rank undertone of meat.

It was some time before Robin could move and when she did, she sat wakeful, staring through the slats of the window by the futon at the small visible patch of sky. Robin's idea of stars was of a faded, pale dust strewn above the western sea, and none were visible now, so close to sunrise. Her imagination ran riot in the dimness of the kitchen. She was sure that she could hear the thing, rooting about again, until the shadowy glow from the street told her that this was only the recycling collector's cart out in the back alley. It was now well past dawn. Robin got up and walked stiffly about the apartment, back and forth. Her legs felt heavy and leaden and her head was furry with lack of sleep; when the videolink sounded, she sat and stared at it for a moment before springing to answer.

"Yes?"

A thin, ascetic face appeared on the little screen. "Citizen Yuan?" it said with faint distaste.

"That's me."

"Giris Sardai. Deveth's father."

"Oh." Robin felt hollow inside, as though her stay of execution was over, but the voice was cool and polite.

"I'm looking for my daughter," Giris Sardai said. "I understand she's a friend of yours." A brief expression of bemusement crossed his features, as though he couldn't understand why this should be.

"She is, yes," said Robin cautiously. "But I haven't seen her for a week. I'm afraid I don't know where she is."

Giris Sardai was silent. The black eyes bored into Robin's own. At last, Deveth's father said, "My wife and I would like you to visit us. Discuss the matter further"—as if this were simply a business proposition and not a question of a missing daughter. His tone made it apparent that this was not open to choice.

"I—that is, I've got to go to work."

"Yes, I'm aware of that." Sardai was patient, as if reasoning with a child.

"Well, when?" Robin asked, feeling feeble and hating herself for it.

"This afternoon would be convenient. I'll talk to your employer. Paugeng, isn't it? Very well. I'll send a car."

And before Robin had a chance to speak, the system closed. Robin, wondering, dressed and left to catch the downtown tram.

蛇警探

She got into Paugeng early that morning, the unreliable tram running like clockwork this time. It seemed much later, the result of rising at dawn. She found Mhara still sleeping. One arm sprawled above his head; the gentle face seemed vulnerable and, somehow, younger. Robin did not want to wake him. Instead, she went to sit at the edge of the cot. His fingers were bound up, as usual. Robin wondered: *Why doesn't he try to free them?* The dangerous clawed hands were limp in sleep.

"What the hell is going on?" Robin whispered, consulting her sleeping oracle. "Can you tell me?"

The blue eyes opened suddenly. The face was one she did not know: animal and alive. Then the experiment was yawning. There was no reproach in his face for waking him up.

"Did you say something?" he asked politely.

"No," Robin whispered.

"Then I must have been dreaming," the experiment said, and smiled. They ran through the tests and checks in silence and then Robin tidied the lab. She wanted to establish some degree of order, somewhere.

Jhai paid her a visit halfway through the morning.

"Could I have a quick word, Robin? Thanks." Her face was calm, concerned, neutral.

"I had a call from Giris Sardai," Jhai said. "He wants to see you—did he call?"

"This morning. He said he'd speak to you and that he'll send a car. Is that okay? I'm really sorry, Madam Tserai—Jhai. I didn't know how to refuse."

"It's all right, Robin. It's not your fault. I told him we'd be glad to help. I gather there's a problem? Their daughter's missing—your friend?" Robin nodded, dumbly. Jhai purred, "That's *such* a worry. But you mustn't let it upset you. I'm sure everything's going to be fine."

"I'm sorry I'm taking time off—" Robin began again.

"It isn't a problem. George Su can cover, it's just an afternoon and you've got the link if anything happens, haven't you? Anyway, I won't be able to see you again today; I'm flying to Beijing later. So don't worry. Go and get this sorted out. And obviously, Robin, there's no wage payback, or anything. I'll square it." She left in a flurry of silks, leaving Robin standing in suspicious gratitude behind her. Jhai had been very decent, really. Jhai was always so sweet, and yet—there was always something so calculating behind it. Perhaps Robin was just envious of her employer's wealth and beauty and talent, but still… Jhai never quite rang true. Anyway, Robin told herself, firmly, that wasn't her problem.

SIX

The forensics lab had come through with a positive ID on the murdered girl. She was, scandalously, one Deveth Sardai: the daughter of a prominent socialite with links to half the city's aristocracy.

"Went a bit off the rails, if you ask me," Sergeant Ma said lugubriously.

"You knew her?" Zhu Irzh's elegant eyebrows crawled upward; he had not pictured Ma's social circle as being so elevated. Ma looked slightly abashed.

"Only from the papers."

"What papers?"

After some evasion, it turned out that Ma was a fan of the cheaper, glossier press: the sort of magazines that turned up in supermarket racks, their pages displaying film stars' lovely homes. Deveth Sardai, it seemed, along with her artfully Bohemian lifestyle, had featured regularly. Ma took an example from his desk drawer. Zhu Irzh stared down at a strong, willful face with heavy brows: Malaysian, he estimated, with a Westerner's blue eyes. Unless she had worn contacts.

"She isn't married, it says. Any mention of boyfriends?"

"No. Girlfriends, though."

"She was a lesbian?" Zhu Irzh asked, vaguely intrigued.

"Fashionably so," Ma told him. Zhu Irzh smiled; it wasn't the kind of comment he expected from Ma.

"Well, any of her contacts could prove helpful. Better start making a list. I suggest you ring the magazine. Meanwhile, I suppose I'd better ask the captain to break it to her parents. Though since they haven't reported her missing, I don't suppose they were that close, but even so…they'd probably like to know what happened to her."

In his office, Captain Sung regarded Zhu Irzh with his usual inexpressive gaze and the demon found himself fidgeting, like a child on the carpet of the principal's study. The captain made Zhu Irzh uncomfortable; he could not shake off the impression that Sung was thinking back to the days of his ancestors, who had ridden the Mongolian steppes, sweeping all before them. Including demons. With Chen, who was after all married to a former citizen of Hell, Zhu Irzh was allowed to feel almost human, or at least, not noxious. With Sung, he had no doubt as to where he stood in the hierarchy of lower lifeforms, but the captain never let his animosity show and that unnerved Zhu Irzh more than anything.

"Seneschal," Sung said formally.

"Captain. Good morning."

"So. We have an identity for the victim, I believe? Just as well."

"I'm sorry?" Zhu Irzh frowned. Of course it was "just as well." What a strange thing to say.

Sung's gaze grew colder and heavier. "You haven't heard? Word hasn't filtered back? I suppose that's encouraging. Usually I'm the last one to hear the rumors."

"Heard what?"

"It is just as well that the lab got a positive ID from the samples it took from the body, Seneschal Irzh, because now the body is gone."

The demon gaped at him. "Gone?"

Sung nodded. "It disappeared from the morgue last night. No signs of forced entry, no locks tampered with, nothing out of order except that the body of the unfortunate Ms Sardai is simply no longer there."

"Could it have walked by itself?" was the first thing that occurred to Zhu Irzh. "Let itself out?"

"You tell me."

"It *is* sometimes possible to raise a corpse," Zhu Irzh said, frowning. "But it's not easy. You'd need a very powerful piece of necromancy to do that, and anyway, I wouldn't have thought that the body was in any real shape to walk… Crawl, maybe. But it wouldn't have been able to see. She didn't have much face left."

"Could someone have spirited it out by magic?"

"Possibly. But that would have entailed opening a gate between the worlds, and that's not so easily done."

"Think about the possibilities, would you? I've put Exorcist Ghi on this particular part of the case; he'll be liaising with you in due course. Try and be co-operative, please."

"I'm always co-operative," Zhu Irzh protested. Sung gave him a long, level look. "I suppose you'd like me to alert the family?"

Sung sighed. "Actually, no. Look, don't take this the wrong way, but I'll have to put some of our top people on the Sardai case. It's high profile. It was one thing to send you out on a murder investigation when we didn't know it was such an important victim, but now—"

The demon bridled. "It's an embarrassment to have me on the case, is that what you're saying?"

"I'm not saying you haven't been useful, Zhu Irzh. The fact that not everyone can see you is often to our advantage, but you can see how it might be a bit of a handicap if I were to put you in charge of the investigation. Besides, your specialty is really vice, isn't it?"

"I see." Impossible to resent it, really. Sung's reasons were good ones and now that Zhu Irzh thought about it, he couldn't see a couple of socialites wanting a demon investigating their daughter's death.

"Although how we're going to tell this extremely rich and powerful clan that we've managed to mislay their daughter's mutilated corpse, I have no idea. I suppose I'll think of something. Leave it with me." For which small mercy Zhu Irzh found himself extremely grateful.

Leaving the captain's office, he returned to the more amiable company of Ma.

"Very helpful, that magazine," Ma said. "Gave me several names, they did." His face wore a small, smug smile, somewhat foreign to Ma's usually anxious countenance.

"Well?" the demon asked. He'd break the news about the body in a minute; why spoil Ma's moment of triumph.

"I think we might have a lead," Ma said.

"What, already?" After the news that the main piece of evidence had gone astray, this was welcome.

Ma nodded. "Deveth Sardai was a close friend of Jhai Tserai." He glanced expectantly at Zhu Irzh, as if anticipating explanation, but the demon was ahead of him.

"The Paugeng heiress. Even I've heard of Jhai Tserai." He grinned. "Most of Hell has, as a matter of fact. She's got a number of interesting contacts down there."

"Do we go and see her?" Ma asked rather hopefully. Zhu Irzh caught his lip beneath one pointed tooth.

"Tserai's one of the most powerful industrialists in this city, even if she is only in her twenties. She's got a lot of clout. I know for a fact that some of that extends to the police department…I think I'll pay Jhai Tserai a visit, Ma. Alone. Sort of off the record." There was no need to tell Ma about his conversation with Sung just yet. It would show initiative if he were to go and see Tserai. He paused, still smiling. It didn't hurt that Jhai Tserai was also remarkably beautiful, and—according to persistent rumor—unattached. But perhaps she wasn't interested in the opposite sex. Fair enough, Zhu Irzh thought, but then again, he enjoyed a challenge.

SEVEN

High in the Paugeng tower, on the terrace of the penthouse, Jhai sat and gazed out over the twilight city. The penthouse was silent; her mother was visiting one of her innumerable charities and the servants had been dismissed for the evening. Jhai wanted to make sure that she wouldn't be disturbed. After the difficulties they'd had with Deveth Sardai, it seemed reasonable to downsize a bit, proceed on her own rather than using hired help. She'd been a fool to rely on Deveth, though. She should have realized that the woman was unstable. Deveth had not possessed limits, that had been the trouble. Jhai's own limits might lie far beyond the edge of human morals, but nonetheless, they were carefully and precisely defined.

She looked down at the little, black capsule in her hand, weighing it in her palm. It was as light as air, yet for Jhai it was a burden as heavy as a world. If anyone ever found out… She and her mother, and her grandmothers as far back as the seventeenth century, had taken such care, such pains. They had bred selectively, never marrying, always choosing the most auspicious elements of the gene pool, revealed through reliable oracles; treading a fine line between power and discovery. Technology made things a lot easier. If Paugeng's genetics division got its research right, then the next generation would be simply cloned and the knife-edge dangers of breeding would lie safely in the past. But that, Jhai thought with a thin smile, was the fallback position. If her plans worked out, then her heritage wouldn't matter any longer anyway. It would not be necessary to merely pass.

Jhai weighed the capsule again and left the terrace, closing the door softly behind her. She headed for the penthouse's lavish bathroom, ignoring, for once, the invitations of the gilded jacuzzi or the sauna, and put her hands on the porcelain basin. She stared hard at her own reflection in the mirror, willing it not to move. It remained fixed, the perfect mimic, and Jhai breathed a sigh of relief. She did not like taking the drug. She played a game of cat and mouse, leaving it as late as possible before the next dose, but this time she had almost overstepped the line. She could feel the change starting within her, itching to be freed from the remains of its neurochemical shackles. She let the silk robe rustle to the floor and turned to examine herself in the mirror.

Naked, she thought without vanity, she was close to perfect, as long as the drug kept the changes at bay. But as she scrutinized her own reflection, she could see the faint tiger stripes along her ribcage, a golden light behind her eyes. Sliding a hand behind her, she felt the tug of growing bone at the base of her spine and for the thousandth time she was tempted to just let it happen, go all the way, see what the result would be... But she already knew. The collection of Keralan miniatures that her mother kept locked in the safe had shown her that. Warmth crept between her legs and Jhai crossed her hands over her aching breasts and arched her back. That was another reason to stop taking the drug: to exchange frigid humanity for unnatural desire. What an irony, Jhai reflected bitterly. The very source of her charisma and her legendary sexual appeal had to be kept in check, otherwise it would get her banished down to Hell. She was human enough not to want that, and if she kept taking the drug, she could have it both ways, even if she was unable to enjoy the results of the attraction she generated. She could retain enough of her ancestress' glamorous powers to keep the corporation and her fortune together, and still pass as wholly human. You *can* have it both ways, Jhai told herself grimly, swallowing the black capsule at last and watching the stripes fade from her flanks and the fire from her eyes. But you can never have it all.

EIGHT

Normally, Robin would never have gone anywhere near Bharcharia Anh. Her little beat was confined to Shaopeng and Battery Road, with occasional trips out to the countryside along the delta to visit her grandparents, who were proud of their made-good granddaughter. Robin had never been this far up into the heights. The car avoided the congested town center, sweeping out beyond the city limits and then rumbling back onto the fast arterial road. It reached Bharcharia Anh close to three o'clock.

The white turret where the Sardai family lived looked wet, as though dew had gathered on the pallid surface, and the grounds were green and lush, dense with imported hibiscus and oleander. The hallmark of the homes of the rich, Robin understood, was not their opulence but their silence. From up here, the rest of the city, the whole squalid, roaring mass, may just as well not exist.

Inside the tower, it was utterly still. A doorman showed Robin to the elevator and left her there. The elevator glided upward and then opened out into the wide atrium of the Sardais' apartment.

To Robin's left, a water sculpture gushed into a pool filled with carp. Before the pool something was being created, molding and shaping itself on a plinth. Robin watched, fascinated, as it became a running horse, a rose, and at last settled into the figure of a shark-monkey, flat face astounded, thin little hands waving and the long tail beating and twisting against the surface of the plinth. Nanotech art, anything you wanted, moment by moment. The monkey melted down into a nebulous mass, and out of the writhing substance Robin's own suspicious face emerged. Robin watched in fascinated revulsion.

"It's a mischievous toy," Sardai said, stepping into the atrium. He was very much like his daughter: the same harsh, aquiline face, but with an ascetic cast which Deveth, the puritanical hedonist, had never possessed. He was dressed in a white Mao jacket and loose dhoti, and leaned on a cane. "Come forward."

Obediently, Robin walked through into the main lounge. Far away on the horizon, the gibbous moon was visible, floating about the hazy curve of the world. The tower blocks of Tevereya rose up to the left, the buildings glinting in the sunlight. Beneath the moon, a smudge of peaked land arose, tiny in the expanse of sunlit water: Lantern Island. Such were the lives of the wealthy, Robin thought again: silent and high.

"This is my wife, Malian." Sardai made punctilious introductions. Deveth's mother was a big woman, but her face was sunken and hollow-cheeked. She did not look well. Neither of them did, come to that. Without really thinking about it, Robin had assumed that when you were that rich you could afford all the health that money could buy, but evidently this was not so.

"Come and sit by me," Deveth's mother suggested. She patted the cushioned chair by the side of the couch. Robin sank into it and thought she might never rise again. Giris Sardai unobtrusively disappeared. Malian dabbed her broad face with a handkerchief. Robin wanted to say: *I'm so sorry. I don't know where Deveth is.* She was still convinced that, somewhere down the line, they would have her arrested, or thrown out. Something bad, anyway. She did not belong here.

"Tell me about my daughter," Malian said. "You probably know her better than I do." She gave Robin a mock humorous look to take the bitterness out of her words.

"I've been wondering whether I know her at all." Robin said. With a vague sense of dismay, she found herself telling Malian Sardai everything: about the embarrassing parties, the way Deveth always promised to phone and never did, how they used to go round the market together. She felt her nose start to itch and tingle with imminent tears, and thought furiously, I'm not, I'm *not* going to cry. She was saved by the arrival of a quiet drone, a slender young man dressed in a green dhoti, with perfect Dravidian features except for his lack of a mouth. Robin tried not to stare. He put a tray down before her: tea and fruit, cut into elegantly carved pieces.

"Thank you," Robin said. Her nose was about to run. "May I visit your bathroom?" She followed the drone down a twisting corridor. Movement, almost imperceptible, kept catching the corner of her eye. The bathroom, containing a mercifully copious amount of tissues, was larger than her flat. If Deveth had given up all this to go and live in artistic squalor on Mherei Street, she was a fool, Robin thought, impatient with the indulgences of the rich. The poor couldn't afford to experience ennui. Deveth had talked a lot about how important it was to follow your creative instincts, whatever the cost, and Robin had sat silently among her lover's admiring friends and thought what it must be like to have such a choice. And she was one of the lucky ones: with her own place, no need to live with her four brothers and two sisters, and her good job at Paugeng.

Robin wiped her eyes and nose in front of the wall-sized mirror and repaired what remained of her minimal make-up. Her eyes looked frightened and vast in the small paleness of her face. She wanted to hide in the luxurious bathroom in this enclosed silent place and never go back to her cramped flat or that good job which involved feeding a supernatural captive experimental drugs every day. The wish was so strong that it was a moment before she realized its impossibility. This scared her: *Starting to crack and go paranoid, Robin?* In the mirror, her eyes were rimmed with crimson. On impulse, she rummaged in the tidy medicine cabinet and found a familiar blue phial with the red Jaruda bird on the label and a list of instructions. Paugeng should dole them out free to employees. Robin wasn't going to spend good money on headache pills otherwise. She swallowed two of the flat, white painkillers ("suitable for headaches, toothache and muscular disorders") with a handful of water scooped from the tap. Surely the water would be all right up here, she thought, surely there was no need for filtering and boiling in this part of town? Hastily, and somewhat guiltily, she slipped some of the pills into her bag in case the headache started up again, then put the phial back in the cabinet and slid the door shut. She should go back to Malian. She stepped out of the safety of the bathroom into a wide, bulb-shaped hallway. What had happened to the corridor? Robin, disoriented, stood quite still and watched the floor crawl slowly away. It moved like a slow wave, a thick liquid, ebbing toward the steps. Beside Robin's ear, the wall bulged outward and rumpled back. Robin thought: *Oh god, those weren't headache tabs.* I've taken something else. I'm *tripping*. Her head felt muzzy and her vision swam. She took a step forward. An opening appeared in the wall and, like a child, Robin went through. She was in an unfamiliar small room, yet there was again the statue on the plinth. The drone appeared in the melting doorway behind her and placed a tactful hand on her shoulder. She let him lead her out, and back to the lounge. Malian Sardai was all apologies.

"I'm terribly sorry. The nano-decorator's set on a cycle; it just comes on and we're so used to it…"

Once she knew that she wasn't hallucinating, Robin felt better.

"The whole apartment's like that?"

"So *clever.*" Malian gave her a smug too-much-for-little-me-to-understand look. Robin had not realized how wealthy they must be: the entire apartment was nanoed up. You wouldn't ever have to move, you could do your own interior decoration just by reprogramming the setting. She also realized, without a word being said, that Malian Sardai had become bored with her. Malian didn't really believe that anything could happen to her weird daughter: they were too rich, whatever lifestyle Deveth had chosen to adopt. Malian didn't think anything could really befall people like herself, she truly could not countenance it, and so nothing did. They remained in their secure, fashionable lives up here in Meriden, quite safe, entertaining the most delightful lifestyle options, while the rest of the world battled and struggled below. Except that Deveth was still missing. Robin gave Malian an artificial smile.

"Thank you so much for seeing me. I feel better, somehow, getting it all off my chest." She felt like an artless little liar, but Malian gave her a sad, brave smile in return and clasped her hands.

"Thank you, Robin. It makes me feel better, too, knowing Deveth's got such loyal friends."

She called the drone, who took Robin down in the elevator and showed her the very obvious way out through the garden. *Making sure I leave the premises,* Robin thought. She thanked the drone, who, mouthless, could not smile, and made her way to the waiting car. At least she got a lift back into town. But if Deveth's parents didn't care what had happened to their daughter, then Robin did.

蛇警探

Later that evening, the downtown tram dropped Robin at the foot of the ruined temple of Shai. She glanced up at its squat, forbidding walls, its huge dome, wondering whose temple it had once been. It rose up like a fortress, made of dark gray stone shot with odd black streaks. She knew little about Shai, only that it was old, much older than the surrounding city, and rumored to be haunted. This evening, with the temple looming above the buildings around, Robin had no problem in believing in those rumors. She could almost hear the place whispering to itself. Resolutely, Robin turned her back on its dark bulk and made her way along the litter-strewn downtown platform.

At the bottom of the platform steps, a snick of an alleyway led into Mherei Street. She hurried through, and found herself in the forbidding confines of the old town. They had been here how long, these houses, that temple?—the remnants of the little settlement that had made way for Singapore Three. The narrow streets rambled about the central spine of Mherei, black glass and dark wood, imported or grown in the southern plantations, angled, charmed roofs to fend away bad luck. Since these early glorious days, Mherei was rather low on luck, however, getting seedy despite the solid old houses. It was very much the bohemian quarter now, the haunt of artists, creatrixes, writers and the pharmo-technicians who bracketed themselves alongside, fellow creators of the mind's visions. Deveth had loved it here, though she complained incessantly about the infighting and spite. It was a community, despite its closed, cold appearance now and the dark temple squatting at its heart.

Robin did not belong here, and she knew it. She had visited parties once or twice, with Deveth, and had made herself unpopular. These were the spoiled children of the wealthy, Deveth's friends, the ones who didn't need to work, who could afford to play out their fantasies of Paris or Vienna. Robin had worked since she was fifteen, down in the mining labs in Bharulay and then scoring, making it into Paugeng. She could never afford to live here. Deveth, sardonic, had watched her make a fool of herself arguing with a neosocialist at the last party they had attended together.

"It's all very well for your friends," Robin had said later, in frustration. "They're living in a—a *cushion*."

"This isn't an affluent neighborhood, Robin. None of them are very rich."

Deveth lit a cigarette as she spoke and the brief light flared up around her face, the harsh cheekbones and hawk nose illuminated and then gone, back into the dim, comfortable light of her apartment. She sounded loftily understanding, as though Robin couldn't really be expected to comprehend these sophisticated ideas.

"Don't be stupid," Robin said with contempt, forgetting now how eager she had been to impress this glamorous woman. "Your families are."

She saw the expression on Deveth's face change from languid amusement to wariness: mustn't wind the peasant up too far. Robin had never criticized her before. Until that night, she had behaved as though Deveth were quite perfect.

"I'm sorry you feel that way," she'd told Robin, neutrally. "Maybe, it isn't meant. Maybe we should end it here." And then off-course, Robin, stricken, had stammered apologies while Deveth, sad-eyed, watched.

And now, Robin thought, in a fury, she's probably just dumped me in favor of some little sweetheart whose dad lives in Meriden, no doubt, who stays up all night and talks about her *art*. She stormed along, realizing suddenly that she had gone past Deveth's house. She retraced her steps and made her way into the entrance hallway. Deveth had given her the code to the main door, but not the apartment itself: not the key to her heart.

The hall opened out into a wide atrium, once the fashionable home of palms and a carp pool, but now full of old divans arranged in a rough square. The air was musty, stained with old incense and the breath of dampness. The pool had been drained, and now featured as a sort of conversation pit, studded with candle ends. Robin eyed it with distaste. They had held the party here. Ghosts of the young and pretty stared at her from the rotting divans, mocking, smiling at Deveth Sardai's bit of rough.

"Are you looking for something?" An uncertain voice came out of the gloom.

Robin jumped.

"I'm a friend of Deveth Sardai's... I came to see if she was in."

"Oh, it's you," the voice said, without enthusiasm. She came further into the wan light from the street and Robin recognized her: Tarai Alba, who lived on the floor above Deveth. She had been at the party, too; Robin remembered her in a steely sheath gown, blonde hair on a lattice of struts and pins. Every time she met Robin's eyes, she had given her a thin, little smile. She had once, Robin knew, been Deveth's lover, and probably still was. Robin said, "Is Dev here?"

"I don't know," Alba replied. She looked smaller and thinner than Robin remembered her. The sheath had been replaced by a ripped silk dressing gown; she was barefoot.

"I'm sorry," Robin said automatically. "Did I wake you up?"

"It doesn't matter. Deveth's not here. The last time I saw her was several days ago, I can't remember exactly. I don't know where she's gone. And her phone keeps going and going—I can hear it."

Her small voice was lost.

"Have you been in her apartment?"

"No, she wouldn't—she didn't give me the code." *You, too,* thought Robin with a breath of satisfaction. She led the way up the stairs to Deveth's apartment. The door was firmly shut. Even out here, it felt empty.

"She might be in there." Alba whispered. There was no way they could force the door. Reinforced steel does not give way easily to a kick.

"What about the windows?" But the side of the building was sheer, and the double windows wouldn't open from the outside. They went out with a torch to have a look, but there was no sign of a forced entry. The lights were off.

"There must be some way in," Robin said. "What about the waste disposal?" She and Alba, shivering, went down to the basement and investigated. The base of the disposal unit was a narrow, snaking pipe that entered the main collection unit. With difficulty, they detached it.

"I'm not going up there," Alba said firmly.

It was not pleasant. The pipe stank, and its serpentine sides were slimed with refuse. Like going into someone's intestines, Robin thought. She could climb by gripping the latches; fortunately, the house was too old for a modern chemical valve system. She counted as she climbed. At the second floor, a voice, echoing loud and sharp in her ear, said, "What's that?"

Light seeped around the edges of the disposal hatch.

"Rat, or something."

"That's revolting. You mean they live in the system?"

"You're never less than twelve feet away from one, they say," the voice floated away as Robin climbed on. When she reached the third floor, she located the back of the hatch in Deveth's kitchen, praying that she'd got the right apartment. She did not find the idea of tumbling, covered in filth, onto the floor of some sneering neobohemian's kitchen, an appealing one. She had to force the hatch. An unpleasant ten minutes ensued. She couldn't dislodge the hatch, and she could feel the struts beneath her heels starting to give; they were never meant to bear so much weight. Robin pushed and tugged, certain that at any moment the struts would give way and she'd fall down the pipe, only to get stuck fifteen feet down where it narrowed. Then, the hatch gave way with a crack and she fell headfirst into the kitchen.

It was Deveth's. There was a terrible smell of rotten meat and old cigarette smoke. Robin retched over the sink. Clutching a washcloth, now dried and stiff, to her face, she made a quick tour of the apartment. She knew what she'd find: Deveth's murdered body, cold and rotting, flung against the wall. But the apartment was dark and quiet. The dreadful smell lessened as she entered the bedroom. Deveth was not at home, alive or dead. Robin found the main switch and turned all the lights on, discovering the culprit in the kitchen: a large and ancient steak sitting on the worktop. Robin picked it up with a fork and flung it down the waste disposal, unfortunately forgetting that they had disconnected it at the bottom. Someone hammered at the front door. Robin opened it to see Tarai Alba's white face floating like a balloon in the dim hallway.

"Is she—"

"No, no," Robin said, to stave off what might turn into hysteria. "She's not here."

"What's that *smell?*"

"She left a steak out in the kitchen. It rotted, what with the heat. Or," Robin said suddenly, "it might be me." Her vest top and canvas jeans were covered in the mold from the pipe. Filth nested in her hair. Alba regarded her with horror.

"Look," Robin said patiently, "I'm going to find something else to wear."

She went back into the bedroom. Deveth was several inches taller, but Robin found a pair of clean trousers that she could roll up at the cuffs, and a baggy shirt. Inside the wardrobe, she found a whole collection of little packets of pills and herbs. She recognized none of the herbs: strands of crimson and black, as though the contents of the packet had rotted and then dried; a musty yellow substance that smelled of old fish. The herbs were somehow sinister. Going back into the kitchen, Robin stuffed the dirty clothes in the washing machine and padded into the bathroom in her underwear.

"What are you doing?" Alba called.

"Having a shower!" At least the water was on. She caught a glimpse of herself in the bedroom mirror as she dressed, a short, pale-faced person under a wet bob of dark hair, wearing huge clothes. *Where are you, Deveth?*

Alba was hunched on the sofa, smoking sourly. *Deprived of her audience,* Robin thought.

"What are we going to do?"

"Well, I don't know." She wondered if Paugeng security, Tserai's private troops, could be roped in. An ice-cold thought made her shiver: What if Deveth was dead? What if the Sardai family thought she'd killed Deveth? She wasn't the same class...you didn't know how these people might behave. Robin had been brought up to consider that the rich were all mad.

"Could you call her parents?" Tarai said, doubtful.

"I don't think they'd trust me," Robin replied. She didn't want to talk about the earlier visit. "I'm not good enough for Deveth."

Underneath the posturing, Alba had a kind-enough heart. She protested. "I'm sure they wouldn't think that! I mean—Dev and I were never real lovers, we had a thing sometimes but it wasn't—we were friends."

She stubbed the cigarette out, and Robin, relieved to be leaving this sad, empty place, followed her down the stairs.

MING I:
THE DARKENING
OF THE LIGHT

NINE

In the fashionably muted atrium of Paugeng, Zhu Irzh found that Jhai Tserai was unavailable. The young man behind the reception desk seemed entirely unfazed by the demon's presence. He smiled warmly at Zhu Irzh. The subtext said: *We're so happy to see you. What a welcome visitor you are.* It made Zhu Irzh smile. They all got it from Jhai Tserai, who was apparently picky about details, especially those regarding quality management. Top down.

The young receptionist told Zhu Irzh that he was most welcome to stay and wait. Perhaps he would like to wait in the guest suite? There was a pool (green, cool, a length of water submerged between the fronds of ferns; you could swim with the soothing carp in the pond). The demon's mouth watered at the thought, a surprising physiological reaction, but some perversity made him decline.

"No thanks. I think I'll go and explore the port."

The receptionist managed to convey to Zhu Irzh that this was absolutely fine. If the demon had announced his intention to immolate himself on the front steps he would, he presumed, have evoked a similar response. He smiled and left.

Outside, a wall of sticky heat hit him. At the edge of the port, a battered tin sign announced the presence of a café. The demon hesitated for a moment, then went down some steps and was disorientingly out in the open again, in a small and dusty side street. Two boys were cooking something in a large, flat pan over an open fire. Both of them looked up and wary recognition flickered across their faces. They could see him, then. That betokened some evidence of magical training—Paugeng and the police precinct could afford expensive wards to bring visibility to supernatural intruders; out here in the slums, you were on your own. But there was a vacancy to the boys' faces that suggested they were simple. Under a corrugated iron awning, an old woman dozed, her seamed, beige face nodding above a stiff, black collar.

"It's all right," the demon said. "I'm not here to hurt you." The boys grinned up at him. He estimated they had about six teeth between them.

"Tschai?" a boy said without preamble. After a moment, this made sense.

"Thanks. I'd love some tea." The demon squatted on his heels beside them, fastidiously flicking the skirts of his silk coat out of the dust with his tail. The older child pottered to the back of the shop and produced a vast iron kettle, from which a thick, chocolate-colored liquid emerged. He handed the warm glass to Zhu Irzh, who thought of ice: ice and mint and pale green drinks. Actually, the tea was refreshing, although there was a peculiar aftertaste which he couldn't quite get hold of. He smiled and nodded at the boys; they smiled and nodded back; the grandmother woke up and everyone smiled and nodded at everyone else. It was all very friendly. He sipped the tea and consulted his watch. One of the boys came to with a start. He spoke to the old woman. The grandmother retreated into the depths of the shop and staggered out again with a large box. The demon watched curiously. She set the box in a niche, where some of the plaster had been gouged out of the wall, gave a bouncing bow and opened the hinged doors of the box. Inside, a portrait gazed out at Zhu Irzh: dark, upturned eyes beneath elegant brows, an aquiline nose, a smiling mouth. The earlobes were stained red. Grandmother picked up the stub of a scarlet candle and lit it. Fake flowers surrounded the icon, along with a greeting card featuring violets, a chocolate bar and a small blue bottle. The grandmother noticed Zhu Irzh's transfixed stare.

"Yes!" she croaked at him. "You know her! Everyone does." She pointed to the Paugeng tower, the home of the object of her reverence. *Imperial Majesty!* thought the demon. The corporate executive as religious icon. He must remember not to underestimate Jhai Tserai.

On returning to Paugeng, he was told that Jhai was now available, and would see him shortly. Zhu Irzh was whisked into the upper reaches of the tower in a mirrored lift, which gave him the opportunity to correct any minor details of his person that failed to pass muster. It was fortunate, the demon reflected with a trace of distaste, that his particular brand of Hellkind did not sweat. Humans were really quite *unfortunate* in that respect. He plucked a stray hair from his silk collar, and the lift came imperceptibly to a halt. Zhu Irzh stepped out into a leafy atrium, almost as large as the hallway below. A demure, smiling secretary, his hair fashionably long, greeted him. Zhu Irzh glanced at the young man with approval; it seemed Tserai had excellent taste.

"She'll be right with you," the young man said.

"Excellent." Zhu Irzh was ushered into a pleasant lounge overlooking the port. A hazy afternoon sun shimmered through tinted glass and there was a clean smell, partly antiseptic, partly floral. A bank of orchids stood along one wall, engineered into fantastic creations. At the far end of the room, a voice said, "Seneschal Zhu Irzh, I understand?"

The demon turned to see a young woman stepping through the double doors. He recognized her immediately; he had, after all, just seen her face in iconic representation. In person, however, Jhai Tserai seemed to glow. She wore a saffron sari; gold sparked at her wrists and throat. She glided, smiling, down the length of the room and extended a languid hand in the Western manner. Zhu Irzh took her long, cool fingers and immediately felt as though someone had slipped a soft, gentle hand against his groin. The sensation was unexpected, wonderful, and entirely inappropriate. Jhai Tserai's hand closed briefly around his own fingers, but the touch was experienced somewhere else entirely. How did she do that? Zhu Irzh wondered through the red mist in his head. Some kind of pheromonal enhancement perhaps. Still, he wasn't about to complain.

To his intense relief, Jhai released his hand and stepped back. Desire receded to a part of Zhu Irzh's mind where it could be unpacked later and examined in detail. He took a deep, shaky breath. The industrialist was regarding him with some amusement; he realized, with dim horror, that Jhai Tserai was well aware of the effect that she had just achieved. Flustered, the demon said quickly, "I've come with regard to a sad matter, I'm afraid. Do you know a young lady named Deveth Sardai?"

Jhai's eyebrows rose. "I do indeed. We were in school together. I've known her for years. In fact," she added in a murmur, "I'm pleased you're here." She leaned forward confidentially to meet the demon's eyes and Zhu Irzh was astounded to find himself blushing.

"Are you?"

"I was beginning to worry," Jhai said, suddenly earnest. "I couldn't help feeling that something might have *happened* to her. Deveth and I keep in irregular touch—sometimes we see a lot of each other; sometimes our social lives take us in different orbits; you know how it is… We're all so busy these days and it's hard to catch up with old friends, no matter how much one might want to. But a young girlfriend of hers told me that she hadn't seen Deveth for days, and naturally, I was becoming rather concerned." She reached out and put her hand briefly over Zhu Irzh's own, as if readying herself to be brave. "Tell me. What's wrong?"

"I'm afraid she's dead," the demon said, watching Jhai narrowly. It was hard to concentrate. His hand was still warm where she had touched him.

Jhai stared at him. "Dead? How? Oh Goddess, don't tell me she overdosed." She put a hand to her mouth in dismay.

"Was she in the habit of using drugs?" Zhu Irzh asked, evading the question.

Jhai frowned. "I don't like to speak ill of a friend, but I must be honest. I knew it would get her into trouble one day. She took a lot of opium, sometimes coke, sometimes the new, more experimental stuff…" She sat down on one of the overstuffed leather couches and patted it, inviting the demon to sit by her side. *"Can* I be honest with you?"

"I'd rather you were," Zhu Irzh replied dryly.

"The girlfriend. Robin Yuan. You see, Seneschal, I believe in giving the more *disadvantaged* members of our community a chance, and Robin's been a good, solid worker. But I do keep a very close eye on my personnel, and lately, well, she's been behaving a little erratically. I made a few discreet enquiries, and there have been suggestions—nothing more than rumors, mind—that Robin has a history of dealing. Nothing on the police books, she's never been charged, but there are—rumors. Now if this has led to poor Deveth's death—"

"Is Robin here today?"

"I'm afraid she's off sick at the moment," Jhai said firmly. "Seneschal, please— don't think that I'm casting suspicion on Robin. It's just that it's better to be *open* about these things, even if it casts doubt on myself as an employer."

Her beautiful eyes were guileless, but Zhu Irzh was left in no doubt that suspicion was exactly what Jhai had intended to cast. His admiration rose. The girl would do well in Hell, no doubt about it. And she was still having this unfortunate effect upon him... desire was washing over him in waves, making it difficult to think. If the interview got protracted, he'd have to make an excuse to visit the bathroom and do something about it, undignified though this might be. Any notions he might have had of dominating this particular interview were well past their sell-by date.

The secretary glided in with tea. Zhu Irzh sipped it, wondering absently what variety it might be; it had a faint sweetness, like decay, but it was not unpleasant and it helped to clear his head a little.

"I'm terribly sorry," he heard himself saying. "But in fact, it wasn't an overdose. I'm afraid your friend was murdered."

Jhai went cold and still. "Tell me what you know," she whispered. Zhu Irzh gave her an edited version of events, omitting the missing body. Despite the ache in his groin, he managed to extract from her a reasonable summary of her recent movements, but it was a formality and they both knew it. The woman who owned Paugeng would have little trouble in buying an alibi. The demon wound the interview to a close, and rose to leave.

"I'm very grateful to you," Jhai said softly. She reached out and touched his arm. He looked down into her eyes, and saw a dark golden glitter in their depths. She leaned forward again. His mouth brushed the air, and she stepped back. "I know you'll find the person responsible for this," she said, as the secretary appeared to show him to the door, and even through the haze of need and desire, Zhu Irzh thought he glimpsed the unmistakable odor of a threat.

TEN

Robin was wondering, vaguely, why she felt so dreadful. She had started feeling ill some time ago, the morning after her visit to Deveth's family. It was an actual, physical pain lodged in her muscles: a burning, flulike ache. Her head pounded, and there was a tight constriction in her chest, which made breathing painful. She sat up and was seized by a fit of coughing, which rattled alarmingly in her chest. Heaving her reluctant body out of bed, she rooted in the bag for Malian Sardai's headache pills, and took one. There were several left. It seemed to abate the pain in her head a little, but she felt so tired, yet she must have slept for a good nine hours. An appalled glance at the dial of the clock showed her that it was much longer than that: she was already an hour late for work. If she took the day off, she was sure she'd be fined. One afternoon, with Jhai Tserai's permission, was all very well, but calling in sick immediately afterward was not a good idea. The fines were comparatively minimal—Paugeng was a caring company—but Robin couldn't afford it anyway. She took a shower and felt marginally better.

She left the flat early, wrapped in a parka against the day, which was already becoming hot. She couldn't seem to get warm, in spite of the weather and the thick coat, yet she was sweating. She forced herself past the Shaopeng stop, and walked on to Embaya Street, where the herbalists were opening. The man wanted to do a full analysis, but Robin did not have time.

"What's good for everything?" she asked.

"What's your constitution?"

"I haven't the faintest idea. I think it's water."

He grumbled, but Robin forced him to give her a twist of flat, white pills. He told her that they would cure fever and aches. Robin studied the ingredients, which seemed to represent a diverse range, paid him and left. She swallowed two of the pills at the downtown stop. There was no discernible difference;

she still felt awful. She would see the resident doctor when she got to work, money or no money. They might be talked into giving her an installment plan, if her luck held. This did not, however, seem to be her lucky week.

Mercifully, the downtown was not excessively crowded. Robin fought her way to a seat and stayed there, leaning her hurting head against the dirty pane. The city rattled by: Phikhat, Battery Road, Semmerang Anka and at last the Ghenret platform for Paugeng. Robin got off and stood on the platform, trying to clear her head. It was a pearly, damp day, a sudden return to spring after the summer was almost over. A light mist from the sea wreathed the harbor, and the heights of Paugeng were lost as though in cloud. Looking up made Robin dizzy. She walked carefully to the Paugeng steps and as she climbed up into the perfect atrium, she thought she heard something laughing, faint and far away.

She crept in through the Paugeng atrium, hoping no one would see her. For once, the place seemed quiet, and she went straight down to Y lab. George Su would know she was late, because of the log-in readings, but hopefully he had enough to do without worrying about her timekeeping. Robin was flooded with guilt. It was such an important experiment, even though this was a routine phase. For the previous few weeks, Jhai had put her top crew on it, only handing off the testing to Robin for follow-up once they'd finished the main runs.

Nonetheless, the experiment was her responsibility and now here she was, deserting Mhara again and again. She went through the checklist on the main screen, even though it blurred before her vision. She felt as though someone was watching her, sensing an implacable gaze on her back, but when she turned to look at the experiment he was lying serenely still in the bunk. There was no sign that he had moved.

Robin sat down beside Mhara and checked the readouts on the monitor. The experiment was as close to normal as he'd been for some time. He was lying on his side, the pointed face half-buried in the pillow. His skin seemed even paler. The illness was making Robin maudlin, in need of comfort. She stroked the soft, indigo hair behind Mhara's neck. It just showed how little Jhai Tserai really understood people, for Robin's neutrality had been hopelessly compromised on the day that she had first had to administer a half-developed drug to a bound and helpless otherworldly captive. She tried to stifle her feelings: this was her job, the one she'd worked so hard to get, and that was that. She didn't have the luxury of moral choices, she told herself. So she had compromised, made the experiment's limited life as comfortable as possible, and did as she was told.

Mhara's eyes looked dark in sleep, but at her touch he stirred and the eyes flooded with light, like the sun over the sea. Robin felt the cough begin in her throat, and hastily turned her head away to avoid choking over him.

"Robin? You're ill?"

"It's the flu, or something," Robin told him hoarsely. "It came on a little while ago."

"And you still had to come to work?"

"Unfortunately, yes."

"Are we going to do more tests today?"

Robin coughed again. "No…just your shots." She fumbled in the drawer and got the sterile packets, then went through the range of jabs. He submitted placidly. She seemed all thumbs today; her fingers would not obey her.

"You might as well try and sleep," she told him. It was what Robin herself wanted to do. She tried to go through the test checklist but nothing seemed to make much sense. She could make coffee though, and drank cup after cup, stumbling back and forth from the machine. The heat was comforting, and she could wash down the hourly painkillers, which still did not seem very effective. She could not face lunch when at last her breaktime dragged around. The coughing fits were becoming more frequent, and by midafternoon, she took refuge in the lavatory and gave way to a bout of choking which seemed to go on for hours, stifling it in a wad of tissue. When she took the paper away from her mouth it was bloody. Robin stared at it in disbelief. She should not go near the experiment in this state, but the thought of going off work scared her. It would cost too much: she might be fined, and now it looked like she had something serious and that would mean more expense. She could not afford medical insurance either. *Come on,* she thought furiously. *You drag yourself in there and give the poor thing the four o'clock jabs, and then you go home.*

She stood up and the tiled room spun. Somehow, she got back to the office, took the right jabs out of the canister and went in to the experiment.

"Just me again," she muttered. She sat on her usual place by the bunk, and took out the little syringes. Nothing seemed to make sense. She stared at the labels, hoping they would become clearer. Everything was very dim and furry around the edges. She looked up and saw that the experiment was watching her, raised on his elbows. The blue eyes were very clear, and very bright.

"Mhara," she said.

"Yes?"

"That's your name," Robin whispered. "You have a name."

Mhara said softly. "But you knew that."

"No," Robin said. "I didn't understand it, not until now. Not really. Mhara, I think I'm really sick."

"Sick?" His eyes seemed to fill the world. She began to fumble with the activation unit for the bonds that held him to the cot. "Robin? What are you doing?"

"Setting you free. Doing something good. Before I die," Robin said, and then she felt the cough beginning deep in her throat. It took hold of her and she bent over double, spluttering. She felt a gentle hand on her back, stroking and soothing, and oddly it stopped the cough.

"You're in pain, aren't you?" the experiment said, gently.

Gratefully, Robin turned to him.

"Yes, I—" and then she realized what she had done. Her head swam with panic and elation. *But he wouldn't hurt me, not after I've helped him!* was her first confused thought, and then: *Why not? You're his torturer.* She tried to get up from the bed, but her legs would not obey her.

"Please—" she started to say.

"Goodbye, Robin," Mhara whispered. His hand gripped her wrist, keeping her pinned to the bunk. He was much stronger than she would have expected, after all the testing. The frail patient in the bed was not so fragile, it seemed. Robin stared at him without understanding and tried to pull her feeble hand away. Her experiment gave her his sweet, vague smile and kissed her on the forehead, and then she felt his fingers close gently around her sore throat.

ELEVEN

"They've found another body," Ma said, sounding almost cheerful.

"Have they indeed?" Zhu Irzh murmured. He put down the copy of the *Hell Morning News*, which was delivered promptly to the station house every day, took a sip of blood tea, and gave Ma his full attention. "Who and where?"

"It isn't a woman this time, but it's in pretty much the same condition. Looks as though something tore it apart, and it's a few days old, probably about the same time of death as the first. They found it up on a mining site, dumped in a landfill crater. It was sheer luck that the foreman spotted it; they were about to fill in the hole when he noticed the foot."

"The foot?"

"They found the rest of the body nearby."

"And have they figured out who it was?" Zhu Irzh rubbed gritty eyes.

"As a matter of fact, yes, they have. It's the body of a local *feng shui* man, named Hsu Ko. Seems he was undertaking some dowsing on the site, to check for minerals. He's one of a number of *feng shui* experts on contract to the mining companies."

"Any obvious suspects?"

"No, apparently he was liked well enough, kept to himself. He was brought in to replace someone who was having problems with their license—" Ma frowned. "A man called Paravang Roche. Didn't you have a run-in with someone of that name?"

"Yes, I was the one who got his license revoked. He hadn't paid his bribes. It was a trivial affair."

"Maybe not to Roche. These people can get very jealous with one another. My cousin used to work for the Feng Shui Practitioners' Guild but he packed it in, said there was too much backstabbing. Anyway, the foreman said that Ko was the last person he'd expect to turn up murdered."

"And we're expecting the DNA results on the last body this morning, right? Perhaps there'll be a connection," Zhu Irzh murmured, though he could not bring himself to be too hopeful. Things just didn't work out like that. But to his surprise, Ma nodded.

"Yes, there is. The mining company's owned by Paugeng."

"Paugeng?" Zhu Irzh glanced up with renewed interest. "Jhai Tserai's company. Well, well. Paravang Roche worked for Paugeng before his disgrace. And Tserai was a friend of the murdered girl." He sipped his tea, lost in momentary contemplation. Jhai was starting to feature heavily in this investigation, not to mention Zhu Irzh's dreams. The previous night had been restless and disturbing, filled with images of Jhai in his arms and the sweetness of orgasm running through him like water. Demons were renowned for their sexual stamina, but everyone had their limits and morning had seen Zhu Irzh exhausted. It would have been worth it if Jhai had actually been present in the bed, but Zhu Irzh rather resented so strong an attraction being placed upon him from afar. It put him at a disadvantage, and wounded his pride.

"I think we'd better take a look at the site," he said now. "And the body."

But Captain Sung, it seemed, had other ideas.

"I told you, Zhu Irzh. I don't want you too involved with this investigation." Zhu Irzh held his breath, but Sung made no mention of his trip to see Tserai. "However, there is something you can do. I'd like you to check the *feng shui* of the site itself. See if there's anything peculiar about it. Sometimes meridians can attract elemental spirits, and they're often dangerous. We should take another look at the place where Sardai's body was found, too."

"All right," the demon said. "I think I can handle that."

When told of the plan, Sergeant Ma frowned. "Do you know much about *feng shui*? Because I don't."

"I don't either," the demon said thoughtfully. "Only what I learned from my tutor. But I know someone who does."

"Who, Paravang Roche? You can't involve a potential suspect in the investigation of a murder!"

"Why not? It'll be interesting to see how he reacts. And there's no question about his skills, just his finances."

"I really don't think—I mean, Captain Sung told me what he said to you and—"

"I know what Sung said. Look, Chen left me in charge of you, didn't he? I'll take the blame if anything goes wrong."

He was expecting further protests, but Ma merely muttered.

Fortunately, it was still early, even by the time they had collected a protesting Paravang Roche from his little apartment and driven up to the site. The scars and tears in the earth were shrouded in the clouds that boiled down from the top of Wuan Chih. The damp air was refreshing after the humid heat of the last few days, but Zhu Irzh knew that it wouldn't last. Before noon the sun would swim up and burn out the mist in a burst of heat, and by midafternoon the humans would all be sweltering and sweating.

"Nice morning," Zhu Irzh said to Paravang, who just grunted. The dowser's face was sourness itself. Paravang had gasped when he saw the demon once more standing on his doorstep, and Zhu Irzh's sensitive nose had caught the unmistakable odor of guilt. Interesting, the demon thought now. What had the dowser been up to, then, apart from unpaid license fees? Murder, perhaps? But he couldn't see what Roche thought he might achieve by murdering the man who had replaced him: it wouldn't get his license back, after all. Well, there was plenty of time to find out. It was always useful to have a dowser on board, given the ever-shifting *feng shui* of Singapore Three. Paravang would be working for him, now. Without pay.

They surveyed the squares along the eastern margin, Paravang's dowsing rods twitching infinitesimally. At least he appeared to be taking his professional responsibilities seriously. Zhu Irzh, hands in his pockets, strolled around the segmented edges of the square, then stood, a shadow in the morning mist, and looked enquiringly at Paravang.

"The meridian's running through here," Paravang at last volunteered, grudgingly.

Zhu Irzh swung around, staring. "So the body was found on the same meridian, is that correct?" He glanced down the hill to where police tape marked off an orange square. A sheet concealed what remained of Paravang's luckless successor. Irritably, Paravang nodded.

"And you're quite sure about that, are you?" The demon frowned, thinking back to an early lesson in the precepts of *feng shui*. That had been over a hundred years ago now. It was a long time to keep anything in your head, and Zhu Irzh believed in remembering only the essentials.

"What do you mean, am I 'quite sure'?" Paravang asked, with some belligerence.

"Well, I thought we might be getting confused with the lesser land lines." Zhu Irzh frowned at the ground. The *ch'i* meridians glowed with a very faint light, only dimly discernible even to a demon's enhanced gaze. "It's not wholly clear…"

"What isn't?" The dowser glared at him.

"The meridian goes down here and then up under this boulder, yes?" The demon's long fingers made undulating motions, like someone emulating the flight of birds.

"I suppose so." Paravang conceded.

"Here, where the thing starts to descend again, is where I thought there might be a join. There's a meridian coming in from the southwest. There's a lot of water under here, too."

"There's no join." Paravang Roche spoke with absolute finality.

"I see," Zhu Irzh said.

"I suppose you can sense a sort of knot?" Paravang lectured.

"Actually, as far as I can see, it's more like a seam."

"The *knot* is produced by the presence of the mountain line to the north-west, which pulls the meridian out of shape. Anyway, what of it? What am I even doing here?"

"The mountain line is muted by water, surely? Look, Paravang, we don't know whether the site's *feng shui* actually does have anything to do with the murder, but since the dead man *was* a dowser, and since dangerous elementals can sometimes be conjured by disturbances to the earth, and since those same elementals are forced to travel along *ch'i* meridians, it's worth investigating, surely?" Did Paravang's manner suggest guilt, or only irritation? Zhu Irzh wished he had paid a little more attention to studies of human body language, but it was not an area that greatly interested most of Hellkind. He turned back to the site without waiting for a reply. "There's a substantial spring down there." He pointed.

Paravang said loftily, "I doubt that very much. It's entirely the wrong sort of terrain."

Zhu Irzh made a universal both-hands-in-the-air gesture.

"I can't help that. I can see it! There it is. Go and get your little stick and take a look."

"It is not a little stick! It is a dowsing wand!"

"My apologies."

Paravang stormed down to the carrier. When he returned, trudging up the slope, Zhu Irzh had not moved. His attention had been caught by something beneath the earth. The taste of water was suddenly fresh in his mouth, and he could hear it running, bubbling up underneath the dry stones. Zhu Irzh stood still and listened.

"Where do you think you are?" Roche snapped. "A bloody cocktail lounge?"

Zhu Irzh favored the disgruntled dowser with an uncomprehending gaze. He said, "Sorry, I was listening for something." This was interesting. He'd always known he possessed these powers, like most demons from the first levels, but he'd never actually bothered to put them into practice before. Could such skills, Zhu Irzh wondered, be used for locating something less boring than *ch'i* meridians? Buried treasure, perhaps?

"Never mind!" the dowser snapped.

On further investigation, they discovered that Zhu Irzh was right. There was a big spring, gushing out of the gap between the hidden strata. Paravang's fury that it had been the demon and not he who had discovered the spring was manifest. Moreover, he would not admit his error, subsequently acting as though Zhu Irzh had been somehow abducted into the netherworld from which he came. When forced by circumstance to utter, he spoke into the air.

By now, the sun had broken through the clouds and the suburb of Wuan Chih spread in a tarnished glitter far below. The earth of the site was covered in condensation; droplets lying like spider webs over the rumpled russet soil. Zhu Irzh turned and gazed down the slope with pleasure. He may have a few frustrations with this world, but he could not deny that it had its charms. He watched the clouds settle over the distant hills, dimly aware that Paravang, directly in his field of vision, had flung down the dowsing rod.

"What are you staring at me for?" Paravang shouted. All the dowser's control was evaporating like the risen mist.

"What? Oh, I'm sorry, I didn't mean to put you off."

Paravang was not appeased by the apology. Before Zhu Irzh's startled gaze, the dowser snapped. He began to rave: shouting about imported labor, filthy creatures who weren't even foreigners but worse, something conjured up from Hell, taking his job and his money away from him, stealing his secrets, and it all got much worse. By this time a small and curious crowd had gathered. Zhu Irzh blinked. He could feel a stream of pheromonal hatred emanating from the dowser. Heat began to swim in his blood and drive a spike behind his eyes. He blinked, trying to keep a sudden, overwhelming fury at bay. It was too powerful for Zhu Irzh to reflect that this was not normal behavior for him, that it was utterly irrational…

"—who summoned you up?" Paravang shrieked. His round face was distorted with rage.

"I was not summoned," the demon heard himself say, very softly.

"—just because you're some spawn of Hell you think you can lord it over the rest of us, come here and take my living away—"

The crowd made a little convulsive motion forward, as if pulled by a sympathetic string. Zhu Irzh reached Paravang in three strides. He appraised the ranting dowser for a moment, then reached out, as contemptuously as a cat, and swiped Paravang in the ribs. His sharp claws cut through Paravang's shirt like butter and sent him sprawling to the ground. Paravang looked aghast at the parallel bloody grooves in his flesh and wailed. All movement stopped. Zhu Irzh watched him with a dreadful interest. Everything became inverted, the sky darkened and the ground underneath him seemed horribly bright. Zhu Irzh reached down a clawed hand, hauled Paravang easily to his feet, and hit him again across the side of the head. He could smell the enticing scent of fresh blood. There was a series of meaningless noises away to his right, which, if he had been able to understand them, would have resolved into the voice of the site manager, shouting. He glanced down at the ground and saw that the meridian at his feet was glowing white hot, all the way down into the city. Then something hit him in the ribs and bowled him over, knocking him away from the meridian. The rage was abruptly gone, melted like snow, but in its place was a dull, burning ache in his side that kindled into blazing pain. Zhu Irzh's vision blurred, but through the fading landscape of the site, he saw someone sprinting toward him. A woman: tall, and wiry, dressed in Paugeng security team fatigues. And in her hand she was holding a remarkably large gun.

TWELVE

The lab team did not find Robin for some hours. Her erstwhile experiment had not bothered to gag her and when she came round, she cried for help until the coughing stopped her. She tried to get out of the bonds, but they were tied too securely and the fever weakened her. She lay for a long time in a daze. Faces swam above her: Jhai, Deveth and Malian Sardai, her own mother, and always back to Mhara's well-water blue eyes. At first she thought they were real, but soon realized that they were no more than illusion.

Eventually, George Su found her, having heard her coughing uncontrollably. He acted promptly, releasing the bonds and sending a priority call to Jhai, who had just arrived back at Paugeng. She came straight down. Robin was too ill to speak by now, running a red-hot fever and coughing until she couldn't breathe. Tserai called the medics and got Robin into a ward. On the way, Robin was vaguely aware of Paugeng's private troops pouring out into the atrium. It was then about nine in the evening and the light had gone. *They won't find him now,* Robin thought, elation running under the fever. *He's long gone.* She was too ill to worry about the consequences. The medic kept trying to bring her round, and she knew Tserai was hovering over her to find out what had happened. She tried to tell them, but could not stop coughing, and eventually she felt a sedative prick her forearm and the ward became a woolly haze.

蛇警探

Under the sedative, Robin dreamed. It was a small, clear dream, like a sequence of images, very finely drawn. She was standing on a hill in a hot place. A dark red sun was setting over a line of sea. Beneath the hill lay a city, walled and crowded with tall houses, each with a curling edge to the roof, and bearing a lacy fretwork of balconies. The air smelled of blood. Smoke drifted up from the buildings and drifted across the steaming air. She could see immense towers in the distance, reaching almost to the crimson sky.

Then she was inside one of the tall houses. It was warm and shadowy, a small room with a fire in the grate. The window was made of some kind of paper, with a curled catch that cast a precise shadow against the lacquered pane. She was waiting for someone. She looked down and saw a cup filled with something thick and red.

And then she was outside again. A great wall of mountain rose up before her, a remote and rosy edge of snow in the dying light of the sun. She was running, faster than she'd ever run before, leaping the boulders and sliding down a long apron of scree. The air tasted of frost, and stars filled the sky. Robin had never seen anything so bright. Before her, the spotted, doglike creature leaped and pranced clumsily. It looked at her over its shoulder and said in a harsh human voice, "Come with me—"

—and they were back in the ward. It was dim and quiet. Robin, still dreaming, followed the animal out through the door of the ward and down the stairs. Their way was illuminated by a pale, unfocused light, which grew stronger as they neared a doorway. Robin thought they must be somewhere on level eight, below the atrium but above the main labs. The beast led her into a room full of lockers, like an old-fashioned chemist's store. It squatted by a cabinet set into the wall.

"Why don't you open it?" it said. Now its voice had become seductive, enticing.

Why not? Robin thought. She pulled the heavy drawer and it rolled forward smoothly under its own momentum.

She found herself staring down onto a woman's body. The corpse was covered by a sheet of stiff, slightly oiled plastic. Its face was gone. In the dream, Robin, cold with shock, pulled the sheet down and saw that the breast was marked with long, parallel rips, the flesh on either side ruffled and frayed. Below the ribcage, the abdomen had been torn away to reveal the internal organs; very neat, like an anatomical model. There was a strong, synthetic smell. Robin pulled the sheet back up with shaking hands. The animal pushed sympathetically against her bare shins. *It's only a dream,* Robin's mind whispered to her.

"It's me," Deveth's voice said, filled with malice. "Not so pretty now, am I?"

The animal was suddenly nowhere to be seen, but Deveth's spectral face hovered over the ruined visage of the corpse for a moment, a snarling mask, before it faded. Robin could not seem to bring herself out of her trance, and as she stood in wonder and revulsion over the corpse it dawned on her that she was awake.

Robin slammed the drawer shut. The noise reverberated throughout the narrow room and there was a little click. Looking up, Robin saw the red monitor eye swivel and focus. She bolted for the door, shut it behind her and started to run through the warren of corridors. It all looked the same. She came upon a perspex-paneled door…Looking through, she saw row upon row of beds, like a dollhouse, each containing a subject attached to dripfeeds and monitors. The wan ambient light, set at constant for the duration of the experimental run, made each face look the same. Much more distinctive than personalities, histories, names: the individual neural and biochemical basis of the organism. What is it to be the same, to be different? Robin could not have cared less. She knew where she was now. She turned right at the end of the corridor and came out by the elevator, directly underneath the wards. She thought she would get her things and go, leave forever, but the exertion made her legs shake. Her skin was clammy and hot. The fever had returned, and all Robin could do was sit on the edge of the bed trying to clear her streaming vision and eventually passing into unconsciousness.

THIRTEEN

Zhu Irzh blinked up into the anxious face of Sergeant Ma, which hovered over him like an untethered balloon.

"Where am I?" he heard himself say, croaking feebly, but it was not Ma who answered.

"You're in a cell," a crisp voice said. Zhu Irzh turned his head, to see the woman in the fatigues sitting on a nearby bench. Her pale green eyes were as cold as a winter's night, set in a thin, drawn face. Painstakingly, Zhu Irzh reconstructed what had happened and said, surprising himself, "Fair enough."

"Seneschal, what came over you?" Ma pleaded. Painfully, Zhu Irzh hauled himself to a sitting position and leaned back against the white plastic wall of the cell. It was some kind of mobile arrest unit; he'd seen them before. The woman's hand stirred in her lap. He could see the glint of the gun.

"Good question," said Zhu Irzh.

"And the answer is?" The woman's voice was as arctic as her gaze.

"I have absolutely not the faintest idea. One minute I was fine, the next—I was freaking out. I'm as amazed as you are. I had no desire whatsoever to kill Paravang Roche. He might be a pain in the ass, but if I attempted to murder everyone in a similar position, I'd have no colleagues left."

"You're a demon."

"I might be a demon, madam, but I'm not a maniac. I don't slay people at random, I'll have you know. Killing people requires finesse, it requires style—you can't just leap on someone and start trying to butcher them."

"What, like you just did?"

The woman's voice was a razor across his senses. Zhu Irzh closed his eyes, to see if that made the pounding in his head any easier to bear. It did not. He murmured, "And you would be?" He wanted to hear her say it, though he already had a fair idea what the answer would be.

"Colonel Ei. I'm in charge of security at Paugeng Mining. And Paugeng Mining owns the site on which there is one slaughtered body, and damn nearly another."

"Is Paravang all right?" Zhu Irzh asked, not really caring, but feeling he should ask anyway.

"He'll live. He's clawed and shaken, but he'll be okay. He's had the relevant biotic shots, apparently, so you're unlikely to have infected him with anything." Colonel Ei stood and crossed the cell with a long, lithe stride. She leaned over the startled demon, gazing down into his face. He could smell soap on her skin, as though she'd scrubbed at it. She took the demon's chin in her hand and gave a death's head smile that, to Zhu Irzh's horror, made his skin prickle.

"I've placed you under arrest."

"You can't do that. I'm an officer. I—"

"I don't care which department you're with. You're on Paugeng territory now. You're subject to our regulations." She gestured toward someone unseen and the engine of the arrest vehicle roared into life. "I'm taking you to the nearest secure unit."

"Wait a moment," Ma said. "You can't just arrest another officer, there are procedures, and—" But the woman turned and strode through the door into the driver's cubicle, closing it behind her with menacing care. Ma exhaled a long breath and rolled an anxious eye in the demon's direction.

"What now?"

"I think," said Zhu Irzh, pulling what remained of his fragmented dignity about him, "we're going to have to do what she tells us."

FOURTEEN

When Robin woke, it was morning, with the warm sunlight of the port falling across the floor. She felt perfectly well. Her cough had gone and so had the fever. She got out of bed and looked through the door. She met the enquiring gaze of a nurse, typing reports at a desk.

"There you are!" the woman said inexplicably. "I'll call Madam Tserai."

Robin caught a glimpse of her face in the mirror on the back of the door before she went back to the bed, and wished she hadn't. It was sallow and pinched, smudged with the remains of her fever. Her eyes were bloodshot. She looked remarkably hung over. Jhai, on the other hand, was positively glowing with health, in a simple dark green sari and slippers.

"Robin, you're better," she said, with a parody of concern. Then she sat down on the bed and started to laugh. There was a grim note in it that did not augur well.

Robin waited to be told what was so funny. At last she said, "What's the matter with me?"

"Nothing. Not anymore. What was it, Robin, were you trying to be hip, or what?"

"What?"

"Whatever did you take that shit for?"

"I'm sorry," Robin said. "I'm not following this at all."

"Well, you don't give yourself tuberculosis for no reason."

Robin thought of the garbage bags rotting in the summer alleys, disease running through the city, changing, mutating…

"I've got *tuberculosis*?"

"Not exactly. We couldn't work out what it was at first, then Saira got hold of the hallmarks. Anyway, we found some of these in your bag…" Jhai opened her hand and the flat, white culprit lay on her palm.

"What, those? They're our headache tablets!"

Jhai looked at her narrowly.

"Light begins to dawn, Robin. This isn't a headache pill. This is something you take to give yourself the non-fatal, no-long-term symptoms of the more romantic set of illnesses. Like TB, and like anorexia, and Shenan fever, and AIDS."

"*What!*" Robin said again.

"They're called Geneva pills, after the old conventions over chemical warfare. People take them because it's fashionable in certain more decadent circles of society to look beautifully wasted. So you get the symptoms, for a short time, but you don't actually have the disease. There's no need for a cure, because you're not really ill. You just feel and look like death, at whim, which is a prerogative of the very rich. When you get tired of it, you stop taking them."

"But I was coughing blood and everything!"

"Yeah, they're an effective little number. Minor hemorrhage. I begin to perceive that this was not a matter of choice, Robin, which I should have guessed because they're also very expensive. But then, Deveth Sardai is an heiress, isn't she, wherever she's got to?"

A heavily ironic use of the present tense, Robin thought. The skin along her spine crawled. "Deveth didn't give them to me. I got them from her mother. When I went to see her, I wasn't feeling too goo—"

"Deveth's mother has that effect on a lot of people."

"—and so I raided her bathroom cabinet. They were in a Paugeng bottle. I thought they were para-codeine."

"She probably didn't want the old man to know," Jhai mused. She fixed Robin with a gimlet eye. "Anyway, you're all right now. For the time being."

Desperately, Robin explained to Jhai that the experiment's hands had been bound, that she had not aided his escape. Her employer proved noncommittal. Eventually Robin nerved herself to ask Jhai if she would be fired.

"I'm sure we'll work something out, Robin," Jhai said ambivalently, and then her wrist phone hummed, mercifully distracting her attention away from Robin. Jhai read the text message scrolling on the tiny screen, and Robin saw her face tighten with displeasure.

"God, it's going to be one of those days," she muttered. She gave Robin a cold glance. "I've got to go. We'll discuss this later." She left. The nurse came in soon after and gave Robin a sedative; before she had time to think, she was asleep once more.

Later, awake, Robin considered facts and tried to stifle panic. She would lose her job. They had Deveth's dead body concealed in the morgue room (and something far away within her wailed at that thought) and she was sure she had been caught on the monitor. The experiment had gone missing; a dangerous, angry demon at large in the city who had legitimate grounds for hunting her down. She was going to get out of here *now*.

She dressed with haste, fumbling into her clothes, and stood waiting until she heard the nurse go into the adjoining room. There were two technicians in the elevator, neither of whom she knew. Both of them ignored her. Unobtrusively, Robin made a long detour through the palms in the atrium and as soon as she was clear of the entrance bolted into the warren streets of Ghenret. She had no clear idea where to go. She could not go home, nor to her mother's, and there was nowhere else. She wandered through the dusty back streets, feeling eyes on her spine, eyes everywhere as far as the downtown stop. By noon Robin had crossed Ghenret and the canal district, and was into Shaopeng, merging with the lunchtime crowds and losing herself in the malls and markets near the station. She stayed there all afternoon, pretending to shop and lingering in teahouses. She had gone to the bank, and drawn out as much cash as she could from the autoteller, but she did not like to use her card in case Paugeng had put a trace on it. Robin, in times of stress, operated according to an instinctive sense of survival, which so far had not failed her. She told herself this now: *Remember when you stayed in that bar all night until the man at the opposite table, the one who'd tried to pick you up, had left with another woman?* His date had later been found floating in the Taitai canal. *Remember when you decided not to take the ferry, or walk down that dark alley, or talk to that person?* All those times, she realized, had been a rehearsal for this one. She moved among the crowds, inconspicuous, at last coming out into Shaopeng as the last green light of the afternoon fell in the strip of sky above her.

As the evening wore on, she bought a takeout and then made her way to the silent warehouses at the back of Shaopeng. You could lose yourself in here forever, if you were lucky: hidden among the little, private go-downs, the maze of back alleys. Robin did not know where she was going, only that as she walked she realized that she was becoming more herself. Every moment that she had lived, since childhood, she had been striving for something else: to better herself, earn money and security. She had molded her personality to make sure that she achieved these things, and now she looked back on the person she had been with a kind of wonder. Robin with the wealthy girlfriend, who only once had dared to criticize and say what she felt. Robin the loyal employee, who had acquiesced in someone else's torment, administered it, lessened it in only little ways. Conscience was something that you had to be able to afford, and she had never been able to do that, until now. *If I die tonight,* Robin thought, *at least I've been able to admit that I was wrong, and I did one good thing. I let Mhara go.* Even if he was a demon. Her animal was dancing in front of her, Robin saw without surprise. She followed where it led.

FIFTEEN

Lights blazed from Paugeng, the whole place lit up like fireworks, lights exploding out across Ghenret and transforming the harbor into a puddle of flame. Jhai Tserai, just returned from Beijing, was on dyamentex to help her think, and it was making her grind her teeth, a sure sign that she'd got the dosage wrong. This annoyed her almost more than everything else. She'd invented it, after bloody all, and now she had given herself some ham-fisted quantity of the stuff. So, she thought, dragging her unruly thoughts back to the central problem. The control had escaped and now so had Robin Yuan, basically because Ei was too stupid to keep a hold on either of them. She did not blame Robin for the Geneva pills or the control's flight, nor for her running from Paugeng, which had been an intelligent move. Jhai recognized the hand of Hell in this somewhere, the characteristic sulphurous reek. She was determined not to have to be rescued by Heaven at the last minute, however, no Faustus she. She wouldn't rat her co-conspirators out. She would not deal, no matter what her contacts in Hell demanded.

The dyamentex stopped her from feeling the possible failure of her plans too deeply, but she knew it would hurt when the dosage wore off. She had instructed Ei to find the control and bring him back here; there was no need to do anything else just yet. They were supposed to find Robin, too, but she had not returned to her apartment, understandably. Tserai thought that she might head for Deveth's old place. She was having that watched as well.

"We will see," Jhai said to herself, and started grinding her teeth again. "We will see."

The link rang and Jhai switched it on to find Ei's grim visage staring back at her. "Colonel?"

"I think you should come downstairs, Madam," Ei said. "We've had to take the detective into custody."

"What?"

So Ei explained, and with growing interest, Jhai listened.

SIXTEEN

Apart from his arrest, the last thing Zhu Irzh remembered with any clarity was standing at the edge of the site. Then Roche had turned on him in a fury, and that was the last thing that was clear. He retained a confused impression of the man beneath him on the ground, his face bloody and contorted with rage and fright, and after that there was only blackness and silence. His arm stung, and his head felt thick and heavy. Ei must have drugged him when she bundled him out of the transport vehicle. Experimentally, he tried to move, and discovered that his limbs were restrained. His head seemed to be held in some kind of brace, and a strap passed underneath his chin and between his teeth, cutting into the sides of his mouth. They had muzzled him.

"He's moving," someone said, above him.

"Make sure he's still tied, for God's sake," a second person—Ei?—replied. "I don't want him breaking out in here."

Zhu Irzh tried to shake his head, to reassure them that the episode was over, but this had the result of a tighter pull on the gag. They seemed to be passing along a corridor: there were a series of lights that illuminated a high, narrow strip of ceiling. He reached out and lightly touched the mind of the man at the back: a slow, stupid brain. It was like touching something stuffed with flock. The one at the front was a different proposition. He could see the back of a blonde head and the mind within was quick and subtle, as though he tried to catch an eel. That was Ei, then. The demon lay still and let himself be carried. He heard the hum of a door, and then was taken through into somewhere that smelled of water, rank and saline. They lowered the stretcher to the floor and moved away. The door closed again, and he heard a series of clicks. The bonds removed themselves from his wrists and ankles, drawing back into the edges of the stretcher. The gag remained. He lay still for a moment, flexing toes and fingers until the circulation returned, and then he stood up.

He was in a small, curved cell, the shape of a comma. He could feel the spit and crackle of warding spells, but not, he thought, terribly strong ones. Zhu Irzh grinned to himself. He loved being underestimated. In the bulge of the comma was a plexiglass opening, beyond which his captors stood, gaping at him like people in front of an aquarium. Ei rapped on the glass. "Can you hear me?"

"Yes."

"Good. I want you to be aware of a number of things, demon. Firstly, you're in Paugeng's prison unit. Secondly, you're being held for unprovoked assault, which carries an extensive sentence under local corporate law: three years, according to city statute. No remission, and no diminution. Thirdly, your employer has been notified and will be obliged to pay for your board. If they refuse, the money must be repaid within thirty days of leaving this building, otherwise you're back inside. It's not very fair, but you should have thought of that when you attacked Dowser Roche."

"Have you spoken with Jhai Tserai?"

"*Madam* Tserai's gone to Beijing, on business."

"When will she be back?"

"I don't know. That's up to her," Ei said primly.

"I see," Zhu Irzh remarked. He sat down on the molded bench that extended from the wall. His new position had not yet sunk in; the remains of the trank still fumed within his brain. With an effort, he tried to get a grasp on the situation, but he was starting to fade and soon, they were all gone again.

蛇警探

Somewhere in the recesses of imagination, Zhu Irzh was distantly aware that he dreamed. He was floating deep in the airless, starry depths of the Sea of Night. Globes hung close by, like glowing fruit. Zhu Irzh thought they might be worlds. Warmth sang through his veins with the heat of a sun; its grip took him with a force beyond orgasm and he gasped. It punched him through the membrane between death and life, Heaven and Hell. He could feel all the worlds at once. A great red eye, many times his own height, gazed at him for a moment and then the crack through which it glanced closed up. The sound of his own blood beat in his skull like a drum. All was silence for a moment, then a wave was upon him. He stood surrounded by it, like a man on an island, and despite the roaring in his ears he heard the tinny clatter of metal. Looking down, he saw that the coins of the *I Ching* lay at his feet, scattered across a web of light. It was curiously familiar; bending down, he saw that it was a map of the meridians of the city, as faint and fragile as one of the skeins of silk that the spiders draped across the hibiscus hedges.

Then the vast rushing tide was gone. The demon turned. Out of the shadows a speckled, doglike creature padded, and looked at him with human eyes. The beast opened its mouth and exhaled a great sour breath of rotten meat.

"Look what I have become," it said.

"What are you?" the demon asked. "What were you?" And the beast sighed.

"Only a human woman, but I wanted more. I risked everything," the beast said, with a laugh like a hiss. "And I lost everything. I should be in Hell, but instead I am here, between all the worlds that are."

Zhu Irzh remembered a crack, opening between the worlds, and a crimson eye, watching. Memory made him shiver and Zhu Irzh, a demon after all, did not like this added humiliation. He crouched beside the beast and said, "What is happening, to this world and Hell? Can you tell me? Why should you be in Hell? What is this risk that you took?"

The beast gave its long lipless smile.

"Someone is gambling for high stakes. As high as Heaven itself. I was told that my help would buy that prize for Hellkind, the greatest prize of all. So that all the worlds would become one world, beneath the thrall of Hell. I was told that my power would be limitless. Instead, they killed me once my role was over."

"Someone. Who?"

The beast said, "The goddess Senditreya. She who is the patron of dowsers. She has fallen, in Heaven. She is no longer one of the great ones. She wants her rightful place back again, even if it involves the betrayal of her world to Hell. And she has human help."

"Who?" the demon said again, pressing.

"Myself, when I lived. Jhai Tserai, who lives now, but for how much longer? Tserai lied to me. She told me I was at her own right hand, that I would rule Earth alongside the demon and herself. She told me that together we would open a gate between the worlds and so we did, but the price was my life and my soul. Now she and Senditreya plot while I walk the waste between life and death. This was not," the beast added pathetically, shaking its brindled coat, "what I had planned." It glanced uneasily over its shoulder, as if something might be listening. "You can save the city, if you choose, demon. You who have less allegiance to it than any human." It grinned, beginning to dissolve and coil into the air.

Zhu Irzh stepped hastily back and as he did so, he woke up. He was once more confined in the cell. His head beat like a giant, unnatural drum and his mouth tasted of ancient socks. He had been given answers, but were they even real, or simply the product of a monumental hangover? Well, Zhu Irzh thought grimly, there was only one way to find out.

The cell was dim and translucent, almost ghostly. He raised a hand, and summoned his strength in order to cast a spell. He was by no means sure that he would succeed, but he was damned if he was going to be confined here indefinitely. He'd had enough of being at the mercy of involuntary whims; it was time to take control. Taking a deep breath, he pressed the plexiglass wall and released the spell. The spells that had warded him gave way and then the wall itself shattered, soundless and slow. The demon stepped through. Time slowed in the spell's wake. There was a man at Zhu Irzh's shoulder, his mouth opening and closing in underwater languor, and as the black muzzle of the gun came up the demon swatted the man casually aside and strode through into the hallway. Voices whispered through the air. He could detect the familiar iron smell of blood, and it pulled him toward it, faster and faster until he was running down the corridor. Shadows streamed past him. Two carved double doors stood before him; he flicked them open and stepped through. Abruptly, the voices stopped.

蛇警探

As the demon stepped through the door, the guns came up to greet him. Time glided to its normal speed as the spell faded. Zhu Irzh did not raise his hands but stood watching the security detail as they looked nervously to their employer for guidance. Jhai Tserai was standing behind by a desk, mouth open. It was the first time, the demon thought, that he had seen her genuinely surprised. An interesting combination of expressions crossed her face: momentary fear, supplanted by confusion, and, unless he was greatly mistaken, a trace of guilt.

"How did you get out?" Jhai said.

Zhu Irzh shrugged. "I walked through the window."

"The—? Oh, the plexiglass. You're not supposed to be able to break that," she said. She bit her lip in consternation. She suddenly looked about ten years old. "We'll have to get that mended," she added.

"In time for the next incumbent?" the demon suggested blandly.

"I'm not going to waste a perfectly good cell," Jhai told him, then glanced at the ring of guns as if for the first time. "Oh, put those away," she told the security detail impatiently. "You won't need those."

A brave gesture, Zhu Irzh thought, inviting trust, but he saw that her right hand remained below the level of the desk. Jhai was looking at him curiously. "I gather you had an—episode—of some kind?" She was giving him a chance to explain himself, which was, Zhu Irzh supposed, more than he deserved. He paused for a moment, considering. He could tell Jhai the truth: that it had been involuntary, atypical, inexplicable. But it sounded like a weak excuse, and perhaps it would not hurt for her to see him as a little dangerous. At the moment, she had him at a distinct disadvantage. He was a demon, after all, and Jhai was nothing more than a human girl. Time to regain some ground, Zhu Irzh thought.

"I'm afraid I lost my temper," he said coolly. "I really must apologize. Inexcusable, but my kind are often like that. How is the unfortunate Mr Roche?"

"He'll live. He's not badly hurt. But I want your assurance that it won't happen again." She gave him a stern look, like a schoolteacher faced with a recalcitrant child. It was not how Zhu Irzh had expected to be treated. Jhai blinked innocently under his stare. He thought: *What have you been up to, Jhai Tserai? What are you planning to do? If what the beast had told him was true…* Everything seemed to lead back to Jhai and Paugeng. Zhu Irzh walked across the room, and as if the guards were not even there, he put a gentle hand to her cheek. She stared up at him, wide-eyed. The demon smiled.

"Only if you come and see me," he murmured. "To talk things through." And after a moment, Jhai nodded.

"I'll ask Ei to take you home."

Colonel Ei was clearly unhappy with this state of affairs. With her gun drawn, she accompanied Zhu Irzh to a vehicle waiting in a compound behind the building, keeping a narrow gaze upon him all the way. He could feel that gaze boring a hole between his shoulder blades, as though Ei had stabbed him with an icicle. He supposed that he could not blame her. Ei motioned to the vehicle, a long, black limousine, with the gun.

"Get in."

"Thank you," the demon said politely. He felt that he ought to make up for his earlier lapse. Ei's face became even more pinched and sour, like a collapsing lemon.

"And shut up."

Zhu Irzh started to say something, but nodded instead. He climbed into the vehicle and Ei got in behind, still with the gun pointed unwaveringly at the demon's throat. She knew where to strike, then. And he was also sure that Ei felt herself to be good enough not to miss. The limo set off through the Paugeng compound and out into the port area. Zhu Irzh studied the vehicle with interest: it was certainly a fine car. He was tempted to play with the gadgets on display, but thought better of it.

There was a carton on the seat next to the driver, filled with sticky pink glop. Zhu Irzh tried not to concentrate on the insipid odor of warm shrimp congee that filled the vehicle. Zhu Irzh's stomach contracted in longing. The muzzle of Ei's automatic remained pointed at Zhu Irzh's throat. Ei watched him with an impassive lizard's gaze, and Zhu Irzh saw her fingers tighten rhythmically against the butt of the gun.

"We're nearly at your home," Ei said. "Don't think that I don't know already where you live. I know everything about you, demon. I have made it my business. I'll be watching you."

"Madam," Zhu Irzh informed her as the limo slowed, "I wouldn't doubt it for a second." He suspected that Tserai had chastised her, but why? Why have him arrested in the first place, then let him go? Because Tserai knew that she couldn't hold him? Or was there some other reason. Zhu Irzh was getting the distinct impression that Ei had acted on her own initiative, and that she was somehow not quite in the loop.

The door snapped open, releasing Zhu Irzh into the day. He decided that it would give Ei too much satisfaction if he watched the limo slide away, and so he turned his back on it and went into the local chophouse. Congee porridge, he thought, would do nicely for breakfast. Perhaps with a side dish of blood.

SEVENTEEN

The hospital wing had fixed Paravang's ribs and bound up the scores in his flesh under a protective coating of synthetic skin. They kept him unconscious for a day or so, to let him mend, and woke him up on the following day. He was sore, but his ribs had healed and his worst afflictions were a severe itching and an unpleasant harsh taste in his mouth, soon removed by several cups of tea.

"You can go home now," the nurse said. He smiled brightly at Paravang, who grunted in reply. They had sent round a car, and so he traveled back to Bharichay in comparative splendor. Once he was back in the safety of his small flat, he breathed a sigh of relief. Perhaps things would quiet down now. He spent a peaceful couple of days or so, reading and practicing Hsing-I to loosen his aching muscles. Paravang's neighbor fed him throughout his indisposition, producing bowls of chicken breast soup and noodles on the hour. Paravang grinned grimly at the thought. She probably wanted something.

He had just returned from one of his exercise sessions in the local park when the doorphone rang. Paravang got stiffly to his feet to answer.

"Who is it?"

"Jhai Tserai," purred the phone. He was so startled that he pressed the button to admit her.

"Mr Roche," she said, once inside, and her voice held that low note of concern which Paravang so much distrusted. "I'm so *terribly* sorry."

She sat down in his armchair and proceeded to explain a number of things. Everyone knew how much stress he was under, what with the temporary removal of his license, and it was completely understandable that he had reacted negatively to what he perceived as provocation. She'd done that herself on occasion, she confessed, it was very natural. The demon detective, too, was under a great deal of pressure, a long way from home and so on, and although his attack on Paravang was unpardonable, she hoped that Roche would manage to rise above it. A complaint had been made to the police department. Paravang was still a part of Paugeng—they didn't forget old employees, even under currently embarrassing circumstances—and Tserai wanted to recompense Paravang for his dreadful ordeal and offered him: three days' worth of trauma counseling, which he could select as he chose, a bonus for his sterling work over the past six months and, of course, the sickness pay he would normally be charged would be waived.

Paravang Roche, his voice trembling, told her how grateful he was to have worked for such a caring company. He accepted her generous offer and remarked that his training in various spiritual disciplines had given him the inner serenity to discount what the world would regard as a painful episode. His former employer patted his hand.

When she had left, Paravang fell back against the couch and sent a fervent prayer to Senditreya that Jhai Tserai would suffer a prolonged, painful and eventually fatal accident before the year was out, accompanied in her death throes by Seneschal Zhu Irzh. He had expected the attempt to buy him off, and had enough native cunning to anticipate what might happen if he made a fuss. The last site manager for Paugeng had been a man with little or no sense of personal danger, some sort of genetic mutation, Paravang supposed, and had not only taken Tserai to task over medical related staff problems once, but several times. The man had an extensive opportunity to explore such difficulties, now, having come down with an unusual kidney disease after a visit to Tevereya. There had been considerable speculation as to its cause, never satisfactorily resolved. Fortunately, Paugeng looked after its own, and had provided medical treatment at a discount rate.

So Paravang determined to take what was offered and make other arrangements to regain inner serenity. He made more tea, and after he had drunk this he took the downtown to Air Street and headed for Senditreya's temple, where he demanded to see the priest-broker and spent an hour pouring out his woes. The broker opened his eyes wide at the sight of the ragged scratches that were healing slowly underneath the synth skin and was suitably and gratifyingly horrified. Paravang could not resist milking this unfamiliar sympathy.

"Unprovoked!" he told the broker. "First, the foul creature revokes my *feng shui* license. Then he forces me to work for him, without pay, and in the course of my duties—during which he never stopped arguing—he attacked me. Why? It must be some kind of curse. An enemy has conjured him from Hell to persecute me."

The broker nodded, sagely. "I know the being," he had told Roche. "I have made enquiries. He is attached to the police department—an unorthodox but legitimate arrangement. Putting an end to his persecution of you will undoubtedly attract attention."

"What are you saying? I thought you wanted to help me?"

"That is correct. My sympathy for your plight is as bottomless as the pits of Hell itself. I am not suggesting that there is nothing that can be done. Merely that it will not be cheap. Legal fees can eat money like candy."

Paravang shot the broker an incredulous glance. "Who said anything about legal fees?"

The broker favored Paravang Roche in turn with a lengthy and considering look.

"Then there is a man…" he began.

The broker had set it all up for Roche, deducting a token payment from the practitioner. The bulk would be paid once the exorcist had carried out his work. Then they had gone together into the temple and Paravang had gazed with bitterness at his fickle, beaming goddess. Senditreya's bovine face betrayed nothing. Useless to rely on such an apathetic deity. He was glad that he'd had the wit to turn to human help.

"Will it not be too soon? Look obvious?" he had asked the broker.

"Not if it is carefully done. Leave it to me."

Paravang caught the tram back to his neighborhood: the row of crumbling tenements that lined the suburban hills. He was tired and angry, and he was not pleased to find a neighbor, an elderly, vituperative woman, waiting outside his apartment. Not wishing to lose face, however, Paravang forced himself to be polite.

"Good evening," he said with a small, stiff bow.

"Citizen Roche! You have to do something about it!" the old lady said without preamble.

"What?" asked Paravang, bewildered.

"The Third Commercial Bank! What else?" his neighbor said. Paravang listened as patiently as he could while she explained at length and volume the wickedness of the new Third Commercial Bank for pointing their sharp and nasty roof right at her kitchen window.

"Spoils my dinner!" she shrilled. "Brings bad luck!"

This was the problem with being a dowser, Paravang reflected. Everyone expected you to be able to solve their problems for them, especially when some organization decided to get the drop on their neighbors by manipulating the energies that lay beneath the city and altering the surrounding *feng shui*. The neighbor was quite right. Throughout Kuen, Rama and Wuan Chih, a *ch'i* war had snaked across the city. The whole thing had started in Shaopeng, where the Eregeng Trade House had erected its monstrous new headquarters: capped by a devilish pagoda roof flaring out in all directions, but directed principally at the northeast. Everyone directly beneath its baleful influence had called in the builders—at night, so as not to lose business—and had their premises tweaked and tucked to accommodate the energy flow of beneficent *ch'i* and malignant *sha*. The battle lines had shot from Shaopeng and radiated east, all the way to Paravang's neighbor's kitchen ten miles distant.

In the days—so sadly recent—when he had still possessed a dowsing license, Paravang would simply have recommended some lesser practitioner. Fixing his neighbor's *feng shui* would not have been worth his while, but now, he was forced to take what little he could get. He accepted the meager dollars that the neighbor shoved grudgingly into his hand, and, grinding his teeth, fixed her culinary trauma with a set of judiciously positioned *bagua* mirrors to halt and deflect the unlucky energy.

Now, he stood in his little kitchen, angling more octagonal mirrors to deflect the malevolent *sha* lines that were still running off from the Eregeng Trade House. He had hung red tassels around the windows and over the door and the entrance to the disposal chute, and set up a complex array of *bagua* mirrors. Gradually the sense of oppression had begun to lift, but he could still feel it, hanging heavy and ominous, like a storm cloud just beyond the horizon.

Eventually the mirrors were arranged to his satisfaction, and Paravang turned his attention to his dinner. He shredded ginger and spring onion, pounded it with the garlic that he grew in pots on the windowsill, and chopped Chinese leaf, bean sprouts and shrimps. He doused the mixture in soy, rice vinegar and sesame oil and set to making neat little packages with the won ton wrappers made by his neighbor. Arranging the won ton in the bottom of the steamer, he put the water on to boil. The lights were beginning to come on across the district, and Paravang's neighbors were starting to straggle home. Paravang looked out the window, filled with sudden doubt. Seedy though it undoubtedly was, he liked living here. In the evening he could go down to the small, dark bar at the end of the street, the one that always had washing hanging outside, and sit with his cronies. They were not practitioners. *Feng shui* men tended to keep aloof from one another, fearing rivalry. These were local businesspeople who respected him. Once a week he took the tram out to Bharulay to see his elderly father, and they went for long, silent walks along the canal. His mother, the shrill, quarrelsome Mrs Roche, had long since passed into one of the more pleasant neighborhoods of Hell, if that wasn't a contradiction in terms. She sometimes telephoned, a tinny, distant voice in her son's ear, demanding to know why he was still unwed. Since he was now fifty, he thought that she'd have given up hope long before now, but not so. She had always been a most determined woman. Apart from this maternal irritant, his life had been good enough until the arrival of the demonic intruder and the revoking of his license. But now… had he really done the right thing in hiring an—an exorcist? He thought of the demon's blank, menacing visage, and the terrible ripping claws. What if the exorcist—Paravang shied away from the term "assassin"—messed things up? What if Zhu Irzh came after him again? He needed a fallback plan, Paravang decided, staring sightlessly out over the lights of the city. He needed serious help.

EIGHTEEN

The world had become a dream to Robin, a circus of wonders, and nothing could touch her. She had followed the beast along the turning alleys of Shaopeng and Ghenret until they had come out into a place that she recognized. They stood in a wide square, but the towering compartments made it seem as though Robin and the animal stood at the bottom of a well. At one side an oblong of night sky was visible, above the much lower roof of the Battery Road teahouse, and Robin had gasped. She had never seen such stars, such brightness. They fell in a great burning coil over the teahouse roof and she recognized none of them.

At the center of the square stood a stretch of trees, as though a wood grew in the middle of the buildings. Robin knew, however, that this patch of acacia and thousand-flower concealed the Shaopeng cemetery. The cemetery boundaries seemed to be much more extensive than she remembered, and this made perfect sense to Robin. It was night, after all, and she had only ever visited in the day. All at once she understood what was happening, here so close to the eve of the Day of the Dead. The world was dreaming, the city re-creating itself in sleep, and changing itself to its other form, the form of its counterpart in Hell.

"Isn't that right?" she said aloud to her companion.

And it replied, "What do you think, Robin? Tell me what you see."

"I can see the temple roof," Robin said obediently, "and the trees, and look, they're coming into flower." She could see the starry white blossoms of the thousand-flower swell out from their buds and burst outward the petals curling like a ghost's soft hand, expanding to propel pollen in a dusty shower into the night air. A great breath of sweetness came from them, engulfing Robin and the animal in its perfume. The petals fell in a pale shower to the earth and the process began again, petals budding, shaking out and falling, until the ground beneath the trees was covered in a snowdrift of flowers.

"Perhaps we should go in," the animal told Robin, murmuring, and when she looked at it, it was no longer a beast, somehow, but something else, a form of darkness, strangely vivid yet undefined. Robin nodded, and stepped through the ornamental gate of the cemetery. The petals were still falling, but more slowly now, and the air was filled with sweetness. The cemetery was full of light, lamps and votive candles set upon the tombs, beckoning through the scented dark. Robin could see the little temple at the center of the cemetery, and its curving roof seemed to hold the stars. Something shot over the temple roof in a burst of light and buried itself alarmingly close to Robin's feet. A firecracker? Robin's companion bent and plucked it from the ground, digging with animal swiftness in the damp earth. Steam rose from its indistinct fingers. Robin felt something placed in her hand. She looked down. It was a small piece of metal, glossy as though wet, and still warm. She felt her companion smile. Teeth glittered in the half-light.

"Heaven's falling, Robin," it said, and the voice was now thin and old. Robin put the meteorite in her pocket.

"Are we going to the temple?"

"It's not a temple. It's an exchange." And Robin thought, *How stupid of me.* It was indeed a money-changing kiosk, with the little metal slot in its side through which a slip of paper was expelled after the completion of the transaction. Together, they walked to the exchange. Someone knocked on the door, from within; a ritual three times.

"Yes?" Robin's companion said.

"May I come out?" a very small voice asked. The animal looked at Robin, and smiled.

"Up to you, Robin."

Robin opened her mouth to call it forth, but she surprised herself. She heard her own voice from somewhere, high and frightened.

"No," she said, "No, you may not!" and her companion's smile vanished.

"Ask him to come *out,* Robin," it said. It sounded sweet, as sweet as the petals of the thousand-flower that now blew around them, a white whirling cloud to settle in Robin's hair. Robin felt a hand caress her spine, running lightly down the vertebrae, leaving a trail of warmth behind it.

"Ask, Robin, ask," and it was the experiment's voice murmuring in her ear, gentle, whispering. Do this for me, Robin...

"No, no!" Robin shouted, and broke away, running blindly through the graveyard. She caught her foot and fell, landing across a granite barrier. She felt a hot burst of pain shoot through her knee and something fiery licked her cheek. She thought that she had fallen against one of the votive lights, but then she felt it again and knew it for the animal's tongue, sliding affectionately across her face. It stung and she cried out.

"Get up, Robin," the creature said. Robin clambered to her feet and stumbled against the tilted stone, half-falling. She had broken her knee, she thought. The sensation seared through her, a pulsing lump of pain. Someone put their arm around her waist, and it was longer than a human arm, and stronger. She looked up fearfully. Her companion's voice rasped in her ear like a tongue.

"*Ask,* Robin," and then suddenly it dropped her and sprang away through the snowy petals, a heavy, bolting form, four-legged. In the little exchange, someone started to weep, softly at first, and then louder, until it was a voice that boomed out across the graveyard, filling the sky and bringing down a hail of stars, hissing from the heavens into the damp soil of the cemetery. Robin cowered by the grave marker, her arms bent ineffectually over her head, pain throbbing in her knee. She felt hands beneath her and then someone lifted her up.

"No more," she cried, and struck out. A hand caught her wrist and held it.

"No more," someone agreed, and she relaxed. She was hurried from the cemetery, half-lifted to help her limping gait. Behind them, the green shoots of thousand-flower began to lift through the soil, in each place where a star had fallen.

NINETEEN

After a long and difficult conversation with Captain Sung, Zhu Irzh had been given a couple of days off work. Long and difficult conversations with the captain were becoming a habit, he thought resentfully. Next morning, therefore, he locked up the houseboat and walked across to Haitan market. He needed provisions, after his time away from home, and he also wanted to consider Jhai Tserai. He had to admit that she was highly entertaining, whatever demonic bargains she might have been engaged in. He grinned to himself, causing the few fellow shoppers who could see him to shuffle nervously or find something unexpectedly fascinating on the fish counter at the opposite end of the row. Zhu Irzh didn't notice; he was too busy thinking about Jhai. His longing for her was, he reluctantly conceded, more than desire; it was opportunity.

Even if people could see him, they tended to find him sinister; including the not very alluring women who hung around the Ghenret go-downs and the slightly more attractive boys in Shaopeng tram station. If he allowed himself to become closer to Jhai, there might be an opportunity to find out more about whatever she had been doing. This, he decided, was a reasonable plan. Sung might have sidelined him in the course of the investigation, but that altered nothing. He was hot on the trail, he told himself. He was *dedicated* to upholding the right of the law. He forced away the knowledge that it was nothing more than an excuse.

The market was crowded today. Zhu Irzh was obliged to queue for everything, and submitted to being elbowed in the ribs by fierce elderly ladies. At last he came to his final purchases. He had bought enough for two or three days, a diet that emphasized meat, as befitted someone with Zhu Irzh's carnivorous teeth. The meat here always tasted slightly strange, not horrible, but a bit flat. He had seen cattle in the city, roaming through the vacant lots

78

like huge, tethered shadows, and had been wary of them until Ma reminded him that they were herbivores. In Hell, nothing was a herbivore.

Zhu Irzh reached the boat and fumbled the round key out of his pocket. Inside, the boat was dim and stuffy. The badger-teakettle sat on its shelf, in its inanimate form. Zhu Irzh watched it warily for a moment, trying to work out whether it had moved since the morning. It seemed to have given up being a badger, at least while he was around. He opened all the windows, arranged the food in the small refrigerator, then swung himself up onto the windowsill to watch the regular Tevereya ferry sailing past, silently across the sunlit bay. The coins of the *I Ching* rattled in his pocket; fishing them out in a sudden whim, he shook, and threw, and threw again. The sunlight flashed up from the water, dazzling him, and for a moment he could not tell whether the light had come from the sea or from the coins that now lay so innocently beneath his hand. It was the configuration of *Hsiao Kuo. The Small Get By.*

Encouraged by this, Zhu Irzh went to the cupboard and found a bottle of Hell's finest brandy, which he had been saving for medicinal purposes. He was feeling a little off-color still, not quite himself. This, he thought, was as medicinal as it got. The liquor seared an icy trail down his throat, bringing a semblance of clarity in its wake.

"What is wrong?" asked a thick voice behind him. It was as though Earth had spoken. Zhu Irzh turned to see the badger-teakettle, Inari's family familiar, standing four-square on the deck.

"I attacked someone today," Zhu Irzh muttered. "For no reason, with no warning, and in an embarrassingly uncontrolled manner. I'm never going to live this down." And what would Chen say? The demon realized with a degree of amazement that he actually cared what a human thought of him. He groped for the bottle and poured another measure.

"You do not know why?" The badger's dark gaze was as opaque as obsidian.

"I haven't the faintest."

"Perhaps you are changing."

"Changing? What do you mean?"

"Those who have visited the lower levels find that their form begins to alter after a while. A demon countenance forms a muzzle, small eyes, thicker blood. Humans change, too, become more bestial."

"I know, but I've come to Earth from Hell. If any changes were to occur, you'd think I'd become more human—oh." Zhu Irzh stopped.

"Is that not what humans do? Demons are cruel, rarefied, cunning. They devise magnificent punishments, vindictive and baroque. Is that not the very essence of Hell? While humans are merely slaves to their instincts. Perhaps your instincts are changing."

"Perhaps," Zhu Irzh said dubiously. It was a possibility, but not one that he really wanted to entertain. He gestured toward the bottle.

"Want some?"

The badger's pointed head shook from side to side.

"I do not take such drinks. Only blood."

Zhu Irzh regarded the creature with a sudden spark of speculation.

"Human blood?"

But the badger did not reply. Change shimmered the air, and Zhu Irzh blinked.

When the demon once more opened his eyes, there was only an old iron teakettle sitting on the deck.

"Suit yourself," Zhu Irzh remarked to the weighty air, and turned disconsolately back to the bottle.

TWENTY

When she got back to the penthouse, Jhai went straight to the bathroom and spent twenty minutes in the jacuzzi, soaking away the day. Then she walked slowly into the dim expanse of her bedroom and stood before the mirror. Her reflection captured her movements, and nothing more, but in the depths of her own gaze, she could see something golden and old. She smiled, a quick grimace, knowing that Zhu Irzh had seen it, too. She could still feel the warmth of his hand on her cheek.

"For fuck's sake," she said aloud, disgusted with herself. She'd realized what Zhu Irzh was as soon as she'd set eyes on him: a combination of things, all intriguing.

A potential enemy: the person who could, if he chose, bring all of her plans crashing down around her.

A possible ally: the person who could, again if he chose, secure those plans and help them become real.

A hunter: uniquely placed to track down the missing experiment that Robin Yuan had so disastrously let slip through Paugeng's fingers. Whatever Zhu Irzh might be, Jhai knew that he would be of use. How stupid Ei had been to capture him and attempt to bluster. Jhai had been furious to discover this on her return from Beijing.

But all those useful things that Zhu Irzh might be had completely gone out the window, now, because… Jhai sat heavily down on the bed and put her head in her hands. How ironic. She knew what the demon must be thinking: she'd used some form of pheromonal glamour, hormone enhancement, on him in a calculated attempt at teasing seduction to throw him off balance. She had done it before, after all; the city was littered with Jhai's conquests, male and female. She'd gained the reputation of South China's most heartless flirt, bringing entire boardrooms to their knees. Literally, in some cases. But boardrooms weren't bedrooms, Jhai reflected bitterly. This time, the glamour with which she'd dazzled Zhu Irzh had not been intentional; he had summoned it forth all by himself, and there was nothing she could do about it.

On the few times when she had allowed relationships to get as far as the actual bedroom, her abilities had deserted her. She'd had to pretend, to avoid the threat of a rumor that she was nothing more than a frigid cock-tease. It was the drug, of course, that held her power, and therefore her sexuality, in check. Without the drug, she could be as uninhibited as she chose, but without the drug, she wouldn't be quite human any longer, either. She knew what her ancestresses had been, long ago in ancient India. They had been *devas*: demon courtesans, wielding enough sexual and sensual power to control emperors. In the Hell that corresponded to Singapore Three, Jhai would be an Imperial whore. Here on Earth, if she gave her powers their full rein, she could have an empire of her own to control. It was illegal for demonkind to live unlicensed on Earth, yet Jhai knew for a fact that there were more than a few magnates who possessed unnatural concubines. But such a role wasn't good enough for Jai. She wanted her own empire; not just to be an adjunct, some kind of supernatural *grande horizontale*… And now that Paugeng was established as one of the principal corporations of Asia—and perhaps, if her plans came to pass, the world—Jhai was about to blow it completely by getting involved with a policeman. *No, she wasn't,* she told herself sternly. Zhu Irzh was dangerous: to Jhai, to Paugeng, to the schemes that she was so carefully nurturing. She would stay well away from Zhu Irzh in the future, if she had any sense.

She got up from the bed and crossed to the wardrobe.

"Open," she murmured, and the doors slid smoothly aside. Her saris hung in a neat, multicolored line along one end of the spacious closet; she preferred them for work. The Indian dress was like a badge, setting her aside from the mainly Chinese personnel. But she had plenty of Western clothes, too, ordered from New York and Paris over the Net. She would not be wanting any of those tonight, Jhai thought. Soon, she would be going back down to the office, and working. Her hand snaked out and plucked a little spangled dress from its perfumed hanger. Thousands of tiny beads rustled as she pulled it over her head. Unbidden, the image of Zhu Irzh sidled into her mind: pale, handsome face alight with amusement, the gilded gaze fixed on her face and leaving no doubt as to what was going through his mind. He was taller than Jhai, too; surrounded by short men, she had reason to appreciate the fact. And he as a demon…she'd heard stories, erotic and disturbing. A policeman, Jhai thought, shaking her head. How in all the worlds did someone like that get to be a *policeman?* He looked as though he should be propping up a couch in some seraglio. Her thoughts drifted away into uncharted territory. She took some trouble over her make-up.

When she had finished, Jhai looked at herself and abandoned all pretence that she had any intention of working. Before she left, she looked in on her mother, dressing for the opera.

"You're dressed very smartly tonight," Opal had replied, without even looking round. How did she do that? It unnerved Jhai.

"I've got a meeting with someone. Anyway, I think it's good for company morale if I dress for the evening." It was a pathetic excuse, an attempt to stave off the lecture which inevitably followed.

"This is foolish! He is a demon, like—well, anyway, not a stupid man, even if he is not on our level, Jhai. He knows what you are doing."

Her daughter took a deep breath. Once again, her mother, who had been nowhere near recent events at Paugeng, had proved that she knew exactly what Jhai was up to. "I know what I'm doing."

"There is nothing there for you—just lust. It is not clever." Opal segued into the wider argument, a hardy perennial these days. "You should find a nice girl and settle down."

"Oh, for God's sake, Mother!"

"You're twenty-nine years old."

"I'm sorry, Opal, who did you say was primitive?"

"I am talking about a political connection."

"I know what you're talking about. You want to fix me up with Aily Pardua. Last year, I seem to recall, it was Beth Murriday from that oil company, and look what happened to that. I'm not going to be a laughingstock just because you start parading every available young woman in town in front of me."

"It's not as though you don't *like* girls…" her mother mused, brutally. "But all the ones you choose seem so…so…"

"Poor?"

"Perhaps not very appropriate. But at least they were female. Not some unhuman gentleman from who knows where."

"One presumes that my father is out there somewhere."

Her mother bridled. "I chose very carefully from the implant clinic. Your grandmother and I went to the cache together, the most selective place. I was twenty-three, a very good age."

"I don't see why it was a better age than any other. I mean, I wasn't in you for long, was I? I was in some test tube!"

Her mother's artfully outlined lips compressed.

"Oh, look, I'm sorry." She put her arms around Opal's shoulders.

"I know." Opal's face became indulgent. "You want to enjoy yourself a little. Well, so did I." She kissed her daughter on the cheek. "Go on. Go and have fun. But be *careful*."

Downstairs, Jhai called for a car, asking for the anonymous black Mercedes coupe, without a driver. She picked up the car on the Paugeng forecourt and took the coast road to the address that Ei had given her. She left the car at the side of the wharf.

The houseboat floated some distance away, and she would have to negotiate a series of pontoons to reach it. Jhai slipped off her heels and stepped gingerly off the wharf. The first pontoon rocked gently beneath her slight weight. The last of the sunlight sparked from the lapping water. The far islands were blocks of twilight shadow. With high heels in hand, Jhai took a deep breath, and clambered across the row of pontoons.

"Zhu Irzh?" she called when she reached the houseboat. There was no reply and she froze, thinking: *the bastard has stood me up.* Then a familiar voice came from below deck.

"Hello?"

"Zhu Irzh? It's Jhai."

There was an unnervingly long pause. "Come down."

When she reached the bottom of the steps she saw that the room was dark. After a moment's adjustment, she saw the demon sitting on the windowsill. She shut the door behind her.

"Turn the light on," he said mildly. He involuntarily ducked his head as the light went on and Jhai saw a dark membrane slide across his eyes and back, like an animal's eyes. Like her own. She went to stand by the window. Beyond, the harbor lay like a field of shadow, sparked with the lights of ships.

"Do you like sitting here?" she asked, and instantly regretted it. What a fatuous thing to say.

"I can watch the ships, sit in the breeze. You can see Lantern Island from here. Come here, I'll show you." Reaching out, he drew her close. Jhai stiffened for a moment, then relaxed against him. It felt alarmingly natural to be so close to him. His skin was smooth and cool, and the silk jacket was soft against her skin. Zhu Irzh bent his head, and kissed her. There was a familiar tightening deep within her; she stepped quickly back.

"Would you like a drink?" the demon asked, after a slightly bewildered pause.

"Yes." Jhai said shortly. She felt as though she'd been hit by a sledgehammer.

"Wine? Brandy?"

"Whatever." She leaned back against the windowsill.

Zhu Irzh came back with a bottle.

"It's brandy. Hell's own. A little rough, perhaps, but it grows on you. Here." He held out a generous measure. *Trying to get me drunk,* Jhai thought, but suddenly it seemed like an excellent idea.

"You look very nice," the demon said admiringly.

"Thanks." She took a large swallow of brandy and choked. Tears streamed down her face, so much for the make-up. She'd look like a panda.

"Are you all right?" Zhu Irzh asked, in some alarm. Jhai leaned against him, mastered the coughing with an effort, then reached up and pulled the demon's head down to kiss him. Zhu Irzh put the bottle on the windowsill and responded with enthusiasm. Then the tension was back, lust jerked into submission by the iron pull of the drug, and Jhai found herself struggling.

"We don't have to if you don't want to," said Zhu Irzh reproachfully.

"Don't we?"

"I mean, I may be from Hell, but I can still behave like a gentleman if the occasion demands it." He looked as though it had cost him quite a lot to say that. Doubt assailed Jhai. She used people so much that she wasn't sure anymore whether she'd know if they were using her: this is the trouble with power, the small voice said in the back of her mind. Zhu Irzh was watching her, his golden gaze shadowed, and it had been a bad idea to drink that brandy, because she wasn't sure what was real and what was not, and she had given him control. She turned away from him and stood looking into the room, and felt his hands take her by the shoulders and run lightly down to her waist, making her shiver. Then he turned her around again and drew her against him.

"What do you want me to do?" he whispered against her throat. "Tell me what you want." *Anything,* she wanted to say, *anything you want,* and shut out the voice inside her head and the insistent wire-taut singing of the drug. "Do you want to go and lie down?" he asked, and she nodded against his shoulder. Zhu Irzh put his arm around her waist and led her to the bed, where he sat beside her.

"What do *you* want?" she asked in a very small voice.

The demon considered this. "Apart from the obvious? I'd like you to enjoy yourself." He kissed her, and she put a hand over his. As she did so she felt the claws slide out from his fingertips. Her hand jerked.

"What's wrong?"

"Zhu Irzh, I'm afraid of you," Jhai said, horrifying herself.

There was the sudden glitter of teeth in the dimness.

"That," said Zhu Irzh softly, "is very wise. Now, will you let me make love to you?"

So she lay back and let him. He was very gentle, taking a lot of time, and eventually she was amazed to find that his hands and his mouth were drowning out the tug of the drug. Lost in desire, she ignored the fact that its control was slipping away until Zhu Irzh rolled over, pulling her with him so that they were both half-sitting. He cupped her breast in one long hand and reached behind her with the other, stroking her back.

"Well, well," the demon said softly. Jhai felt a twinge at the base of her spine, and then something…unrolled. It happened very fast, with a twinge not unlike neuralgia. Jhai and the demon looked down. A tail was coiling around the demon's wrist. It was not like Zhu Irzh's own whip-thin tail. It was sleek, and tiger-striped. Jhai glanced down. Her rib cage was banded with shadows. She opened her mouth and her incisors slid neatly down behind her upper lip.

"I must say," Zhu Irzh remarked, as if commenting on the weather. "This does explain a lot."

"Zhu Irzh—"

"You," said the demon reprovingly, nipping her throat, "are a *very* bad girl."

"Don't patronize me! I didn't mean—"

"I don't suppose you did." Zhu Irzh hissed. His erection slid along her thigh. A swift movement took her onto her back, tail lashing, and then the demon was hard inside her. She'd had no idea that demons would make so much noise, snarling and growling like that, but then Jhai glanced up into Zhu Irzh's abstracted face and realized that it wasn't him, it was her. And that was the last thought she had, for some time.

When it was over, she sat up and looked at him. Zhu Irzh was lying with one arm flung up over his head, staring at the ceiling. She ran her hands down his chest. His breathing began to deepen.

"Why do men always go to sleep?" She could feel his body starting to shake. It was a moment before she realized that he was laughing. He pulled her down beside him and stretched out. She thought he was watching her but his breathing slowed again and she realized that although his eyes were open and reflecting the starlight, he slept. And after a few moments, with her tail entwined with his, so did Jhai.

HSIAO CHU:
THE TAMING POWER
OF THE SMALL

TWENTY-ONE

Robin must have fainted, because she could not remember leaving the cemetery. When at last she regained consciousness, she was lying on something soft that smelled familiar, a warm, reassuring smell, and the bags beneath her were full of something scratchy. She perceived that she was lying on a bag stuffed with hay, and the dusty darkness about her was a cattle shed of some kind. She could see the beasts themselves: horned, matted, with long, ruminative faces.

Someone came through into the stall and the cattle stamped nervously, tapping their hooves against the rough concrete. Someone murmured something. A calm blue gaze shone through the gloom.

"It's you," Robin said. Her victim had come back, free and predatory, and she was aware only of relief.

"I came back," Mhara agreed. The blue eyes were wells in the darkness, the color of the indigo washing powder that spilled across the market stalls.

"What happened to me?" Robin asked. He had bound up her knee, which was stiff and sore.

"I don't know. You were with—people, I think, but the dead. Ghosts." Mhara took her chin in his hand and turned her face to the light from the street that crept in between the slats of the go-down shed.

"Your face is burned. I don't know how it happened."

"It licked me," Robin whispered, remembering. She heaved herself to her elbows and looked at him. "Oh, Mhara," she said, before she could stop herself. "I'm so sorry. For what I did to you."

"I know. It's all right."

"Why did you come back?" she asked in a small voice. "You should kill me, by rights. I tortured you."

"Do you think so? Not as much as you fear, perhaps. You don't know much about me, Robin, the kind of person I am." The predatory hand stroked her hair. "Do you want to rest some more?"

"No… I think we should make a move. Paugeng security will be looking for you. And me." She stood and the bound knee gave way. Mhara caught her arm.

"I'm sorry," Robin whispered. "It really hurts. I think you'd better leave me, Mhara." He gave her a long, contemplative look. She amplified: "I can't walk very far. And we can't take a taxi or a tram."

"Then we will take a boat."

"What?"

"We're at the back of the Shaopeng canal. Once we get on the canal, all we have to do is follow it until we reach—that is, until we find a place where I can return to where I belong."

Robin gritted her teeth. She was determined not to ask him to stay. She remained, nursing her knee, as he vanished. He was gone a long time. Robin was hot and every time she moved a burning ache ran along her shin. The stuffed sacking was making her nose run and her eyes itch. She had never known such a week for being ill. The beasts stamped in their stalls. Mhara was coming back, she thought with an uplift of hope, but they refused to settle down and he did not come into view. One of the cows kicked out, and the sound echoed around the stalls like a hammer blow.

"Robin? Where are you?" a soft, familiar voice said. Robin kept still. She could see it flickering against the wall of the shed, like a shadow, no shape or form, just movement. Then it collapsed back into its normal being, the powerful hindquarters swaying against the sacks. Wise, orange eyes looked at her.

"There you are."

"Go away," Robin cried.

"Oh no," the beast said.

Do not look at it, she thought, *it is not real, it is not there, a spirit,* but she felt her head, suddenly bursting with pressure, turned around to meet its gaze.

"Well," Mhara said softly from the door, "whatever are you?"

The animal looked up at him and whined. It gave a little purring laugh.

"So you're the one," it said. "Have you told her yet? What you are, and what they made you?"

Mhara crouched down on his heels and regarded the beast with some interest. He was smiling his vague smile but Robin saw his fists clench slowly. His spine was taut.

"Not yet, no."

The animal laughed again, and scratched one ear with its heavy, hind foot.

"Better do so then," it said. Mhara growled. His thin, amiable mouth drew back from the long, sharp incisors and narrowed the blue eyes to a slit. The cows, fretful, shuffled in their stalls. The animal bounded forward and Mhara rose and stepped swiftly from its path. It bounded through the door and was gone. He looked after it.

"Found a boat," was all that he said.

He helped Robin through the door and down a small set of steps, strewn with dried grass, onto the street. They were, she saw now, outside a long range of warehouses. From here, the go-downs looked like separate buildings, when in fact they were a single long barn. The derelict lot to the side of the sheds was blowing with grass, a pale golden haze in the darkness, and the night air was filled with pollen and dust. This, presumably, was where the beasts were kept in their city pasture, contravening the zoning regulations.

Holding onto Mhara, Robin hopped the remaining few yards to the bank of the canal. This was not the main Shaopeng canal itself, but a narrow tributary. The boat was roped roughly to a post. It was a small, nondescript craft, barely big enough for two people, a flat raft rising slightly to a squared prow and half-covered by a semicircle of canvas. It was the boat of a poor person. Robin's liberated social conscience protested.

"We can't take *this*. This must be all someone's got."

"It's all right," Mhara soothed. His eyes were shadows under the single wharf light. "I paid for it. Fifteen hundred dollars in gold."

"*How* much? Wherever did you get all that?"

"I don't think we should stand here, Robin. We should go."

Robin acquiesced as he jumped from the wharf and turned to lift her down. When he had untied the boat and had started its small inadequate engine, she said, "Who did you take the money from?"

Mhara squinted narrowly ahead. "I did not take it from anyone. I just happened to have it."

"What, you just 'happened to have' fifteen hundred bucks in gold?"

"Yes. When I found the boat, it was roped to another one, and I thought perhaps I shouldn't just take it, so I left the money in exchange. That's what you do, isn't it, with money? I don't understand it very well."

"Yes," Robin said, staring at him. "Basically, that's what you do." She was beginning to wonder whether she had done the right thing, going quietly along with him, her victim, whether she should not try to escape and raise the alarm, perhaps try and get her job back. But then Deveth was there, dead in the corporate morgue. Then she looked at him, the peaceful, oval face, the veiled eyes, a braid of hair tapping between his shoulder blades, and demon or no demon, job or no job, she knew she could do no such thing.

"You should sleep, Robin," Mhara said. "I will drive the boat." So she lay uncomfortably down on the damp slats, and watched the walls of the canal slide by, and the watchful face above her, gazing ahead.

By degrees, they came to the lock that joined the tributary of the canal to the main branch of the Jhenrai. Mhara left Robin in the boat and went to investigate the lock. Robin watched as the demon, moving economically, wound down the lock and then rejoined the little boat as it sailed down to meet the canal. To the east, the sky had taken on a watery tinge with the coming day. The lock opened and the boat slid out into the main channel. Mhara steered to the left, and when Robin looked up she met the yellow eyes of the creature that had been pursuing her, pacing along the wharf.

"You are very persistent," Mhara said, reprovingly.

"I have all the time in the world," it replied, and yawned, displaying jagged, tartar-stained teeth. It chuckled at the demon and trotted off toward the waking city.

TWENTY-TWO

"So," Zhu Irzh said, smiling at Jhai. "How was it for you?"

She twisted round in his arms. "How did you know I was awake?" The first of the dawn's thin light was coming through the little window.

"I could tell." The demon, though horizontal, managed to effect a shrug. The memory of the previous evening, hazed by sleep, returned to Jhai in a rush and she sat up. The tail was gone, and so were the teeth. Zhu Irzh nuzzled her neck. There was a now familiar twinge at the base of her spine, eclipsed by rising desire. Zhu Irzh's pale fingers were almost skeletal against the sudden dark barring of her stripes.

"A *deva*," the demon murmured. "I've never met a *deva* before."

"You know what they are?"

"I *have* read the *Kama Sutra*, darling," Zhu Irzh said reproachfully, adding, "several times. Now, hush. I have things to do."

An hour later, restored to a semblance of human, Jhai lay in his arms.

"Zhu Irzh?"

"Mmm?"

"Did you know what I was? Before I changed?"

He squinted round at her. "No. I thought you were using pheromones."

Jhai exhaled a long, pent-up breath. "Good."

"So why do you hide it?" the demon asked, then answered his own question. "Because you'd be put on the next boat to Hell, I suppose. But plenty of businesspeople have demonic associates."

"Associates, yes. They're not actually running corporations, as far as I know. I don't want to spend my life in Hell, Zhu Irzh. No offense, but Earth is my home. Besides, I'll end up there soon enough."

"It's not so bad. Anyway, you'd be very popular. An exotic, in a Chinese Hell—I'm presuming that's where you'd end up? Maybe not." He frowned in

92

momentary theological speculation. "You'd rise straight through the ranks, with your looks." He smiled reflectively. "And skills."

"That's what worries me. I don't want to end up as some kind of tart, Zhu Irzh."

"And what's wrong with that?"

"You were with the vice squad in Hell, weren't you?"

"That's right."

"I see." She wriggled over so that she could look down at him. The golden eyes were dreamily glazed.

"What do you take?" he murmured. "To keep your true form at bay?"

"Both are my true forms, my mother told me. But certain—circumstances—bring out the *devic* characteristics. There's a compound of various drugs that inhibit neuroreceptors. I've been taking it since I was a child."

"That transformation must have taken a few lovers by surprise, though. If what I remember about *devic* biology is right, then no drug can withstand the powers of arousal."

Jhai was silent.

"What did they do, hide under the bed?"

"It was never an issue," Jhai told him, and could not believe she'd said it.

"What do you mean, not an issue? You're not a virgin."

"No."

"So that means—what? Don't tell me you've never become sufficiently aroused."

Jhai felt her face flaming. "No, never. Because I was so uptight about it, I suppose. I thought it was the drug, holding it back. But now it seems that it might not have been that at all. Also, you're a demon."

"But that's *terrible!*" Zhu Irzh said with honest indignation. "You must have felt so frustrated." He caught sight of the look on her face and fell silent.

"I don't want pity," Jhai snapped. A brief war seemed to cross the demon's countenance, and tact apparently lost.

"So it was that good, was it?" If there had been more than a trace of smugness in Zhu Irzh's voice, Jhai would have hit him then and there. A fleeting memory of the previous night, and morning, made her betray herself.

"Yes, if you must know, it was, actually," she said through gritted teeth.

"What, waves crashing on the shore? The earth moving? Curtains fluttering in the—" He caught her striking hand and laughed. "Anyway," he added, sobering up. "You can have your cake and eat it, now."

"Meaning?"

"Well, you can dispense with the drug, for a start. Tell your mum it's obviously all been a huge misunderstanding and what generates the instability between your two states is simply that you haven't got satisfactorily laid. Then, when the change starts regenerating itself, all you have to do is—"

"Oh, for God's sake!" Jhai rolled off the bed and reached for her underwear. "That's so typical of a man. So all I need to sort me out is a good fuck, is that it?"

"I couldn't have put it better. Obviously, you'll need someone to supply that particular aspect of your cure, and I will nobly volunteer my services."

"If you think I'm sleeping with you again after that remark, you've got another thing coming."

The demon studied her for a moment, then appeared to come to a decision. He rose sinuously from the bed, snatching up a silk robe in passing. Knotting it about his waist, he said seriously, "I would like that. You had as great an effect on me as I have had on you, though perhaps a bit more predictable. It's not just about sex, Jhai, or even love. It's about meeting your match."

"Bullshit." She frowned. "Are you proposing?"

Zhu Irzh laughed. "Not yet. But who knows?" He took her by the shoulders and kissed her, gently and lingeringly. "Perhaps when we're no longer enemies."

Jhai took a reluctant step back. "Is that what we are?"

"Two bodies, Jhai. Not ours. Two people ripped apart by something with teeth and claws." He raised an eyebrow, still smiling. "A human wouldn't dare to ask you that, after last night. But I will."

There was a long, arctic silence.

"Are you accusing me of murder, Seneschal Zhu?"

"Maybe. You say this is your first real transformation. Flattering, but is it true, I ask myself?"

Slowly, Jhai sat back down on the bed.

"Yes, it's true. I've never just…changed."

"You're sure?"

"I'm absolutely sure." *That was the truth, anyway,* she thought. She knew exactly who, or what, had killed Deveth and the *feng shui* man, and it wasn't herself. The murderer was even now roaming the city, released by the compassion and incompetence of Robin Yuan.

The demon sat down beside her and took Jhai's chin in his hand, turning her face to meet his own.

"You didn't kill them. Then who did?"

"Suppose I knew. Suppose I told you. What would you do? Go to your masters in the police department, Hellkind that you are?"

"Perhaps. Perhaps not."

"Liar," she said softly.

"No, I am not lying. I don't know if you can trust me, Jhai. It depends how high the stakes might be."

"Pretty damn high." She met his gaze, as golden as her own could be. "As high as Heaven."

"I've been to Heaven," the demon said, with seeming irrelevance. "A pretty place, if you like that sort of thing. Bit insipid."

"Perhaps not for much longer," Jhai said, taking a risk.

"And why would that be?"

"Zhu Irzh, there's something I'd like to show you. Not here. At the Farm."

"The Farm?"

"It's a nickname, for my mother's country estate. It's not far from the city. I could send a car to pick you up."

The golden gaze narrowed. He didn't trust her, Jhai thought with reluctant approval. She could hardly blame him.

"Let your colleagues know where you're going. You can even bring that large sergeant of yours, if you want."

"When?"

"Tomorrow afternoon? I have things to arrange before then. One o'clock?"

"All right." Zhu Irzh stepped forward, and kissed her mockingly on the cheek. "I'll see you then. Send a car to the wharf. I'll be waiting."

TWENTY-THREE

Robin and Mhara had come to the end of the side canal some time ago and were now traveling as unobtrusively as possible along the main Jhenrai. Day was coming quickly, the light spilling out of the eastern sky and turning the flat water of the canal into pale gold. Robin was trying to find her bearings. Everything seemed truncated and squashed at this angle. She could see the unpopular angled roof of the Eregeng Trade House from here, and the First Bank of China rising up through the throng of buildings along Shaopeng. There, suddenly glimpsed, rose the dome of the Opera House, in shadow. Then the chugging boat took them around the next long bend. Beyond the storage piers and warehouses was the bulk of the ruined temple of Shai. As they rounded the turn Robin realized that the great iron doors of the temple were open. The canal lapped against the sluice gate.

"Listen!"

"I know." Mhara's voice held a grim note. They could hear the erratic swish of a powerboat engine approaching up the western stream of the Jhenrai. It was one of the big troop boats, the Paugeng symbol bright along its side, and as it spun to a showy stop before Mhara and Robin, the latter saw a form, indistinct in the morning light, crouched in the blunt prow. The little boat bobbed uneasily in the wake.

"Have they seen us?" Robin asked from beneath the concealment of the canopy.

"I think so." She looked at Mhara, whose face was bright and peaceful as he knelt in the shelter of the canopy. The rim of the sun, blazing summer white, crept over the edge of Wuan Chih and the world was abruptly flooded with light. The canal burned in the sudden sun and above them the temple was thrown into a massive angular blackness. The Paugeng troop boat was no more than a shadow against the water. Slowly, Mhara turned the tiller so

96

that the boat spun into the watery entrance of the temple.

"We can't go in there!" Robin protested, but they were caged and outmaneuvered by the troop boat. The little craft, with Robin trying in vain to see beneath the canopy, began to edge forward. The brimming sunlight ran from the sides of the wharves, spun out of the water. The Jhenrai danced with a fiery brightness and now the edge of the boat was bumping against the sluice. In haste, Mhara spun the wheel and the sluice gate creaked upward. The troop boat surged forward and then Mhara and Robin were through the narrow channel and into the temple vault. Behind them, something gave a low, snickering laugh.

Within, the temple seemed enormous. The top of the dome lay at the edges of sight, though from the outside Robin had always judged it to be a couple of hundred feet high. The vault itself was darkness laid upon darkness, but from the crest of the dome a single beam of light sent the dust motes twirling in the air. The vault was filled with whispering: voices murmured in Robin's ear, borne on a rushing wind like the breath of the sea. The sound muffled the mechanical beat of the boat's engines, churning the smooth, black surface of the cistern into a pattern of dappling water. Slowly the boat slid forward, a toy in the midst of vastness, and by the time the wider Paugeng boat had engineered itself through the cistern sluice, Robin and Mhara had turned the corner and vanished into emptiness.

TWENTY-FOUR

The afternoon found Zhu Irzh in a teahouse, reading among the old men. No one batted an eyelid. Reacting to his non-humanity would mean that they lost too much face, and anyway, as he was trying to catch the boy's eye for more tea, another person walked in, the possessor of a chalky olive skin and a round, beaming face, the eyes like currents in a heavy fold of eyelid, dressed in antique leather armor. He and Zhu Irzh gave one another a polite nod of recognition between Hellkind and then the creature left, having failed to find who, or what, he was seeking.

It was a big teahouse, arranged on four floors, and the shuttered windows were obscured by the usual mass of greenery. Plants were growing in cages, hanging outside the windows, and up here nearer the sun grew ginger and lemon grass, rosemary and sweet basil, fragrant in the late afternoon heat. They made the interior of the teahouse cool and green; Zhu Irzh found it peaceful, despite the chatter of conversation, and, lost in his book, did not realize how late it had become.

When he got back to Lower Murray Street, dusk had fallen and the moon was rising up over Shendei. A figure was sitting on the doorstep of the houseboat, which resolved itself into Jhai Tserai.

"Hello," he said.

"Hello." He let her in and switched the light on. "I didn't expect to see you until tomorrow."

Jhai shrugged. Underneath the dim lighting her amber skin was pale, and her eyes huge.

"Are you all right?" Zhu Irzh said, congratulating himself on having noticed.

"Yes…yes, I'm fine. We had a few problems today, nothing you need worry about." She gave a rather unconvincing laugh. Zhu Irzh took off his jacket and hung it on the back of the door, and when he turned he found Jhai immediately behind him. She wound her arms around his neck and he kissed her, opening her lips with his tongue and stroking the back of her neck. She was not passive now. She made him lie back on the couch and went down on him, and he lay back suffused with pleasure, feeling her take him deeper into her mouth until he realized that he was going to come. He sat up quickly and pulled her onto his lap, pushing up the silken skirts.

She had, in a prudent moment, taken her underwear off and he let her take him inside her. She rode him hard, held tightly within her, sitting back occasionally to stroke his flat belly as he stirred his hips against her, and at last he could not hold back any longer and let go, gasping with release. Before she had time to be disappointed he sat up and rolled over, pinning her underneath him and stroking her hard until she came.

And with it, changed.

蛇警探

Jhai, human once more and putting her underwear back on, gave him a rather shamefaced smile.

"I couldn't wait, sorry about that."

"Neither could I. Are you apologizing for fucking me?" He rested his head on his arm and smiled at her. Whatever tension had been released by that, it was back now. She gave him a nervy grin. A thought occurred to him.

"Jhai? Have you taken anything?"

"No more than usual."

"Ah."

"It's just—I'm a bit wound up today."

"Will you stay?" he said diffidently.

"No, I ought to get back." She evidently didn't want to hang around, and she dressed quickly. Zhu Irzh saw her onto the wharf, and even he, night-sighted and animal-wary, did not see the thing that watched her go.

蛇警探

Next day, Jhai's car arrived early. Zhu Irzh made his way across the pontoons to find it waiting on the wharf; a black Mercedes like a block of night in the afternoon sunshine. As he ambled up the wharf, the door opened and Jhai stepped out into the sunlight. She wore a dark vest and combat pants; her hair fell in a tight braid down her back. Ready for business, thought Zhu Irzh, but what kind?

"Hi," Jhai said. "No back-up?"

"I thought I could handle you alone."

The look she gave him made the demon grin.

"Get in the car, Zhu Irzh." She followed him through the door.

"So," he said, once the chauffeur had taken them out into the lunchtime traffic. "You've something to show me?"

Jhai nodded. "You might not trust me enough to let me, though."

"Oh?" She seemed nervous, he thought. Tension sang in her like a wire drawn tight. For the hundredth time, he wondered what bargains she had made, and how they impacted upon the dead. Detective Inspector Chen would have handled this very differently, the demon knew. A cautious, thorough investigation of suspects: methodical, meticulous, and conducted in the full knowledge that the investigator was on the side of justice. *But am I?* Zhu Irzh asked himself rhetorically. He had been posted to Earth for political reasons, and it was certainly proving entertaining now that he had left that period of ennui behind. But no one, least of all Zhu Irzh, was under any illusions. The only master the demon served was himself. Captain Sung might have kept him on a tight rein, keeping him out of major investigations until Chen's absence, and the station's limited manpower, made it necessary for him to be attached to a real case, but if he was offered a promising alternative, then he'd take it. And Jhai was certainly promising. *As high as Heaven.* A tantalizing remark, but what had she meant by it?

They had left the city behind now, and were traveling through the suburbs. Soon, even these were gone and the countryside became scattered with smallholdings: leafy gardens planted in the yellow earth of the river delta, goats and dogs and ducks.

"Your mother has a place out here?" Zhu Irzh asked curiously.

"In the hills. Another twenty minutes and we'll be there."

Zhu Irzh watched the gentle land roll by and then they were climbing into the barren earth of the hills. Across the hillside ran a fence, triple barred with razor wire. The car slowed. Zhu Irzh heard the hum of an electronic gate and then they were through. The car pulled up at a long, low building. The demon had been imagining a mansion, but this looked more like some kind of dormitory.

"The main complex is underground," Jhai explained, stepping from the car.

"So what do you do up here?" Zhu Irzh asked, not expecting a real answer, but Jhai said, "Lab work. Anything experimental, that needs more space than the city."

"For your mining contracts? Or the pharmaceutical side?"

She smiled briefly. "Both." She touched her palm to a pad on the side of a door. Zhu Irzh saw the blue glow of a retinal scan, and they were through into a kind of airlock.

"High security?"

"It's sometimes necessary." This time, she did not smile.

They passed through into a second airlock, and then into a long, narrow room, clearly a laboratory of some kind.

"Now," Jhai said, motioning toward a desk. "I have a confession to make."

"All right," the demon replied, carefully. "What kind of confession?"

"Not to the killings. I didn't do those, Zhu Irzh. But I know what did."

"What? Not who?"

"Who and what. Zhu Irzh, your aggressive lapse, the other day—I'm afraid I have to take responsibility for that as well."

He stared at her. "You?"

"When you went to the site where the murder victim was found, you caught something from the body. A virus."

Zhu Irzh stared at her. "What was it?"

"Okay. You know that I use a drug to repress my—my other side. It's based on a Keralan folk remedy, oddly enough—a combination of herbs, made into a magical balm. It was once used in exorcisms. The drug I take is the synthetic equivalent. You contracted the same kind of thing, but in a viral carrier, and reversed. A few molecular tweaks here and there, a little refining, and one has a drug that can tap directly into the response centers of the brain. In your case, the drug was on a time-release, just in case anyone made the connection between your visit to Paugeng, and the attack on Paravang Roche."

"That's outrageous," Zhu Irzh said hotly. "I could have killed the man."

"Oh, come on. You're a demon. Don't tell me you've got a conscience, Zhu Irzh."

He didn't want to admit to that weakness, so he said, "No. The attack lacked style. But why?"

"What I have in mind for this particular pharmaceutical range is something—quite ambitious. Come on. I'll show you." She rose and gestured toward the door. "I'd like you to take a walk, Zhu Irzh. It's only a short distance into the hills. Come with me."

Curious and annoyed, the demon followed her. They went back out through the airlocks and into the day. Heat struck the demon like a wall.

"Where are we going?"

"I'll show you."

She led him up a dusty path, through groves of acacia. Looking back, he could see the compound far below, like a child's building blocks. They came to a razor-wire fence, a substantial thing that was also clearly electrically charged—and spell-warded. The demon held out a considering hand and felt the snap of magic along his palm. Jhai halted.

"Is this the perimeter?" Zhu Irzh asked.

"No. This is an enclosure."

"Enclosing what? Jhai, if this is a trap, I think I should point out that I'm wearing a trace. It's embedded in the bone of my arm, so you'll have to have me searched and then cut it out if you want to remove it. If anything happens to me, the trace will deactivate and alert my colleagues. And I have my own wards, too." He was lying, of course, but it wouldn't hurt to make her think a little.

Jhai smiled. "Glad to see you've taken precautions. But this isn't a trap. Not for you."

"For what, then?"

"Go and look."

The demon regarded her doubtfully for a moment, then nodded.

"All right." He wasn't happy about it, but curiosity won out over unease.

"I'll meet you later. Just follow the path up the hillside."

"You're not coming?"

"No," Jhai said. "I don't want to attract attention to myself." She pressed her hand against the gate lock, and it opened. Cautiously, Zhu Irzh stepped through. A tingling sensation ran up his spine like a mouse. At first, he thought this was some aspect of the gate security system, and then he realized. It was natural.

"There's a *ch'i* meridian running along here. I can feel it, under the ground."

Jhai nodded. "You'll notice more of them. This was a sacred place long ago. There's some powerful *feng shui* around here." Gently, she shut the gate behind him, and turned. "See you later."

Wondering if there would be a later, the demon made his way up the hillside. It was very quiet. A single small bird turned in the air above him, spinning on the wind, but only a faint breeze stirred the hillside grasses. Beneath his feet, Zhu Irzh sensed the meridian, its pulsing presence humming under the arid ground. He squatted on his heels and listened. He could hear his own heartbeat, beginning to pound in time to the meridian. There was a change in the wind, beginning to turn to the south, a warm wind bearing the salt-mud smell of the delta, which was just visible in a fan of light through the hills. He could hear the wind and the voices that it carried, once startlingly loud in his ear, speaking a long, liquid language, coming from far out to sea. *Waterdragons.* Zhu Irzh smiled.

Rising to his feet, he walked on. There was a grove of acacia ahead of him. The meridian led directly into it. Following the path, Zhu Irzh brushed the leaves of acacia aside and halted. Within the grove stood a small temple. It was built of pale, smooth stone, and it was very old. It looked as though it had been in ruin for many years; lichen mottled the stone like a scab. But power hung around it all the same. The air glistened. The meridian seemed to shine beneath the demon's feet. As he stood, watching, the world darkened around him; the sky changed from a bone-colored haze to fawn, then amber. Shadows raced by, attached to nothing. Zhu Irzh sank down to kneel in the dusty earth. It seemed to him that he knelt on the skin of a drum, reverberating with the beat of the world, and then the skin parted and let him slip through, dissolving him, so that he was no longer separate from the world but part of it.

To the east, the mines gaped, shattering the surface of the world with parallel scars, and he could see down beneath them in a cross-section of the world over which he was painfully spread. The rifts in the earth were indeed intersecting with the fault lines, as everyone was saying and as the governor, tied into the mining corporations, had strenuously denied. Yet there was something else about the meridians, something wrong—then it was gone, and he could no longer get a grip on it. Both the rifts and the faults ran along the meridian pathways of *ch'i* and *sha*.

Zhu Irzh—stretched, disembodied, smeared throughout the body of the planet—did not care. He was everywhere, simultaneously; unified with the blind, unthinking world. His awareness poured down waterways, felt the delta coursing around him and then was out into the open sea where the waterdragons were still calling, across and over and into the wild country of the southern mountains, uninhabited except for the tiny villages clinging to their bare sides. The stars rang around him and the hard, little moon swung up and over his shoulder like a stone flung into the sky. Beyond, there was only darkness with, very far away, an echo of somewhere known. He could see the shore of Heaven itself, as bright as dawn. It hurt his eyes and he turned within to the world's molten heart, seeking Hell. Fire gushed as the earth's core heaved, and then without warning he was flung back in the familiar confines of bone and blood and sinew. The bleached sky roared over him like a wave. He fell back into the grass, crying out with the shock. He was panting, and drenched in sweat. His mouth tasted of blood; experimentally he licked his lip and found nothing there. Death hung close in the air, making the hairs at the back of his neck prickle and his throat constrict. Claws flexed from the pads of his fingertips.

It was growing dark, yet surely it was no more than three o'clock. He must have been under some kind of spell… He glanced up and froze. Someone was coming out of the temple and walking toward him through the gloom. Hastily, Zhu Irzh scrambled to his feet. The figure was tall, and dressed in a saffron robe. Its hands were outstretched in welcome. Zhu Irzh's hand crept toward the hilt of his sword. He was close enough now to see its face: serene, smiling, filled with peace. The unmistakable scent of peach blossom clung around it. It had come from Heaven and he knew it, now, for one of the spirits that attended the Celestial Court. Slowly, Zhu Irzh relaxed. He released his grip on the sword.

The Celestial being's jaw dropped as though it had been unhinged. Zhu Irzh glimpsed a row of needle teeth, then a probing tongue shot out, aiming at his throat. Zhu Irzh flung up his arm to ward it off and it gripped him by the wrist. The tongue's serrated edge bit into his flesh. Cursing, Zhu Irzh leaped backward and drew the sword, but the tongue as swiftly withdrew. The being threw back its head, making the dislocated jaw flap, and emitted a shrill, shrieking laugh. Then the creature leaped high into the air, displaying long, clawed feet, and bounded like a hare down the hillside. There was a second shriek as it met the fence. He saw a flash, and then the being lay still.

Zhu Irzh became gradually aware that his own mouth was hanging open. His wrist was beginning to swell with a series of painful weals, but the hurt was eclipsed by simple amazement. What, in Hell or out of it, had *that* been? With the sword drawn, Zhu Irzh sprinted down toward the fallen being, but when he reached the fence, there was nothing there. Snarling under his breath, the demon made a swift search of the vicinity but the being, whatever it had been, was gone. At last Zhu Irzh turned and, glancing around him warily, went back along the path to meet Jhai.

She was not there, but just as Zhu Irzh was beginning to think that the whole thing was some kind of gigantic trick, he saw her coming along the ridge of the hill. She caught up with him at the summit. Below, the arc of the world fell away under the green sunset sky, and the sea, by some curious inversion of the light, had changed to a silvery aquamarine, brighter than the heavens. Zhu Irzh stood on a rocky outcrop at the edge of the summit, impervious to the drop at his feet. If he fell, he'd survive, but he wasn't sure about Jhai. His hair, ruffled by the brief battle, whipped in the delta wind. He sensed Jhai come up behind him and found himself smiling: *It's dark… How well can she see?… I'll pitch her over the edge if she tries anything.* She was armed, sensible girl; he could sense the way her fingers gripped the automatic, affecting her balance a little, and the way she moved. His smile widened.

"No need for that, Jhai. I'm not going to attack you, unless you make the first move."

He was expecting protest or anger, but instead she said softly, "Look at the lights." She pointed. Through the haze, the city spread in a blurred star along the delta. From up here, they could see each quarter: Bharulay, Ghenret, Bharcharia Anh, and toward Jhenrai and the harbor, the Paugeng tower spiking up, the highest structure along the flat warehouse district of the port. The warning beacon at its peak flared briefly and a helicopter coming in from the seaward side flipped to turn around it before wheeling at a right angle to the airport. The last crimson edge of the sun slid beneath the horizon, leaving a fiery smear in its wake.

"Look," Jhai said, taking the demon's arm. Deliberately, she was keeping her gaze on the city, so as not to look down and he realized suddenly that she was afraid of heights. It made him feel a little better. "You can see all the way to Orichay. As far as the airport."

"You can see the bridge. And the harbor."

"So you can." Her grip on his arm tightened a little.

"It's cold up here," she whispered. Zhu Irzh turned to her. Her eyes were filled with light, and for a moment no one was there behind them.

"Best go back down," he said.

She nodded. "I'll take you back into the city."

"Do I get an explanation?"

"Yes. But not here. I'll tell you on the way."

He led her down the hill, shivering a little, like an animal or a child. At the compound the driver was waiting, patiently smoking a cigarette. Jhai held the door for the demon; he climbed in, and they set off.

TWENTY-FIVE

The temple of Shai seemed to go on forever. They were in the main cistern now, floating past columns rooted in water. A face looked out at Robin, carved in stone and iron, its mouth fixed in a wide grimace. The stone itself was a dark gray, mottled and speckled like skin. Above them, the ribs of the domes arched upward, vanishing into the soft darkness. The waterways of the cistern were a maze; a pattern that made little sense. It was very quiet. There was no sign of the troop boat. Robin was oddly relaxed, traveling through this silent, melancholy place, as though they had entered some limbo where there was no longer any need to hurry and there was all the time in the world to be oneself. As they rounded one of the numerous bends she saw, without surprise or disgust, the body of an enormous seal. It was little more than a carcass now; the flesh eaten away, the ribs stretching upward and the white skull, with its broad nose and round eye sockets picked quite clean, gazing at the ceiling.

"Who do you think did that?"

Mhara's eyes reflected nothing but the dark surface of the water. "I don't know. The worlds are changing, Robin. You can't feel the change, but it's there. It's going to happen."

"Change how?" Her skin felt icy cold. "How do you know?"

Crouched in the stern of the boat, Mhara, too, might have been carved from stone and iron. He had fixed the tiller and now the craft took them forward, following the canal.

"Mhara?" Robin asked. "Can you see the future?"

He sighed. "A little. But it's never very clear, except for this one vision."

"Can all demons see the future?"

"I don't know." He paused. "I am not a demon."

She stared at him: at the long claws, the sharp canines. "You're not human."

106

"No. But nor am I Hellkind, Robin. My home is Heaven."

"What?"

"I am a—member of the Celestial Court. My mother is Zasharou Selay, Lady of Mists, a maid of the goddess Kuan Yin."

He glanced at her, and when she looked into the calm blue eyes, it made perfect sense. "But—what are you doing here? And—those." Lightly, she touched his clawed fingers.

"I was captured. And changed."

"Oh gods," Robin said, in sudden frozen horror. "The drugs I gave you."

"Yes. The drugs. All unwittingly, Robin, you have been the instrument of my transformation."

She stared at him, aghast. Before them, the vaults of the temple stretched on, arching into night, and they could hear the river now, a limitless rush of water, its currents reaching out to snare the boat and pull it forward.

"Listen," Mhara said. The sound of the river was growing louder, and the air was filled with dampness, a fresh blowing wind that bore rain. The little boat was sucked along the eddying current, spinning from end to end. Robin and Mhara clung on, and then the boat was spun through an open sluice and out into the wider stream. Robin caught a glimpse of the sluice gate, shattered on its hinges and hanging limply above the torrent. She could not see far around her. The mist that had hung over the water had thickened steadily, and now lay in a fog around them, despite the freshness of the air.

"Robin," Mhara said, and his eyes were like lanterns in the dim light, "We are entering the space between the worlds. We are coming closer to the Night Harbor. And I will tell you frankly—I am afraid." His mouth was tightly set. Suddenly the Paugeng troops, presumably still in pursuit, seemed the least of their worries. Robin reached out and rested her hand on his arm.

"Don't worry," she told him. "Don't worry"—as if by repeating it she would reassure herself. Slowly the mist began to pull away, carried into the upper air by the river wind, and as it did so Robin realized that she could see the stars. They were the same fiery spiraling constellations that she had seen above the cemetery, and as she watched, one of them plunged toward the water, hissing as it fell. She leaned over the side of the boat and trailed her hand in the river. It was icy, no longer the tepid, chemical broth of the city, but something clear and dark and cold. It stung her fingers, and she pulled her hand away. The current was taking them quickly, but she couldn't see the banks of the river, only a clouded darkness. Something wheeled above the prow of the boat, crying out in an empty voice, and Robin ducked in alarm. She felt Mhara's arm around her, holding her convulsively close.

"It's only a gull," she whispered, and the white shape whirled up on the wind and away. "Mhara? Don't be so scared."

"I can't help it… When they brought me here, it was like this then, between my world and yours. There was nothing there. It was not real, not a real place, and neither is this one."

"Then where are we?"

"The Night Harbor," Mhara said, so low she could hardly hear him. "Where everything changes."

Light was growing around them, bursting from the cool moist air above the river. It was so dazzling that Robin cried out and shielded her eyes with her arm. Mhara's grip tightened around her waist.

"They're shooting at us!" she shouted, flinching against the expected pain, but although the sound grew louder, she felt nothing. She opened her eyes. The boat had stopped, coming to rest against the side of a weed-slick wharf, and above them the sky was ablaze with fireworks. Not gunfire, but firecrackers, and Robin remembered being a little girl and making the same mistake.

"Come on," she said. They were three or four feet below the wharf, and without stopping to think Robin got a foothold on the wet stone and hauled herself upward. She caught a glimpse of Mhara's tense face beneath her. She reached a hand down and helped him up.

"Where are we?"

The wharf was narrow, surrounded by a rickety nest of warehouses. It looked like somewhere in the city, perhaps Ghenret or Orichay. Fireworks spilled out into the night, chrysanthemum flowers sailing through the darkness, with the smell of gunpowder strong. From not far away, there was a shriek as a rocket soared upward, a moment of silence and then a ricocheting explosion, which rebounded from the walls of the buildings and was echoed a moment later by a burst of laughter. Robin and Mhara stopped. A woman was coming toward them. She had a dancing walk and her pale hair streamed down her back. As she walked, her hair was full of fire, flames trailing behind her, and her long and slanted eyes were empty except for its light. She held out her hand when she saw them and spoke, and the liquid syllables rushed away like water. Mhara's grip of Robin's hand tightened.

"Where are we now?" Robin asked, confused, and the woman smiled, fierce and gleaming.

"You are in the antechamber of Hell," she said mockingly. Turning to Mhara, she made a sign with her hand and then she was gone, taken by the gunpowder air. Mhara took Robin's hands in his.

"Robin, before we go any further, you have to know something."

—and suddenly Robin was walking down Mherei Street, and the night was quiet. Ahead, someone paused, uncertainly, and Robin paced toward her, faster and faster, running now and the smell of fear hot in her throat. The woman turned and her mouth opened wide, Deveth's dark face frozen on the surface of memory, and Robin reached a clawed hand up and tore open her throat. She caught the body as it toppled and dragged Deveth swiftly back, the blood very warm and heavy against her fingers and, curious, she reached down and ripped. The flesh came off in one piece, and even in the warm evening air, it steamed. She sat with the woman's startled head in her lap, absorbed in her prize, and then there was a sharp hiss of air and the dart brought her down, falling over the ruined body, the blood wet in her dark, unbraided hair, warm against her cheek.

Robin looked at Mhara, dazed.

"You gave me the drug," Mhara whispered, "just before you went home, the largest dose yet, and when you'd gone and I was under the long dream, Jhai Tserai took me out into the city. I don't know what I did. I don't remember what happened, only the fragments that you just saw. I escaped from them, the meridians drew me, I don't know what else I might have done, who else's life I might have taken. When I woke I was in the cot, in Paugeng, and it was morning and you were bending over me, so unhappy. Jhai used me, Robin. She used me to kill Deveth. But mine was the hand that did the killing. I am a Celestial being, Robin. Do you know what that means? I deserve to be in Hell. I cannot enter Heaven now, except by stealth. But it's to Heaven that I have to go, to tell them what is happening."

Robin turned and went to stand at the edge of the wharf. Beneath her, the water ran quickly, a haze of darkness dappled with the fireworks' light. She could see nothing beyond.

"We killed Deveth, then, Mhara. You and I and Jhai."

He came to stand next to her on the dock. He had wrapped his arms about himself and she saw that he was shivering, even though the air was warm. Robin said, as if to herself, "You see, there are so many causes… If I had not been so scared of losing my job that I gave up my principles for it, and so scared of losing my lover that I failed to challenge her, and that fear coming from being a child in a poor family and not knowing when or if we'd eat again—I have to set a point somewhere and say, this is where I could have acted, and did not. I can't just look at all the causes and say 'this is where it began.' All stories begin in the middle. But I don't think I've been making the right choices for a very long time."

They looked out over the black, swift current separating worlds.

"Maybe it wasn't my fault that Deveth died, and not yours, either. But that's the result and that's what you have to live with. If I hadn't been too afraid not to run the experiment on you, you wouldn't have killed her and I'd still be back at Paugeng, and so would you."

Mhara sighed and looked up at the gunpowder stars. The flowerburst was reflected in his eyes, and he was no longer shivering. From somewhere, she could smell the scent of thousand-flower, faint and sweet.

"I'll come with you," Robin said. "Wherever you go, in Hell or out of it."

Mhara said, "Come, then." He grasped her arm and drew her with him into the tangle of warehouses. He moved quickly through the narrow streets and although Robin could hear voices all around, in sudden snatches of conversation and laughter from the mild air, no one was visible.

"Where is everyone?" she said, as if to herself. Mhara's long-nailed hand was warm and real in her own, but around them there was unseen life in the windows of the houses: a child crying fretfully, an old complaining voice hushing it still. At last, they came out into a square. The myriad dead crowded around Robin and Mhara. She felt hands lift her hair and stroke the collar of her jacket. She caught glimpses of their faces, the fleeting tilt of a smile, eyes catching the light. A girl's long hair brushed her sleeve and the girl was gone into the air, drifting by. Robin turned her head wonderingly and a swarm of lights sailed up through the eaves; she saw a hand come out of the air and catch a handful. By the sudden blaze she saw a lantern full of fireflies and the patient face of a child, the jaw eaten away, and Mhara was pulling her on. She felt as though she were running through water, the dead flowing past her and then they were gone. The road curved round to a high, carved gate, and then she realized where they were.

"Mhara...this is like Ghenret."

"What?"

"I know where we are. That was Hangsu Square, and there's the Lion Gate."

"The Night Harbor mimics the world sometimes. Just as Hell does."

Sure enough, as they drew closer, she could see the ornamental carved beast high on its lintel, exactly the same as in the world of the living. Mhara put out a warning hand and caught her wrist. Before them, in the portal of the Lion Gate, was a familiar form. It was the non-dog no longer, but the indeterminate thing that had brought Robin to the cemetery.

"Well, Robin," it said to her lightly. "So we've found one another again." It made a quick sidling movement. "Don't you feel it might be destiny, after all? Didn't you always feel that it was meant?" and now its taunting voice had changed, rang familiar in her ears. "But maybe it wasn't meant, after all," the new voice said, sadly mocking. "Maybe we should end it here." Deveth, sitting on the sofa, after Robin had uttered her one word of rebellion.

"It's you," Robin said. She felt a peculiar sense of anticlimax.

"Isn't that what you're supposed to do, haunt your murderer?" The animal shook its heavy, dull coat, and then Deveth was there, just herself, hawk-faced and wearing her old green jacket. "You went to see my mother, didn't you? She still doesn't believe I'm dead; she's still doping herself up with her trendy sickness pills. And my dear friend Jhai's making new friends, or so I've just seen." Deveth's face twisted and slid, dissolving into the air. "But I am dead. Your new friend tore me to pieces. At least it was quick," she glanced at Mhara.

"I suppose I should say thanks for that. And he's prettier than I ever was," she added, turning back to the transfixed Robin. "Well, Robin, aren't you going to say sorry, that you never had the guts to stop tormenting some poor imprisoned thing and turning it into a killer? But you never let principles stand in your way, did you?" Her features slipped and slid once more, and she was half-Deveth, half-something other, shot with lights the color of illness.

Robin suddenly found that she was angry. She spat, "Well, fuck you. Don't think I haven't blamed myself enough. If you hadn't treated me like some little trophy, maybe you wouldn't be here now, so don't get self-righteous with me. I think I prefer you, Dev, as a hyena or whatever you're supposed to be. Maybe that's more real."

"Maybe," the thing said softly. Deveth was gone, and so was the beast. The spirit rose up into the air, a whirling mass of color. Pressure built inside Robin's skull, and there was a sharp bursting pain at the bridge of her nose. Automatically she wiped her upper lip: her nose was bleeding and she felt wetness trickling down her cheeks. Her heart hammered in her ribcage, great, slow beats growing louder and louder until all she could hear was her heart and a thin, high wailing. Through a pinpoint she saw Mhara, on his knees with his arms futilely raised. His face was streaked with blood and the swaying mass was beating at him, each lash laying open his arms and his ribcage. The silvery droplets of blood trailed slowly up into the air and floated away. Something was licking his face as it bled.

TWENTY-SIX

As the car pulled out behind the Pellucid Island Opera House, Zhu Irzh broke a long, tension-filled silence and said, "That—thing—that attacked me. You saw it, I'm sure."

"Yes. Yes, I saw it." Jhai shifted in the seat beside him.

"It was a Celestial being, wasn't it?"

"Yes, it was."

"I thought they were supposed to be nice?"

"They are."

"Well, that one wasn't. It tried to garrote me with its tongue."

"There's a reason for that." Jhai murmured.

"And that would be?"

"The drug you were given via the virus is a neurological enhancer. It taps into aggression and anger. It acts as an override on normal states of consciousness."

Zhu Irzh didn't have a very scientific mind, but he was beginning to see where this conversation was leading. "You fed the drug to a *Celestial?*"

Jhai nodded. "Yes. A while ago, I was contacted by an old friend who had become versed in dark magic. She told me that she had found a way to break the seal between the worlds, an ancient and powerful summoning spell, to bring demonkind and Heavenkind through to Earth. Normally, as I'm sure you know, it's easier to summon demons than the Celestials, but this spell worked admirably."

"And that friend was Deveth Sardai?"

Jhai nodded. "That's right." She gave him a sidelong glance and he could see the flicker of gold behind her eyes. "We activated the spell. And we summoned a Celestial, who was already on Earth for some reason—I never found out why—and bound him here."

112

"Do you know which Celestial?"

"He called himself Mhara. I don't know the name, but then, I'm not very well versed in the hierarchies of Heaven."

"No, I don't expect you are."

Jhai squinted at him. "And are you?"

"No, not really," the demon was forced to admit. "I know most of the major players, of course. But there are a lot of Celestial beings and none of them are that interesting, frankly."

"Anyway, we started experimenting. I told the lab staff that he was a demon, that we were working on ways to protect Earth from another invasion by Hell."

"But, in fact, your plans were somewhat more grandiose," Zhu Irzh said neutrally. "You're planning to storm Heaven, aren't you?"

She smiled. "You're quick. Yes. But not with an army. The original plan was to infect the Celestial with the drug in a viral carrier, wipe his memory and send him back."

"You can do that? Your technology's that advanced?"

"Paugeng's R&D division is cutting edge, Zhu Irzh."

"So Heaven would become infected with an aggression drug, turn against itself, be thrown into chaos. And then—what?"

"Then the people who are paying me to undertake the research would move in."

"And who are they?"

Jhai paused. "Let's just say that they have unlimited funding."

"It's one of the Ministries of Hell, isn't it? Which one? War? Though it's more the style of Epidemics, and they've certainly got reason to try and recapture some of the power they lost earlier in the year." He glanced at her closed face. "You're not going to tell me, are you?"

"I can't. I'm under oath. It would literally kill me to tell you."

"What happened with Deveth? Did she become a liability?"

Jhai grimaced. "She started asking for too much. Power crazy. She knew what I was. I couldn't hide it from her; I started to change during the summoning, and she saw enough to guess the truth. She threatened to expose me unless I handed over control of the project to her. I couldn't risk that, Zhu Irzh. Deveth had no managerial skills; she couldn't have run a bath. So I tried out the Celestial's new-found aggression on her."

"What's that Western expression? Killing two birds with one stone?"

"Exactly."

"So," the demon said, turning in his seat to look at her. He reached out and touched her cheek. "Why are you telling me all this? So that I can take you down to the police precinct and charge you with all manner of iniquities?"

"You think you could make any charges stick? It's your word against mine,

Zhu Irzh. You're a demon from the realm of Hell. And I'm Singapore Three's premier businesswoman. I could *buy* this city. In fact," Jhai frowned, as if trying to remember where she'd purchased a pair of shoes, "I think I already have. If the police department gets too close, I might have to do something about that, but they haven't so far and I've been all co-operation, of course. The Chinese government might have believed Deveth—her father has close connections to it—but I don't think they'll believe you. Anyway, why would you want to expose something that could be to your immense advantage?"

"Then what are you offering me?" Zhu Irzh asked. He did not want to seem dense, but he wanted to hear her say it.

"A partnership. You could be the next Celestial Emperor, Zhu Irzh, if we get this right."

"And if we don't? I could end up consigned to the lowest pit of the farthest level of Hell as something the size of a toe, and you with me."

"That won't happen. My sponsors are protecting me."

Zhu Irzh's eyebrows rose. "You've made a bargain with someone in Hell and you *trust* them?"

"If I go down, I'll make sure they go with me. They won't risk that. And also, remember that my ancestry might be Hellkind of a sort, but it's not from the Chinese afterlife. I have somewhere to bail out to if I have to. So what do you say? Are you with me?"

"I'll think about it," Zhu Irzh said. Jhai nodded.

"All right."

The car slowed at the entrance to the harbor.

"I'll walk from here," the demon said. He gave Jhai a sidelong smile. She hid her disappointment well.

"When am I going to see you again?"

"Tomorrow," Zhu Irzh said firmly. "I need some time to think." Leaning over, he kissed Jhai hard, and was out of the car before she had time to respond. He did not look back, but he smiled again as he heard the car pull away. Well, he had wanted to know what she was up to, and now he did. High stakes indeed. And a great deal of power for someone brave enough, or foolish enough, to grasp the nettle. Zhu Irzh had already become involved in a political battle in Hell, and he wasn't keen to court another one. Besides, he could see that Jhai was making a classic mistake: even in spite of her ancestry, because of her Earthly power, she was tacitly assuming that Hell had little influence over her, as long as she was not actually there. Zhu Irzh knew better. The first slip, and Jhai's masters would make a sacrificial lamb of her.

Zhu Irzh blinked up into the glowing darkness, and wondered what exactly he was going to do about this. Telling the human authorities did not seem to be an option: he believed Jhai when she spoke of her control over the city council. She could make life difficult for him, demon though he was. Nor was he inclined to sell her out; if the plan worked, then there would undoubtedly be something in it for most of Hellkind, and some dark part of Zhu Irzh's demonic consciousness reveled in the idea of the chaos to come. So, he thought, ambling down the wharf, this was one situation that he would simply wait out.

Achieving such neutrality might be easier said than done, given that Jhai had already drawn him a certain distance into her schemes, but Zhu Irzh was confident of the degree of power that sexual authority conferred upon him. The demon rarely underestimated women; Jhai, however, owed him a debt, and he intended to capitalize upon it as much as he possibly could.

He stepped carefully over the pontoons, and halted as he came within reach of the houseboat's ladder. There was a light in the main room, showing through the shutters. The badger had no need of illumination, and Zhu Irzh had left the boat in daylight… His sword whispered through the darkness. Lightly, the demon grasped the ladder and slid up it onto the deck. The door to the main room was ajar. Zhu Irzh listened, but heard nothing. Sword drawn, he kicked open the door and plunged in.

"Glad to see you're on the ball," someone said mildly. Zhu Irzh gaped. Detective Inspector Chen was sitting in the armchair, nursing a cup of tea.

"But—you're in Hawaii!"

"Not anymore. Sergeant Ma called me yesterday. He expressed some concern as to your welfare. I thought I'd cut the vacation short and come home."

"What about Inari?"

"She's enjoying herself with Lao and his wife. She sends her regards." Chen regarded the demon owlishly. "Could you put that away?"

"Sorry." Slowly, Zhu Irzh sheathed the sword.

"Want some tea?"

"No. Yes. Thank you."

In silence, Chen poured him a cup and handed it over. The demon sank heavily into the nearest chair.

"Want to give me your version of what's been happening?" Chen smiled helpfully.

Zhu Irzh reminded himself that he was Hellkind. He was over two hundred years old. He was stronger than almost any mortal man and he had the powers of Hell at his back. So why had he not felt so uncomfortable since being called to his grandfather's study at the age of ten, to explain how he had managed to break each and every window in the Irzh family mansion? Taking a deep breath, he gave Chen a swift, highly edited summary of recent events. He recounted the attack on the dowser Paravang Roche, pleading ignorance of its cause, and told Chen that he had spent the afternoon with Jhai, examining her premises. Nothing was actually untrue, but there were significant omissions.

"That was concise," Chen said when he'd finished. It was impossible to tell whether he believed the story or not. "So let me get this straight. At the moment, we're looking at Jhai Tserai as a chief suspect? And we're working on the hypothesis that she is at least heavily implicated in both murders, even if she didn't carry them out herself."

"Yes, we are."

"And am I to assume that, cultural differences aside, your division in Hell considers such criteria as objectivity, neutrality and so forth critical when interrogating a suspect?"

"Yes, to some degree," Zhu Irzh said warily, not liking the turn that the conversation was taking.

"So having established Jhai Tserai as principal suspect, you brought her back here and spent what is by all accounts an active night with her? In my bed?"

A distant part of Zhu Irzh noted that it was an interesting sensation to experience all the blood draining out of one's face.

"How did you—?" He could not go on. Chen pointed at the silent, accusing presence of the iron teakettle upon the shelf.

"Oh, fuck."

"So I am given to understand. Sergeant Ma is not the only being capable of using a telephone. And why, exactly, did you consider that becoming Jhai's lover was crucial to the course of this investigation? Some disarming ploy, no doubt? A subtle maneuver designed to throw her off guard and elicit the truth from her?" Chen enquired, still terrifyingly bland.

Belatedly, Zhu Irzh resorted to the truth. "No. She has this—this effect on me. When I see her, all I can think of is sex."

It was clear that Chen was sorely tempted to make the obvious retort, and Zhu Irzh winced in anticipation of being told that this was all he ever thought about anyway. But Chen said nothing, and the demon went hurriedly on: "It seems to be mutual; I'll explain why in a moment. She turned up here, one thing led to another, and next thing I knew, we were in bed. And I'm sorry it was yours, but it *is* the only bed here. I promise I'll wash the sheets."

"That would be nice. Why is it mutual?"

"She's not human."

That got Chen's attention. His eyes widened. "Then what is she?"

The demon told him.

"That," Chen said, unwittingly echoing Zhu Irzh on an earlier occasion, "would explain a lot. About her family's origins, about their rise to power… She's in a startlingly vulnerable position, isn't she, even with all her influence? And she's risking that for *you?*" His eyebrows rose.

Trying to ignore the unflattering implications of that remark, Zhu Irzh said, "It's because I'm Hellkind, I think."

"And you know, don't you?"

"Know what?"

"You know, Zhu Irzh, just what Jhai's role is in all this. I can see it in your face. The badger passed on some remarkably disturbing hints, about what Jhai said to you the next morning."

"Was that damned creature spying on me all night?" Zhu Irzh bridled. He had no objection to voyeurism, as long as he was the voyeur. At that point, the teakettle, at which Zhu Irzh had been staring accusingly, blurred and became badger. The night-black eyes were cold. The badger gave a soft, slow hiss.

"Yes," said Chen, coolly. "He was. And just as well. Now. Out with it. What is Jhai planning? I should add, Zhu Irzh, that although I hold you in rather higher regard than you probably think, and I might—under certain circumstances—even view you not only as a colleague but as a friend, I'll have absolutely no hesitation in binding you here and summoning Exorcist Lao back from Waikiki to drag the truth out of you by magical force if I have to. But I'd rather you just told me—not for the sake of the world, or Hell, or Heaven, but for my sake, and Inari's."

Of all the appeals Chen could have made, this was the one that dived under the demon's defenses. Not for the first time, Zhu Irzh had reason to deplore those unnerving elements within his own character, that made him more than demon, yet less than human. Conscience, and affection, and a desire for someone else's respect. Perhaps he should look for a good therapist to eradicate these personal failings when he finally got back to Hell.

"All right then," he said miserably. "I'll tell you."

After what amounted to the demon's confession, Chen sat silently for several minutes. The demon was expecting an outcry: recriminations, blame. But to Zhu Irzh's surprise, Chen mildly suggested that they take a walk. With the badger following, he led the demon down Lower Murray Street to Ghenret and followed the path that led out onto the market wharf. Out on the boards, the walk was slippery with spray: the tide was high tonight. Beyond the harbor the lights of Tevereya illuminated the sky and drained the light of the moon. From this angle, the bulk of the market blotted out the Paugeng tower. The market's wooden-slatted sides were coated with salt and the eaves dangled with *bagua* mirrors designed to deflect the unwholesome *sha* that shot down the side of Paugeng and bounced off the harbor. The mirrors clattered in the little wind high above Chen and Zhu Irzh, and their mirrored surfaces caught the light. The detective and the demon made their way beyond the empty vault of the market and out onto the wider end of the rickety wharf. The Shendei stretched featureless beyond; the only land between here and Luthen Port was little Lantern Island. Zhu Irzh leaned with care on the old rail and breathed in an approximation of fresh air. Chen stood beside him, screwing up his face against the breeze.

"Look," Zhu Irzh said. He was finding Chen's continued silence unnerving. "There are mirrors here, too." He pointed to the end of the dock, where a single octagon hung on a wire, fixed against the wind. Chen shook off his distraction and turned to and fro, working out the angles of *ch'i* and *sha*.

"Yes, you can follow the path of the meridian—comes down the other side of Paugeng and then across the gully between the go-downs…" They both looked at the little mirror. Its dim surface reflected the lights from the shore and then, most oddly, a perfectly reflected face, with eyes like marbles, and a rictus mouth. *How peculiar,* Zhu Irzh thought. He stared at the little face. It was moving.

Zhu Irzh spun and kicked the man's feet from under him. The assassin went down on the deck, skidding on the slippery planks and bounced up again like a ball. The sword whistled past the demon's ear and cleaved neatly through the rotten wood of the rail. It crumbled into wet dust. The demon stumbled backward out of the way and slipped, falling awkwardly on his side and feeling a jarring pain ride up his spine. Chen was balancing on the balls of his feet, waiting for the next rush. While Zhu Irzh regained his footing, the assassin twirled his blade, feinted once, twice, and came at the demon from the side. Zhu Irzh ducked under the blade and slashed at the assassin's throat with his claws. The next minute the demon was off and moving backward. The assassin screamed and rushed him, whirling the sword. Zhu Irzh drew his sword, feinted forward and kicked the swordsman in the kidneys, but the demon was a fraction off and the tip of the assassin's blade sliced across and down, under Zhu Irzh's own blade, catching him under the collarbone. He heard Chen hiss through his teeth. Zhu Irzh and the assassin circled one another. The assassin was gripping the blade with both hands and chanting. He made a start forward and then quite suddenly fell. The sword clattered to the floor. Zhu Irzh saw Chen's silent figure poised above the body. Swiftly, the detective reached down and scooped up the assassin's sword.

"Zhu Irzh, stay where you are. Keep an eye on this one. I want to check if there's anyone else."

The demon ignored this. He hauled himself to his feet and followed Chen. At the end of the market was a sort of hangar, used for storing heavy machinery. The rusty iron lattice of the gate was open. No one was there. Zhu Irzh lowered the sword, very slowly. He rubbed absently at his collarbone. They returned to the body: an unremarkable man in a blue Mao suit. Chen rifled his pockets and found a pair of throwing knives, a garrote and a card bearing the insignia of the Assassins' Guild.

"So, he's a professional." Chen said. "Who wants to kill you? Apart from me, on occasion?"

Zhu Irzh gave him an uneasy glance. "Quite a few, I should think."

"Who, precisely?"

"Jhai Tserai's a possibility. I know too much now. Maybe she started having doubts and decided to take me out of the running. Then there's the dowser I assaulted." Zhu Irzh grimaced. "He's shown remarkable tolerance in not trying to dispatch me before now, if you ask me. There's a whole host of Hellkind—ex-girlfriends and so forth. There's that demon-hunter from Beijing we met earlier in the year—he doesn't like me being here."

"I'd be inclined to think that Tserai and the dowser are the most likely candidates," Chen said, reaching for his cellphone. "I'm calling the precinct. They can deal with the Assassins' Guild."

The rest of the night was spent in tedious and protracted statement-taking. A representative of the Assassins' Guild was summoned. When the woman arrived, she tut-tutted in a perfunctory manner over the body and announced that it had been a freelance contract; there was no record of the attempt on their books, and anyway, the police department knew perfectly well that contracts against law enforcement personnel were not permitted. She and Chen then had an argument about client confidentiality, while the demon sat moodily on a nearby bench, pondering a variety of unpalatable options. It was close to dawn by the time Chen and Zhu Irzh got away. By mutual agreement, they headed for the precinct house.

Even at this early hour, the street was beginning to be crowded and there was a definite atmosphere of anticipation and festivity, a hum of suppressed excitement for the eve of the Day of the Dead. The light was growing, a lemony glow in the east, and the night-lit neon glow of Shaopeng was still bright, fuchsia, orange, turquoise: signs for remedies, soft drinks, drugs, and the screaming stylized faces that advertised the demon lounges near the station. Through the window of the tram, Zhu Irzh saw a lounge client stagger out into the morning and bend double, clutching his head. He looked as though it had been worth every minute, whatever it was. Many of the signs were pushing the latest from Jhai's own commercial labs, the red Jaruda bird symbol above a lightning-bolt spill of tangerine tablets.

Along the length of Shaopeng, the chop and cookhouses were opening for breakfast, already flooded with workers carrying plastic cartons of congee; starting early in order to finish by noon and rush home for the start of the festival. Zhu Irzh found that he was ravenous, but Chen refused to stop for food.

"So," Chen said, when they were within the wards of the precinct house. "If we're to gain any kind of indictment against your new girlfriend, we need to set a number of things in motion. We need proof that she was behind the murder of Sardai, and we need to get Sardai's family on our side. The quickest way to do that, I suggest, is to visit the Night Harbor, assuming that Sardai's spirit hasn't already departed for Hell—and it's likely that it hasn't, since I don't suppose she wants to face the music down there with Tserai's masters. Then it's a question of offering the spirit some kind of deal in order for her to sell out Tserai." Chen paused and took a sip of tea.

"And then?" the demon prompted.

"Then we have to find some way of breaking into the Farm."

"The place is a fortress, Chen."

"Not to someone whom Tserai has already taken into her confidence."

"Perhaps, but she's hardly likely to take me back to the Farm. And if I ask her if I can go, she'll get suspicious."

"Then we'll have to think of something," Chen said. "I have an idea."

"Oh? What?"

"I need to mull it over a bit first. For the moment, I'm going to sort out a permit for the Night Harbor. And another thing, Zhu Irzh. Heaven *must* be informed. As soon as possible."

TWENTY-SEVEN

"No!" Robin screamed. "I'd die for him, Deveth, I wouldn't die for you! I wouldn't die for you!"—and abruptly the attack stopped. Mhara curled whimpering on the ground, the Lion Gate stood silent and empty, and they were alone. Robin sat up and spat blood, wiping her mouth with the back of her hand. She hardly dared to look at Mhara, and when she did she felt a piercing, icy shock. He was curled on the ground beside her, and he was not moving.

"Mhara?" she faltered. She put a hand to his face and his skin was cold beneath the blood. The beast's assault had ripped through the thin shirt and torn the flesh beneath into long parallel grooves; Mhara was covered in blood. A pulse fluttered in his throat. Robin stripped off her jacket and stuffed it against the worst of the wounds, but after a moment she could see the blood beginning to seep through, staining the material with a thin crust. She looked around. No one was to be seen. It was as quiet as midnight in the country. The fireworks had ceased, and it had grown suddenly cold. The four shining heads of the iron lions were furry with frost, and the rime along the steps gleamed. In the open mouth of the beast above her, the metal ball began to quiver, rocking against the lolling, bronze tongue. The dry noise that it made was the only sound. Then the ball fell, shattering on the hard ground into a thousand fragments.

Robin stared as light, golden and calm, spilled from the fragmented ball and surrounded Mhara's prone form. The ragged wounds began to knit together, forming seams in the skin that soon faded until there was no longer a trace of injury. Moments later, the light seeped away, seeming to sink into the earth itself, and Mhara sat up.

"What happened?"

"Something healed you. A ball, from the lion's mouth."

121

"It's an Imperial statue," Mhara whispered. "It must have recognized me."

"Mhara, we have to find a way out of here. Deveth's spirit is roaming around and it obviously doesn't wish you well. We have to get back to Earth, or—"

"Not Earth, Robin. I have to return to Heaven. I told you. Someone must tell them what's happening."

"But you said that they won't let you back into Heaven… Mhara, if you explained to them—no one could blame you for what you did."

"You think so? Heaven is merciful to human souls, but very hard on its own. We are supposed to know better. And there was—an earlier transgression on my part."

"What do you mean?"

"Tserai was only able to capture me because I was already on Earth, Robin. She did not summon me from Heaven. I should not have come here, I was denied permission, but I wanted—" Mhara stopped.

"Wanted what?"

"Wanted to see for myself. I don't think you understand how remote Heaven has become over the last century. As fewer and fewer people believe in it, so it withdraws itself. Celestials are starting to ask themselves why they bother with the affairs of the Human Realms, when they get so little thanks for it. If it wasn't for a bureaucracy that was set up aeons ago, to bring souls to Heaven and reward them for their efforts, then I am not even sure whether the Celestials would bother."

"But what would happen to all the souls?"

"They'd go to the only place that would have them. Hell is always hungry, Robin."

"But that isn't fair," Robin said, aware that she was sounding like a child.

"Heaven thinks that it is taking too long for your kind to learn anything. It thinks that it has given you thousands of years' worth of grace, and that still does not seem to be enough."

"But the woes of the world, the pestilences and the wars and so forth, are so often engineered by Hell."

"The Celestials say that you have a choice, and they're right, aren't they? You do."

And to that, Robin could only be silent.

"If we are to enter Heaven," Mhara said, and she glanced up sharply at his use of the plural, "then we will have to do so by stealth alone."

TWENTY-EIGHT

The temple of Celestial Goddess Kuan Yin held unfortunate memories for Zhu Irzh. He was not fond of meeting the Celestial beings: partly because they were always so smug, and partly because they produced an unpleasant reaction in him—a kind of burning, itching sensation, combined with dizziness. Chen had explained once that it was rather similar to negative and positive particles, but Zhu Irzh had so little interest in science that he tuned out the rest of the conversation and had only started paying attention again when Chen had suggested getting something to eat. And this particular goddess kept treating him not as a powerful and terrifying demon from Hell, but more like a small child in need of a smack. It was with reluctance, therefore, that the demon accompanied Chen through the portals of the goddess' temple and into the courtyard within.

Even granted that it was midafternoon, the courtyard was quiet. Someone had obviously been here recently because a tall, red stick of incense was smoldering in its holder, and Zhu Irzh could detect a faint cold trace of unhappiness on the air, like snowmelt on the tongue. Prayers for the sick, perhaps. To any normal demon, such emotional residue would have been as sweet as candy, but Zhu Irzh found his spirits sinking. He told himself to get a grip. It was definitely time for a therapist when he finally got back home.

"Even though she's not my patron anymore," Chen was saying, "I should think she'd listen."

"Of course," Zhu Irzh agreed. "She'll want to know what's going on."

Chen gave him a narrow look. "And you. Where do you stand on this?"

"Right, well. I think Heaven's boring. A civil war and an invasion by Hell would certainly liven things up a bit, but on the other hand, we'd have to do something with the place when we took it over and it's so *bland*. We'd have to redecorate. And there's another thing, Chen. Without Heaven, we could

123

do what we want, and I think that might get rather dull as well."

"I wouldn't have expected you capable of such theological profundity," Chen said, expressionless. Zhu Irzh tried to decide if he was being sarcastic, and failed.

"I'm full of surprises," he said.

Chen pushed the double doors of the temple aside and stepped through. It felt empty to Zhu Irzh—true, there was no one around, but usually the Earthly homes of the Celestials felt full of presence, as though the gods were keeping an eye on the place, no matter what else they might be doing. This place felt dead. Chen was frowning.

"Wait here." Zhu Irzh watched as Chen walked up to the statue of the goddess and closed his eyes. The demon could see Chen's lips moving in the supplicatory prayer, and braced himself for that unnerving moment when the goddess swam into liquid life. But despite Chen's obviously heartfelt plea, nothing happened. Kuan Yin remained as cool, impervious marble.

"What's wrong?" Zhu Irzh called.

"I don't know. Maybe she's out."

"Out? Gods can't be *out*. They're everywhere."

"Well, she isn't answering."

"Maybe she's busy. Hearing the cries of the world must take up more and more time these days, not to mention doling out doses of compassion here, there and everywhere."

"I would remind you," Chen said rather coldly, "that this is the goddess' temple we're in."

"What's the problem? She isn't listening, is she?"

"Zhu Irzh, could you wait outside for a minute?" The demon was good at judging when Chen was reaching the limits of his tolerance. He complied without demur.

It was more than a minute. Zhu Irzh cooled his heels in the courtyard for just under an hour by the time that Chen re-emerged.

"Any luck?"

"None. And the temple feels—"

"Dead?"

"Yes, as though any deific life that was in it has departed. Something is obviously wrong."

"Perhaps she just doesn't want to talk to you?" Zhu Irzh said hesitantly.

"Perhaps not." Chen looked so unhappy that the demon's heart went out to him.

"There's no way of sending her a message?"

Chen sighed. "I'd just rather speak to her directly. I don't want to take the risk of a message being somehow intercepted, that's all."

"Look, let's go back to the precinct," Zhu Irzh suggested. "We can still try the Night Harbor. Then, if you like, we can come back via the temple, or one closer to the Harbor, and you can see if your lady is receiving guests again."

"If I can't get through to Kuan Yin," Chen said. "I'll try one of the other gods. The Emperor has got to know about this."

"Do you think He'll take it seriously without evidence?"

"By then," Chen said, "I would hope that some evidence, at least, will be in our possession."

TWENTY-NINE

Robin and Mhara moved as swiftly as they could through the Night Harbor, but the chilly air seemed to sap Robin's strength. She should not be here, it was not her time—and the knowledge that she had been here before, passing from one life to the next, in perhaps many different incarnations, was unsettling. Who had she been, in all those past lives? Had Deveth been there, and what had Deveth been to her then? Sister, perhaps, or lover, or mother, or murderer? All lives are connected, Robin knew, the economical universe weaving patterns from the same cloth, unpicking it again, unmaking… But Mhara could not have been there, if he was a Celestial being. Mhara must be immortal, constant, not subject to the forces of life and death.

"Mhara?" she said now. "Where are we going?"

"To find a boat."

"What boat?"

"The boat that takes souls to Heaven. We will have to stow away, Robin, and I do not know if that will be possible. I can mask myself, perhaps, but the wards on the boat are set to sniff out a human soul. I can't expect you to risk that."

"I want to go with you," Robin said. "Even if we get kicked out of Heaven immediately. And besides, it's probably my only chance of ever getting to see the place."

Mhara gave a soft laugh. "Are you so sure, then, that you have not and will not?"

"I'm not a good enough person, I think."

"You see, this is why I left. Whatever Heaven might say, it does not understand what it's like to be human. It doesn't understand the stresses that you live under."

"You said we had a choice," Robin pointed out, "and we do."

126

"But sometimes it isn't possible to see that. Life and living obscures it, makes it disappear. Don't underestimate how hard it is to be alive. I did not understand that before I came here. Heaven entombs itself in perfection; Heaven has forgotten. Perhaps, Robin, it is that Heaven is not good enough for *you*."

"That sounds like heresy," Robin said, with unease. "Whatever religion one might practice."

"Then maybe the heretics are right."

Robin looked about her. This area of the Night Harbor was nothing like the city they had left. Great shadowy buildings rose on either side, but as Robin watched, they shifted, altering into mere facades, some crumbling into ruin before her eyes. Mhara tugged at her arm.

"Robin…"

"I know. I'm coming. Do you know where we're going? Can you tell?"

Mhara's face fell. "I thought I knew. But now I'm not so sure."

Robin looked about her, frustrated. "I don't know the typography of the Night Harbor. Only the superstitions about the journey of the soul—across the razor bridge, through Bad Dog Village, then to the port…"

"We are not near the razor bridge," Mhara said. "That lies close to the entrance to the port, and in any case, we would not be drawn to it—you are a living soul, and I am a Celestial."

"What about Bad Dog Village, then?"

"We will probably have to pass through that." Mhara's eyes were wide in the dim light. "Or around it, which would be wiser."

"Bad Dog Village is not supposed to be a nice place," Robin said, shivering. "The souls of the lost, caught between Heaven and Hell."

"Like Deveth," Mhara murmured. "Talking of dogs."

Robin grimaced. "Or bitches."

The area through which they were now walking was no longer so built up. She could see ahead to what looked like fields, filled with shadow-colored corn. When she looked back, the buildings had melted away and all she could see were the fields, stretching into the distance. The air smelled moist, filled with growing things. It was, Robin felt, the healthiest place they had come to since entering the Night Harbor. The crops, however, varied. Sometimes the fields seemed to contain corn, tall and fringed. Sometimes, the ghostly leaves of pak choi rose stumpily from the earth, and when Robin glanced again, she saw nothing but rice paddies. Then the crops were once more corn. Mhara paused and touched one of the tall, nodding heads.

"It's not supposed to be a good thing to eat when you are in the Night Harbor."

"I'm not hungry anyway," Robin said. The idea of eating any of these shadowed plants was off-putting—then Mhara's hand whipped back. The fringed ear of corn was writhing. Moments later, it split to release a huge moth, which unfurled sticky wings and sailed off into the darkness. The remains of the ear of corn shriveled and withered, and the long stem sank silently back into the ground. A minute later, a sullen potato plant emerged.

"Let's go," Robin said, appalled by this strange fertility. But they did not get far. The corn rustled as if a wind was rushing across it. Mhara drew Robin back, further into the roadway, but figures were already leaping from the corn, waving long pikes. Robin clapped a hand to her mouth. The figures were squat, moving springlike on legs that bent backward from the knee. They wore leather armor, and long fingers tipped with black nails clasped their weaponry. Their faces reminded her horribly of Deveth's new form: snarling doglike masks, mouths gaping behind short tusks. They stank of old meat and piss. They formed a ring around Robin and Mhara, and moved in closer, jostling and yipping at one another.

"So," one of them said in a strangely musical voice, "*you're* the missing boy."

THIRTY

"Good news?" Paravang Roche asked hopefully.

The broker shook his head.

"No news?" Again, the broker shook his head.

"I thought it was to be last night!" Roche said in an urgent undertone. Several people, their prayers disturbed, glanced at him and frowned. The broker was obviously choosing his words carefully.

"So did I. But evidently matters have gone awry. The appointed gentleman did not return to the hiring place, nor was he at his abode this morning. There is beginning to be some concern."

Paravang felt someone draw a long, cold finger up his backbone. He was on the ground again and an expressionless killer's face was gazing down at him.

"What is to be done?"

"Give it another day," the broker said. He rose stiffly to his feet, wincing.

He is not a young man, and neither am I, Paravang thought. His jaw still hurt where the demon had cuffed him to the floor. He was reaching an age where his feet hurt him if he stood for too long, whereas his enemy paced the ground with predator's grace, the walk of a man who dispatched trained assassins without even thinking about it, *and now he might be hunting me.* Why did I do this? The dowser panicked. He should have done what that bitch Tserai had suggested and risen above it, let it rest. Hate had blinded him to consequence. In fright, he clutched at the old broker's arm.

"Can I stay here tonight in the temple? Will that be permitted?"

The broker detached himself with distaste.

"I imagine that for an appropriate consideration..."

"Of course!"

Paravang rummaged in his pockets. He gave the broker a handful of notes.

The old man looked at the money as though Roche had handed him something old and dead.

"I suppose this will have to do. But what will you do after tonight? You can't stay here forever, you know."

Paravang nodded mutely. Senditreya save me… He turned a pleading gaze to his goddess, bowed his head to the floor and spent the first and only night of his life in prayer.

THIRTY-ONE

It took some time for the permit to enter the Night Harbor to come through, during which Zhu Irzh fretted and chafed. Chen remained closeted in Sung's office for almost an hour, leaving the demon in the company of the precinct's indifferent coffee and the badger, which stared unblinkingly at Zhu Irzh with a gaze like a winter's night.

"What's the matter with you?" the demon asked.

"I watch, only. You are a creature of Hell," the badger said in its thick, slow voice.

"What of it? You hardly hail from the Celestial Realms yourself."

"I am a creature of Earth," the badger said.

Zhu Irzh frowned at it. "You really care what happens to Earth? To the human world? They haven't treated you very well, have they? You have to stay as a teakettle half your life."

"It is my nature," the badger said. "Earth and metal. I was forged from the elements of human world. It is as it is. I do not complain."

"You don't normally talk so much," the demon said.

"There is not normally much that I wish to say," the badger replied.

A moment later, to Zhu Irzh's relief, Chen returned.

"Well, the captain's taken care of," Chen remarked. "He was all set to send you straight back to Hell."

"Sung is *always* set to send me straight back to Hell." The demon grimaced.

"This time more than usual. You're not proving to be the model cop, Zhu Irzh."

"I had numerous citations in my previous job!" Zhu Irzh said, stung.

"Quite so. And now you and I are going to the Night Harbor. The permit's arrived."

蛇警探

131

Zhu Irzh had no feelings either way about the Night Harbor. He neither liked it nor disliked it. He saw its necessity, whilst considering it something of a nuisance. Everything to do with it seemed so drawn out and tedious, compared with the comparative ease of shifting between Hell and Earth. However, he was compelled to admit that the majority of humans and, indeed, entities did not enjoy his own family connections and thus there was some need for a kind of clearing house for the majority of the world's population. And the Night Harbor did have its charms. You saw some interesting sights—particularly those unfortunates who had recently departed their bodies and retained the semblance of their last moments of life. Zhu Irzh had once glimpsed someone who had been entirely flat: some kind of industrial accident, no doubt. But he could never get to grips with the place; it shifted about even more elusively than Hell itself.

"At least we know what Deveth looked like," Chen said, as they entered the long, low building that housed the entrance to the Harbor.

"Not if she's still got her final appearance in the body. Still, as I think I said to Ma, all we'll have to do then is to look for someone who's minus their face."

"There can't be that many people in such a condition," Chen remarked.

"Who is to say? The Night Harbor is an odd place."

The young man at the reception desk of the Night Harbor had the air of one who is convinced that he is meant for better things. The sulky, handsome face congealed with disdain as he set eyes on Chen and the badger, mixed with wariness when he saw Zhu Irzh.

"We have a permit," Chen said, and handed it over. The young man stared at it grudgingly, as though hoping to find something wrong with it. But the paperwork was in order. At last the young man gave a martyred sigh and said, "You'd better go through, then."

Zhu Irzh could feel the young man's stare as they stepped through the double doors into a kind of airlock that led to the Night Harbor itself. "What's his problem?" he muttered to Chen.

"Minimum wage, probably. Hell doesn't pay very well. Not if you're a clerk, anyway."

Zhu Irzh frowned. "Doesn't Heaven ever send any personnel to the Night Harbor? It's supposed to be equal, after all. You'd think they'd have a vested interest in guarding the portals to the afterlife."

"The amount of bureaucracy that Heaven contributes to these things has been waning over the last decade," Chen said. "Years ago, when I was just starting out as a policeman, you'd come in here and all the staff would be Celestial maidens. Very pleasant, of course. But gradually they all got replaced. It can only have been with Heaven's agreement."

"Are they short-staffed up there or something?"

"Who knows?" Chen sighed. "There are certainly more souls in Hell than in Heaven. But these days, that's not too surprising."

"Maybe that's why your goddess isn't answering your prayers," Zhu Irzh said. "Perhaps she's given up and gone on vacation."

Chen smiled, but it was strained. They were now standing within the Night Harbor itself. Zhu Irzh could smell the ozony odor of the Sea of Night and hear it lapping against the dockside. Ahead, a maze of low stone walls revealed the tall masts of a ship in dock.

"That's not the Night Boat," the demon said.

"No, it isn't." Chen was staring at it. "I don't know what it is. I thought there was only one boat that sailed the Sea of Night."

"Perhaps it's come in from some other religion's Hell," Zhu Irzh said.

"Or someone else's Heaven," Chen murmured. Looking at it, the demon was inclined to consider this a more likely possibility. The boat was very pale, a pearly phosphorescence in the dim light of the Night Harbor, illuminated by the smoky lamps that burned along the edges of the port. Its sails were folded, but they, too, were white, draping in spectral folds from the high masts.

"Can you see anyone aboard?" the demon asked.

"No." Chen paused. "We ought to be concentrating on finding Sardai."

"Oh, let's just take a quick look," Zhu Irzh suggested.

Together, they walked to the side of the dock. Up close, the boat was smaller than it had appeared from a distance: a delicate thing, its sides completely encrusted with ghostly shells, pale whorls and spirals that shimmered in the uncertain light.

"This is beautiful," Chen said.

"It's a Celestial craft," the demon said. He reached out a hand, but did not touch the sides of the boat.

"It certainly looks as though it might be," Chen said. The demon wrinkled his nose. He could almost smell the offensive peach blossom orchards of Heaven. "But what's it doing here?" Chen added.

"I have no idea. Celestial vessels very rarely leave the Heavenly seas."

Chen reached out and brushed a hand along the shell-embossed side of the boat. Immediately, a gossamer web drifted down and enveloped his arm, imprisoning it.

"Damn!" Chen said, staring at his hand in dismay. "I shouldn't have done that."

"It was extremely foolish," the demon said severely. It was nice not to have been the one to fuck up for a change. "What are we going to do now?"

"Wait," a voice said from behind him. "One moment."

Zhu Irzh turned and found himself confronting a Celestial maiden. She was exactly like all the other Celestial maidens he had seen: beautiful, of course, with a thick fall of lacquered hair and a white ceremonial dress that seemed to catch the light from the lamps and hold it, so that she glowed a faint gold.

"Madam," Zhu Irzh said, and bowed. A pity all these girls were as wan and insipid as their home. Perhaps, if Tserai had her way, that might change. The demon belatedly became aware that he was grinning, but instead of stepping back with a squeak of fright, the maiden simply regarded him with a cool, detached interest, as though he was something she had found at the bottom of a pond. She touched the web that imprisoned Chen and it disappeared.

"I'm very sorry," Chen said. "I meant no harm."

"I know. You were simply curious. And indeed, no harm has been done. You are Detective Inspector Chen, are you not?"

Chen was staring at her. "Yes. But how did you know?"

"You were the protégé of my mistress, before things changed."

"Your mistress is Kuan Yin?" Zhu Irzh could see that Chen was rapidly leaping to conclusion after conclusion. "She's here?"

"Yes. We arrived yesterday, as the Night Harbor reckons these things."

"Then that must be why I couldn't contact her," Chen said. "May I ask why she's come?"

"I think you should ask her yourself," the maiden said. "Come with me."

THIRTY-TWO

"Where are we going?" Robin asked, shakily. It was hard to walk when your ankles had been shackled and your arms were tied behind your back.

"Be quiet," the dogman behind her snapped. She felt hot, reeking breath on the back of her neck. From the corner of her eye she saw Mhara, similarly shackled, hobbling along. They had left the fields far behind them and now walked through a wilderness of sharp stones and jagged outcrops. Through gaps in the rock Robin occasionally glimpsed distant lights, and a vast roiling expanse that knowledge and half-memory told her was the Sea of Night. It made her sick to look at it: a horrible thought, to know that her soul had already crossed that sea many times before. She could not imagine sailing upon it. Small wonder that memories of the life-between-lives could not be accessed, otherwise life itself would be a landscape of anticipatory dread. And now Robin herself would suffer from this suffocating fear of death, having seen what awaited her at the other end. Even Hell would be better than that dark ocean. If she even lived… The boundaries had become too blurred; she did not know what that meant anymore.

Then the rocks clustered more densely around them and the glimpses of the Sea of Night vanished, to Robin's intense relief. She could feel Mhara glancing at her, but she did not want him to meet her eyes and see her fear and dismay, so she stared rigidly at the ground and concentrated on putting one foot in front of the other. But then a howling filled the air: a deep baying, interspersed with wolf-like cries and high puppy yelps. Around her, Robin saw their captors drop to all fours. The armor and the weapons disappeared. She and Mhara were surrounded by the doglike creatures that Deveth had turned into, their little yellow and amber eyes lit by a wicked intelligence. They bounded forward and turned the corner out of sight.

But one remained, in semi-human form: the pack leader. He prodded

Robin between the shoulder blades with a hard hand. "Go on. What are you waiting for?"

Reluctantly, Robin followed the pack. On turning the corner, she saw what lay before them and once more had to be shoved forward. As she had guessed, it was Bad Dog Village.

Rickety roofs showed over a high jumble of palisade. From a watchtower that seemed to have been assembled from roughly cut branches, a lamp burned with a dirty orange light. Architecture was clearly not the dogmen's strong point. The gates to the palisade were open. Robin could see movement within and hear a snapping, snarling argument.

"Do not worry," Mhara murmured, as the pack leader was distracted. "You've been here before." But he did not sound convinced by his own reassurances and Robin, looking at the place before them, felt no sense of familiarity, only an overwhelming dismay.

Within the palisade, it was even worse. The village stank of shit and Robin had to be careful where she placed her feet. Real dogs might have gone outside to shit, but these beings seemed to combine the worst of being human with the worst of the canine, too. The dogs herded them through into a compartmentalized stockade and here she and Mhara were separated. Robin clung to him when she realized what was happening, but it was no use. The dogmen dragged them apart and shoved Robin through the door of a small, slatted hovel, with a pit in the floor. She ran to the wall, but could not see where Mhara was being taken. She did, however, see something else: a small, pallid band of ghosts, hastening through Bad Dog Village with their heads bowed, clutching one another's hands. The dogmen rushed out: one of the ghosts was pulled away from the rest and hauled into the darkness. The others stood, aimlessly lamenting for a while, until reason evidently overcame them and they rushed away. Robin went slowly back into the hovel and sat down on the cleanest patch of straw.

It was impossible to know what the dogmen were planning. Whatever it might be, Robin was sure that she was entirely expendable. The statement made by the pack leader seemed to point to that: *So* you're *the missing boy.* Did that mean that the dogmen were somehow connected to Paugeng? Or were they referring to further back down the chain and Mhara's absence from Heaven itself? One possibility offered hope, the other, ruin, and Robin had no way of telling which it might be. But judging from the nature of Bad Dog Village, ruin seemed more likely.

蛇警探

Later, Robin woke, with no recollection of having fallen asleep. It was completely dark—she could not even see her hand in front of her face—and very cold, with the iron chill of deep night. Her heart was pounding and she was certain that something had woken her, but there was no sense of anything in the room, no murmur of movement. She said aloud, hoping against hope, "Mhara?" But there was no reply.

Next moment, the door to the hovel burst open, ricocheting back on its hinges, and Robin's eyes were dazzled in a burst of light. Something hot and large and panting was in the room, filling it. Robin smelled wet hair and meaty breath. She rolled away against the wall, desperately seeking escape, but the light from the wildly swinging lamp was enough to reveal a glimpse of the dogman: in its semi-human form but bare of armor, the grinning mouth gaping wide, the raw pink phallus between its legs erect. There was no doubt in Robin's mind as to its—his—intentions. She screamed and when the dogman reached down and grasped her hair in his thick padded hand, she twisted round and bit and kicked. She had never fought so hard; revulsion lent her strength. But the dogman gave a cackle of laughter, horribly reminiscent of Deveth, and slammed her against the wall, hands pawing at her breasts, nails tearing her clothes. He jammed the side of a hand against her throat and Robin began to pass out, vision swimming into a sea of light and dark.

Then the dogman was pulled violently away and Robin dropped to the floor. The room was filled with snarling and growling; when she ventured to look up, she saw that the dogman had resumed his doglike form and was rolling over and over with Deveth's beast incarnation. Her teeth were buried in his throat: thick blood sprayed out across the room. Deveth lunged and tore, the yellow eyes devoid now of anything that might once have been human, and the dogman grew slack. The heavy body slumped to the floor. Deveth stepped delicately back, avoiding pooling blood. The dogman's phallus stiffened for a moment, then slid back into its sheath. Moments later, the corpse crumbled into a black, earthy substance and was absorbed by the floor.

"Men!" said Deveth, and spat.

Robin started to laugh and could not stop. She clutched at Deveth's greasy coat and pounded the floor and howled.

"You are hysterical," Deveth said coldly into her ear.

"Thank you," Robin gasped, sobering up.

"You are mine to hunt, Robin, mine to torment, mine to do with as I please. I am not subject to the rules of dogtown. The pack leader must understand that, fool that he is." Deveth was seething with anger. She rose from the floor, shook herself, and surged out, slamming the door behind her with a kick of her hind leg. Robin had never been so glad to be alone. She curled into a ball against the wall, wrapped her arms around her knees and waited grimly for morning.

THIRTY-THREE

"What do you mean, he's dead?" Paravang Roche asked the priest-broker, aghast.

"The man was murdered," the priest-broker said, sourly. "And the Assassins' Guild is claiming that our contract with them misrepresented the situation and the insurance does not cover it."

"What 'misrepresentation'? They knew he was a cop!"

"It appears that the Guild was under the impression that Detective Zhu Irzh was not protected by the full might of the law, being as he is a demon and moreover on assignment from another force with whom the Guild has no contract. However, it turns out that this is not the case and Zhu Irzh is to be regarded as a fully covered member of Singapore Three's law enforcement. Thus they are asking for a compensation payment for some three hundred and fifty thousand dollars."

"But my insurance with the Senditreya Endo surely guards me against attack, doesn't it? Can't I claim under my existing policy?"

"I'm afraid your insurance has lapsed automatically with the revoking of your license. We are obliged under contract to pay and therefore you will have to come up with the money yourself."

"What! But I can't work at the moment, in case that fact had escaped your notice!"

"You will just have to manage. Don't you own property?"

"No, I rent my apartment." Just as well, Paravang thought in dismay. The prospect of being evicted was all that he needed. Then it struck him that it might very well come to that, too.

"Any relatives, any friends who might be able to help you out?"

"Hardly. I don't bother with friends much. I'm not married. My father's been down on his luck—he's barely got two beans to rub together. I help him out when I can. And my mother's dead."

"Dead," the priest-broker remarked reflectively, and Paravang scowled at him.

"Yes, over ten years ago."

"Where is she now? Heaven or Hell?"

Paravang scowled at him. "In Hell, if you must know. There were some… family difficulties involving her own parents. I'm sure she did her best, but the bureaucracy apparently decreed that she missed Celestial entry by a whisker."

"The life-between-lives is often unjust," the priest-broker said smoothly. "And you are her only son, from the sound of it."

"Yes, that's so."

"A loyal son, no doubt. One who honors his mother at the festivals?"

"Well, naturally." You had to keep in with the spirits to some extent, and tradition meant a lot to Paravang Roche, and to his father. They had both been generous, over the years.

"A lot of Hell money bought and burned, then? Sent down to the under-world and your mum in a coil of smoke?"

"Yes, I—" Paravang had begun to see where this was going. "You can't expect me to ask for it back! She's probably spent it by now anyway." He had no idea what sort of retail opportunities existed in Hell but, somehow, he felt sure that they were extensive.

"I'm sure your mother loves you still. And I'm sure she's grateful. Besides, think of it this way—if your mother ended up in Hell as a result of some family embroilment, this is her chance to redeem herself. Get back onto the world's Wheel in a much more fortunate incarnation when her time in Hell runs out. You'd be doing her a favor, really, asking for the money back."

"I suppose you might have a point," Paravang admitted.

"Think about it," the priest-broker said.

"I will."

Troubled, Paravang took his leave of the priest-broker and wandered thoughtfully out into the street. He wanted to have as little to do with his shrew of a dead mother as possible, but in truth, it was the only way out. But it was unlikely, knowing his mum, that she'd simply give him the money, not without a very good reason. If she knew the Assassins' Guild was after him, might kill him—but then she'd have him down in Hell with her, and she'd be knocking on the door every hour of the day and night, demanding this, that and the other. Hell indeed. So telling her the truth was out. That meant a lie big enough for her to return the money he'd burned for her all these years, yet he couldn't think of anything compelling enough.

But then something happened that made Paravang fleetingly reconsider the essential malice of the universe. He turned the corner and ran into the tail-end of a wedding procession.

Marriage! Of course. His mother, when she was alive, had always been on him to get married, and things hadn't changed just because she was dead. From the content of her phone conversations, Paravang knew that it was still her dearest wish. The only trouble was that he hated women and saw no reason to seek out their company unless they were the kind whom one paid by the hour, and even then he wondered why folk bothered. He barely knew any, apart from his next-door neighbor… Paravang sank down onto the bench and contemplated the wedding procession as it meandered by. His neighbor might have a tongue like a shrew on speed, but she was constantly bringing him things—extra soup, leftover dumplings, noodles… And now that he thought about it, she seemed to seek his advice rather a lot, too. Paravang had no illusions about his personal charms. As far as he was concerned, he didn't have any. But the neighbor was a widow, and presumably lonely, and she had presumably also been around the block as far as men were concerned. He balked at actually lying to her, but perhaps if he explained, put the suggestion as a business arrangement and offered her a cut, to be paid once he'd got the Guild off his back and his license renewed… It might even work. Newly inspired, Paravang rose, overtook the wedding procession and headed for home.

THIRTY-FOUR

Once on board, Zhu Irzh took an immediate dislike to the boat. It reeked of Heaven: that sickly peach-blossom odor permeating every crack of its ancient wood. The wood itself was dark and glossy, with a curious sparkle to it as if it contained trapped starlight. Perhaps it did, knowing the ways of the Celestials. The demon ran his hand along a railing and found that it burned his fingers. Hastily, he snatched his hand away.

"So sorry," the Celestial maiden said, though Zhu Irzh reckoned that she wasn't actually sorry at all. No doubt she thought it was nothing more than he deserved.

"Perhaps he should have stayed on the dock," Chen said.

"What, I'm not good enough to be in the presence of a Celestial immortal?" Zhu Irzh asked.

The maiden gave him a long, measured look. "Technically, no."

"Oh, thanks!"

"Well, you are from Hell, aren't you?"

"Hell was where I was born. I can't help that, can I?"

"I suppose not," the maiden said after a moment's consideration. Then she added, humbly, "Perhaps I should be more charitable."

"Yes, maybe you should." But the whole exchange set Zhu Irzh to thinking as they followed the maiden along the deck, with the badger trundling along behind. It was true: as far as he knew, he'd had no choice. He wasn't at all clear about the workings of Hellkind's reproduction, at least, not as far as it concerned the soul. Humans were different: born into the flesh, they served out their time in it, discarded it, and then went elsewhere as if snapped back to their true realm by a piece of elastic. But the Celestials and Hellkind were not like that; they were born all of a piece. There was a limited kind of rein-carnation—when a demon died, it simply remanifested, and as far as Zhu

Irzh knew, the Celestials did not die at all. But did that mean that they could not die, or only that they rarely did? He had heard of demons slaying Celestial beings, but not what happened to them after that. He had assumed that they simply reappeared in Heaven, a bit ruffled. But maybe this wasn't the case at all. Zhu Irzh was starting to feel a distinct theological lack. He frowned as he walked along the deck and was conscious of a sense of nervousness as they approached what was presumably the goddess Kuan Yin's cabin.

When they got to a tall, narrow door, the maiden turned. "Wait here, if you please. I must speak to my mistress." Then she stepped through the closed door, which rippled like water to let her in.

"You know," the demon said. "I don't think I've ever heard of a Celestial being coming all the way to the Night Harbor. I mean, apart from the clerks and so forth. But a goddess?"

"I've been wondering why she's here," Chen replied. "I can't see it as a positive sign, somehow."

"Neither can I." Zhu Irzh glanced up as the maiden reappeared.

"She wants to see both of you," the maiden said, managing to convey an air of discreet distaste as she looked at the demon.

"We'd be honored," Chen said, before Zhu Irzh could answer.

"Then please go in." The maiden opened the door. Zhu Irzh followed Chen into a warm, dark place, confined by red lacquered walls. It reminded him of a womb—that might, after all, be the idea. Smoke curled into the air from several tall incense burners, forcing the demon to stifle a sneeze. As his vision cleared, he saw that the goddess was seated at the far end of the chamber, upon a comfortably upholstered chair. She did not rise as they entered—one would hardly have expected her to—but greeted Chen with warmth. Zhu Irzh received a rather cooler salutation.

"Detective Zhu Irzh. We've met, have we not?"

"Yes, we have. After the—unpleasantness—last year."

"I remember all too well," the goddess said grimly. "And now you are here, on Earth."

"Assigned to the offices of justice," Zhu Irzh said. "Performing good and useful work." He was suddenly aware that he was babbling. He was of one of the aristocracies of Hell, he reminded himself. There was no need to justify himself before the enemy. And yet, looking at Kuan Yin's remote, cool countenance, Zhu Irzh could not help feeling very small.

At last the goddess rose, in a swish of silk and a wave of subtle perfume. "I have come, Chen, to search for someone. Someone who has answers to my questions, and someone who has been transformed."

"With all due respect, Goddess," Chen said. "I'm surprised that you came yourself, and did not send a minion."

"I'm very hands-on sometimes," the goddess remarked, surprising Zhu

Irzh. She hesitated. "Besides, there is a question of trust."

Zhu Irzh could almost feel Chen's mouth drop open. "Trust? Among Heavenkind, I thought that would be automatic."

"Then you would be wrong," the goddess said. "We have our factions, just as you do. Aeons ago, perhaps, it was different—but you know the myths of origin. Creation arises not from agreement, but from conflict and tension. These things are the crucible that generates change. And there are many who hold that this is not a good thing, that Heaven must be more united, more cohesive. They do not believe that a certain degree of disagreement is healthy. They seek to unite us, and they seek to do so by withdrawing us from the ways of the world."

Obliquely, Zhu Irzh understood. Heaven was splitting, Kuan Yin couldn't trust any of her peers, and so she had come all the way down here to get her divine hands dirty. One had to have some respect for that: it was almost Hellish.

"I'm glad you're here," Chen was saying. "I have some critical information for you."

"Tell me," the goddess said, and so Chen did.

When he had finished, the goddess was silent for a long time. She was so still that Zhu Irzh wondered whether she might have returned to her marble form: he'd seen her do that before, the Celestial equivalent of locking oneself in the bathroom and having a long think. But it seemed that the goddess was merely processing, for eventually the life flooded back into her features and she turned to Chen.

"And you say it has already begun?"

"Tserai has already altered at least one Celestial being. My colleague here witnessed its transformation."

"Tell me about this being," the goddess said. Beneath the icy calm, Zhu Irzh thought he detected a momentary unease, but the goddess was too difficult to read. Perhaps he had merely imagined it. He related to Kuan Yin the events at the Farm. When he had finished, she said, "And this Celestial being. Tell me again what he looked like."

She was presumably trying to place the entity. Zhu Irzh obliged and again there was that faint stirring beneath the marble facade, this time one of relief. But why should the goddess be relieved to know that one of her kindred had fallen into the hands of the enemy?

Chen said, "You spoke of looking for someone. May we be given to know who?"

"You may. An enemy. The one who has been trying to bring Hellkind through to the city."

For a paranoid moment, Zhu Irzh thought that Kuan Yin meant himself and was being subtle about it. But the goddess continued: "One who has died and is trapped here. One who was murdered."

"Deveth Sardai?" Zhu Irzh said before he could stop himself. Chen shot him an unreadable glance and it was only then that he realized that Chen himself may wish to keep secrets from Heaven, though he did not understand why.

"She is here, in the Night Harbor. Heaven has had its eye on her for years."

"Surely she's hardly a candidate for the Celestial pastures!" Zhu Irzh remarked.

"I meant, demon, in the sense that we continue to watch our enemies. Sardai's family has long been in league with Hell. And Deveth was one of the most promising sorcerers of her generation. Naturally, we watched her."

"You realize that Deveth is not the prime mover here?" Chen said carefully. He glanced at the demon again, as if wondering whether to ask Zhu Irzh to leave. The demon stood his ground. He knew what Chen was about to say.

"You mentioned the name of Jhai Tserai. I understand that she is the focus of all this. But Tserai is not human, and subject to other jurisdiction. I am licensed only to go in search of Sardai."

"Other jurisdiction? What other jurisdiction?"

"The family is Keralan," Zhu Irzh said. "I'm assuming that makes Tserai subject to other deities."

"We could issue a kind of extradition order," Kuan Yin answered, "but such things are complex and take time. Sardai has all the answers I need for the moment, and her presence and witness is all the evidence."

"You're planning to bargain with her?" Chen asked doubtfully.

"I see no conflict here, Detective. She is your murder victim, after all, not a suspect. You have only to seek out the one who slew her. No, Sardai will be subject to our courts and our justice. There is, however, no difficulty in granting you the right to question her before I take her to Heaven."

The goddess seemed very confident, Zhu Irzh thought, but he supposed that this went with the territory.

"Then if we help you look for Sardai," Chen said, "and she tells us exactly who it was who murdered her, you can take things from there?"

"She can't appear in your courts, can she? All you need is a signed and sealed witness statement."

"Yes, that's perfectly adequate under these circumstances. It isn't possible for a spirit to lie about their death: it's the one thing on which they have to speak the truth."

"Then we are in accord," the goddess said, smiling. "All we have to do now is find her."

But Zhu Irzh, thinking of the vast and shadowed hinterlands of the Night Harbor, suddenly realized that he was unable to share the goddess' presumption of success.

THIRTY-FIVE

Robin knew that no sunlight penetrated into the lands of the Night Harbor, and yet a kind of dawn seemed to come nonetheless. The outlines of the squalid room shimmered into view and she could see once more through the slats of the hovel. Bad Dog Village stirred slowly into life. Robin watched through the slats as dogs bounded from their houses, blurring into their humanoid forms as they did so, scratching, yawning, bickering and occasionally squatting down in the street to shit. No wonder she had no memories of this place. The essential mind-wiping nature of the Night Harbor aside, her spirit had undoubtedly hastened through it as quickly as possible with eyes averted.

She had not expected breakfast and, indeed, none came. This was no hardship, for she was not hungry, but the thirst was dreadful and she was relieved when the door opened and a scruffy, sharp-toothed woman with matted hair entered with a bowl of water.

"This is for you. You'll be thirsty," she said, roughly but not with unkindness. The woman stared curiously at Robin as she awkwardly drank.

"So, you're the brindled bitch's bitch. Not dead, are you?"

"No," Robin said, after a moment. No point in trying to lie: she was sure these people could smell the life in her.

"We don't get many live ones through here. You'd be all they could talk about if it wasn't for the other one."

"Mhara? My friend? Do you know where he is?"

"Oh, I'm not going to tell you that. He's special, is that one. Heavenkind, and they think they know who, too." The woman put on a sly look as though she enjoyed knowing something that Robin did not. "You don't know, do you? He hasn't told you."

"Told me what?"

"Oh, I couldn't say. Tesk would whip the life out of me." She gave a short, harsh laugh. "If there was any in me, that is."

Robin wasn't going to let on that she didn't know what the woman was talking about. She hid her disquiet and said, "So tell me. Who are you people?"

"Us? We're the outcasts. Too good for Hell, too bad for Heaven. People the bureaucrats don't know what to do with. All our cases are pending. Supposedly. But I know what happens—they just shove them in a drawer somewhere and forget about them because they don't want the hassle."

"Can't your families pray—or pay—to have you sent on? Tip the balance?"

"What families? We come from folk who are too ignorant to know and too selfish to care. And so we end up here in Bad Dog Village, little lost spirits whom the land turns to dog-form." The woman's foot thumped briefly on the ground, like a dog scratching. "It's not such a bad life. There's food in the hills, game and such like, though I wouldn't call them rabbits. Too many teeth. And the men are all right once you get to know them, and know your place. It's shelter."

"But you must want to move on, get back into life eventually?"

The woman snorted. "As what? Born back into the same life we left by dying? You don't know what my life was like as a human woman. This might be a shitty life, but it's still better." She rose to her feet and stretched. "Anyway, nice talking to you, but I'd better get on. And, dearie, when you get back to the land of the living, make sure you don't live the kind of life that winds you up back here, eh? I don't need the competition."

When she had gone Robin stared at the empty water bowl and thought. It seemed to her that Bad Dog Village was exactly where she had been heading, up until the point that she freed Mhara, and she only had the courage to do that because she was essentially delirious. But until that point, it had been neither good nor bad, and more of the latter than the former. She had done enough thinking about it, enough self-analysis. It was time to change, but if she was going to escape Bad Dog Village in death, then she had to escape it in life first, and she had no clear idea as to how to go about it.

The bitch-woman's comments about Mhara had been odd, as well. *He's special.* Well, she knew that, but did they mean only that Mhara was Heaven-kind, and far from home, or something more? And if so, what were they planning for her friend?

Resolving to do something constructive, Robin made a thorough search of the hovel, but though the walls were flimsy enough, they were woven in with some kind of tough rush and she could neither force nor unweave her way through. She battered at the door until her strength was spent, but it was of no use. Frustrated, she sat down and tried to think of a plan.

THIRTY-SIX

The goddess did not accompany them back to the Night Harbor, as Zhu Irzh was expecting. Instead, she asked Chen and the demon to remain on deck, then closeted herself in the red lacquered room with her maid. The door remained closed for some time.

"What are they *doing* in there?" Zhu Irzh chafed. The atmosphere of the boat was really starting to get to him, causing a kind of deep psychic itch.

"I have no idea," Chen replied. "Discussing the situation, probably."

But when the door finally opened and the Celestial maiden stepped forth, she had changed. She now had about her an air of grave authority and presence, and her gaze was as depthless and dark as the Sea of Night itself.

"Goddess?" Chen said.

"A seed only," the maiden answered, and her voice was different, too, now having some of the timbre of Kuan Yin's own. Zhu Irzh had seen people download themselves, or parts of their psyches, into other people before, but he had rarely seen it done so smoothly. Usually the possessed were fuzzy around the edges.

"Can we go now?" he asked.

"Of course," the maiden replied, as though there had never been any question about it. Since becoming possessed, she seemed to have also taken on some of Kuan Yin's more fluid and mutable qualities. The maiden moved sinuously from the boat, and Zhu Irzh clambered after her.

The dock of the Night Harbor had filled up in their absence and was now crowded. There must have been a fresh consignment of souls released through the portals while Chen and the demon were on board. The souls looked confused: some wandered up to Kuan Yin's vessel and trailed wondering, wistful hands along its sides.

"We must be careful," the maiden said. "It would not be helpful if some-

147

one were to stow aboard." She spoke coolly, but Zhu Irzh caught sight of the sadness in her possessed eyes and knew that she would save them all if she could. Despite her remoteness, Kuan Yin, the Compassionate and the Merciful, was truly named.

Chen was already at the harbor master's hut, asking questions. When the maiden and Zhu Irzh reached him, he said, "The harbor master thinks he knows who she is. She's not in her original form, however. The dogs got to her when she reached the village."

"I can't understand why she didn't go onward to Hell," Zhu Irzh said. "She wasn't a good person."

"No, but she was murdered and that was probably enough to hold her here," Chen replied. "It gets complicated."

"So what happens now?" the maiden asked. "We go to the village?"

"Yes, but I'm reluctant to walk. It's too far and it's also dangerous. I'll have to try to arrange some transport."

"Leave it to me," the maiden said. She disappeared inside the harbor master's hut. Chen and the demon looked at one another.

"She's the goddess," Zhu Irzh said. "Best leave it to her."

But when the maiden emerged, her head was held high and her eyes were snapping. "Bureaucrats! Come with me!" was all that she said. Exchanging a further round of glances, Chen and Zhu Irzh followed meekly in her wake.

The transport that was to take them to Bad Dog Village proved to be a ramshackle coach, drawn by two mangy kylin lion-dogs. They stamped their fringed feet as the demon approached, tossed their manes and roared, enveloping the party in a wave of fetid breath.

"Lovely," Zhu Irzh said, eyeing them with minimal enthusiasm. "Couldn't they find anything better?"

"Apparently not," the maiden remarked. "I believe that man took actual delight in thwarting a deity. But I have so little jurisdiction here… We must take what we can get." She allowed Chen to open the door of the carriage and help her inside. "You will have to drive."

Chen glanced at Zhu Irzh. "Can you do it? I've no experience with these things."

"I can try," Zhu Irzh said, but he was not confident that the beasts would obey him. Chen hoisted the badger up, then clambered up beside him and watched as Zhu Irzh shook the reins, clucked, and failed to make the kylins budge. Eventually, with a lot of cursing and the use of a small, flicking whip, the beasts were prodded into movement and the carriage set off along the dock at a slow trundle.

"Do you even know where we're going?" Zhu Irzh asked.

"Not really, but apparently Kuan Yin does. Her avatar will give us directions."

"Strange," the demon mused. "You must have come here many times, and yet you retain none of it."

Chen grimaced. "Probably just as well. I don't like the Night Harbor, Zhu Irzh."

"I can see why." Zhu Irzh looked with distaste at the ghosts clamoring alongside them, their spectral hands brushing against his coat and the sides of the carriage. "What good do they think that will do?"

"They can sense the presence of the goddess," Chen said uneasily. "They're drawn to her."

"What, they think she might be able to give them special dispensation? Get them up to Heaven?"

"I have no idea. Maybe they're just like moths to a flame. Maybe it's me they're drawn to. After all, I'm still alive."

Zhu Irzh shook the reins, flicked the whip and the carriage picked up speed as they approached the outskirts of what passed for a settlement here. Chen leaned into the carriage and spoke to the maiden. Zhu Irzh heard a murmured reply.

"We need to head for the mountain road, apparently."

"And where might that be? There's a distinct lack of signs."

"Look," Chen said, and as he spoke the demon could see the mountains rising ahead, huge masses of shadow against the darkness. Somewhere high on a peak, he could see a wan light. "Do you think that's the village?"

"I don't know. Keep on this road and it'll take us into the hills."

As the carriage rolled along, Zhu Irzh saw that they were passing groups of souls, trailing drearily down from the mountains. Some were no more than children, clutching the hands of adult spirits, and many of them were old. Used to the exigencies of Hell as he was, Zhu Irzh repressed a shudder. What an afterlife, he thought. No wonder so many humans tried to make deals with Hell in order to avoid it. You would be much better off going to Hell straightaway: at least it was exciting, not this dull, elusive hinterland.

"Excuse me," he called down to one of the groups of souls. "Have you come from Bad Dog Village?"

"Yes, yes, a terrible place." One of the souls, an elderly man with the ravages of illness still plain in his face, was eager to complain. "We hurried through it, but we lost one of our number. The dogs kept him, it is said they eat spirits or hunt them for sport. And now we head for the boat and the peach orchards across the sea." A kind of peace suffused his worn features, blotting out the anxiety.

"We wish you good fortune and good sailing," Chen called down, and the demon drove on.

Gradually, he became aware that the sky, or whatever passed for it in the Night Harbor, was beginning to lighten. It became easier to see the fields and copses alongside the road, the remnants of farms and smallholdings.

"Who lives here then?" Zhu Irzh asked, puzzled. "Who would choose to farm such changing terrain?"

"I don't think they have a choice," Chen replied. "Some folk just get stuck. And perhaps some people don't want to face the journey, the razor bridge, dogtown—maybe they *do* choose to stay here. I don't know. I thought perhaps you would."

"I understand Hell and its workings," Zhu Irzh said. "But this country... I'm not familiar with it, after all, and why should I have taken an interest before now?"

Chen shrugged. Zhu Irzh drove on and at length the fields faded and gave way to rock and ragged outcrops. The air smelled of dust and decay. Zhu Irzh kept glimpsing bones from the corner of his eye, skeletal heaps by the side of the road, but when he looked, there was nothing there. He had not realized it was so quiet when the roar shattered the air. It reverberated from the rocks, making Zhu Irzh's head ring. The maiden gave a cry, quickly stifled, from within the carriage, and the kylins danced to a standstill and refused to go further.

"What was that?" Chen, his usual composure ruffled, clutched at the demon's arm.

"I don't know. What sort of things are you supposed to find in these mountains anyway?"

"I thought it was the home of the dogmen alone."

"I don't think that was a dogman. It sounded enormous."

"Look, let's just get on," Chen said.

"If I can get these things to move, we will."

Eventually he coaxed the kylins forward, but as they rounded the corner, something bounded down to stand in their path. It moved so swiftly that Zhu Irzh saw it only as a flicker against the rocks. The kylins reared, nearly overturning the carriage. Zhu Irzh and Chen both fought for control of the reins and hauled the kylins back.

"What is it?" the maiden cried.

"A thing," Zhu Irzh called back, with perfect truth.

He had never seen anything like the creature that now stood before them, bouncing slightly on four long legs. It was hairless and white, with a gaunt, tapering body and no sign of genitalia. Its narrow head was eyeless, with a slit for a nose and a gaping hole of a mouth, lined with teeth like a lamprey. Yet despite its unfamiliarity, it felt...known. He had experienced this thing before, and recently.

The maiden, disregarding Chen's warning shout, was scrambling down from the carriage to stand in the road.

"Heavenly Emperor," she said faintly. "*Shur?*" Her face was aghast, and abruptly Zhu Irzh remembered where he had met this thing before. It looked different, but he knew it. He would have paid good money to bet that this was the spiritual remnant of the immortal that Jhai Tserai had captured and held at the Farm. Next moment, his suspicions were confirmed. The thing's razor-sharp tongue shot out in the direction of the maiden and the creature charged.

THIRTY-SEVEN

Paravang Roche went to the temple at the appropriate time. He bought the goddess a bunch of flowers at the station: chrysanthemums tawny in their roll of paper, smelling of spice. A proper show of obsequiousness should help matters along. As he went through the door of the temple he saw that the priest-broker was there before him, kneeling perfectly still, his forehead touching the ground before the outstretched arms of the smiling deity. Roche knelt beside him and waited until he had completed his prayer. The broker uncoiled from the floor and looked at him.

"You."

"Indeed," Paravang said.

"Do you have the money?"

"Of course I don't have the money. These things take time. But I will have it, make no mistake about that." Make a good display of confidence, Paravang thought, and maybe he'll go away without asking too many awkward questions. But the priest-broker's eyes narrowed.

"And how do you propose to manage that?"

"Family," Paravang said, with perfect truth.

He could tell that the broker wanted to believe him, and yet could not quite make the leap. He smiled serenely at the old man, trying to give an impression of untroubled unconcern, and eventually, with a last suspicious glance, the broker shuffled off to the duties of the day, leaving Paravang alone in the temple.

Paravang laid the flowers before the statue of the goddess and prayed for success rather perfunctorily. The rites might have to be duly observed, but his confidence in Senditreya's powers was at an all-time low. He did not spend long in the temple, therefore, but took off down the street to a narrow alley filled with remedy shops and a butcher's. He had first come here years before to defuse a *ch'i* war, and the butcher still owed him a few favors. Before the butcher's door, he paused for a moment and collected himself before going inside.

The butcher was a short, slight man with an unhealthy plumpness. Indeed, it was more than plumpness: Paravang, with a distaste he found difficult to conceal, could see the outlines of breasts beneath the butcher's bloodstained overall, and yet the butcher was unmistakably male. Rumor had it that this was caused by continual exposure to the illicit hormones found in the meat that this particular establishment specialized in, but it had one singular advantage. The butcher was an accomplished sorcerer, and his shifting gender apparently lent him powers that a normal man would have found difficult to attain. Years ago, Paravang had read an article about Siberian shamans who cross-dressed, and he supposed that this was a similar kind of thing.

The butcher looked at him out of reddened eyes.

"Oh, it's you. What do you want?"

"I need your services." Paravang and the butcher regarded one another for a moment with mutual disdain.

"You'd better come in the back, then," the butcher said at last.

蛇警探

The explanation took less time than Paravang had feared. The butcher, Wo Ti, did not bother to ask why Paravang needed the money. Perhaps he'd already heard about the issue of the revoked license: news traveled fast in certain quarters. When Paravang told him that it was essential to conjure forth the spirit of his dead mother, Wo Ti merely grunted and informed him that the time was highly auspicious, given the proximity of the Day of the Dead, but the price would be high. Paravang haggled, and beat the butcher down from outrageous to simply extortionate. He spent the rest of the afternoon in the pawn shop, persuading the broker that a vase really was Tang dynasty and not a cheap knockoff (an episode of some frustration as here, for once, Paravang found himself telling the truth), then returned to the butcher's in the evening with the money.

"I can't summon her here and now," the butcher said. A black cockerel, which Paravang had not noticed that morning, sat huddled in a little cage on the chopping block. "The tides between the worlds aren't right; I'll have to wait till midnight. Go to your temple and wait. I'll send her to you then."

"Can't I wait here?" Paravang said. Goddess knew, he had little interest in witnessing sorcery, but he wanted to make sure that the butcher didn't rip him off.

"No, I don't allow clients to watch except under exceptional circumstances. Don't worry, I won't cheat you. We do have a professional code of ethics, you know."

So did the Feng Shui Practitioners' Guild, but it didn't stop markups and obfuscation, thought Paravang. With reluctance, he agreed to return to Senditreya's temple and wait until midnight.

Over the course of the night, Paravang became increasingly certain that the butcher had indeed cheated him. The temple filled briefly for the evening services, then emptied again. The room grew cold and dark. Even the little votive lamps on the altar seemed to cast no real light. Paravang's chrysanthemums wilted as if touched by frost, even though he had taken care to set them in enough water. Midnight came and went and there was no sign of any approaching spirits. Paravang began to debate whether or not to just go home. The prospect of his own warm bed was exceptionally alluring, and as he started thinking about it, he fell asleep.

Later, he jerked awake as if prodded. Since the temple possessed no windows, he could not see the approaching dawn, but he knew that the sun must be coming up by the sudden activity in the main courtyard. Someone was whistling a jaunty tune, irritating if you have been awake all night, on your knees and frightened. Paravang could hardly move his head from its bowed position. His neck had become painfully stiff in the night, and all his joints ached. Thus he did not look round when he heard footsteps behind him, and a rustle of stiff silk indicating that someone had knelt beside him. It was only when he felt a hand on his shoulder that he turned and found himself staring at a middle-aged woman, dressed in clothes that were fashionable twenty years ago. She was beaming at him, and after a belated moment he recognized his mother.

"God, it's really you," he whispered.

His mother's lips moved, but no sound emerged. She looked about her, gazing up at the shadowy form of the goddess. He remembered now that she had always approved of Senditreya—thought she was a wholesome, next-door kind of deity—and doubtless it was mutual. She was sentimental about religion. She thought it was nice. Paravang gaped at her. His mother had been in her mid-sixties when she had died; the process had evidently knocked a decade or so from her. Her hair was lacquered into a helmet, and she was wearing her familiar dark red jacket. She did not look much like a ghost to her astounded son, until he realized that he was unable to see beyond her eyes: they were flat and without reflection, like the eyes of a mask.

"I'm so glad you're here," Mrs Roche said, reproachfully. "I've been trying to phone your father for *days,* and he wouldn't pick it up, but I know he was there. And you haven't been answering your telephone either, dear."

"I was—I was working."

"Well, never mind, because you're here now. And whoever was that man? I was having ever such a nice read of my magazine and suddenly I found myself in a butcher's shop."

"I'm sorry, Mother. It must have been very distressing for you. But I wanted to talk to you, you see, because I have some wonderful news. I want to get married."

"Oh," his mother said. There was a short, chilly pause.

"Aren't you pleased? I thought it was what you always wanted!"

"It is, dear, of course, but it's just that this has come at a rather awkward time." She rearranged her skirts more comfortably about her. "I wanted to talk to you, Paravang, because I've got someone I want you to meet."

"Oh?" He could have sworn that his mother and the goddess exchanged a complicit little smile.

"Just listen to me, Paravang, and hear what I've got to tell you…"

How can you deny your dead mother? Paravang knelt stiffly on the matting and heard her out, with a growing sense of horror. As one trap began to close, he felt, so another opened beneath his unwary feet. But as she talked on, he began to consider that her idea might have a use, for once. He listened carefully.

THIRTY-EIGHT

Chen leaped down from the carriage and pulled the maiden out of the way. The viperous ex-immortal bounded past her on long, thin legs, swerved, and turned back.

"Zhu Irzh!" Chen shouted. "Get the carriage moving!"

Zhu Irzh obligingly cracked the whip over the backs of the kylins as the ex-immortal raced back. The kylins bellowed with fright and charged forward. Zhu Irzh glanced back to see Chen and the Kuan Yin avatar hauling themselves into the moving carriage. Then the ex-immortal was sprinting alongside, the long tongue flickering out, trying to reach into the carriage itself. One of the kylins shot a glance over its shoulder and screamed with fright. Both beasts changed their shape, transforming themselves into lumbering, over-muscled men who dropped out of the harness and raced, snuffling, into the darkness. The coach skidded on the road, striking sparks.

Zhu Irzh took a deep breath, reached down behind him, grabbed hold of the tongue, which resembled a handful of needles, and pulled. Unfortunately, the tongue tugged as well and Zhu Irzh flew off the carriage and landed in the road with the ex-immortal on top of him. Cursing, he lashed out at it but the stabbing tongue was reaching for his eyes. He twisted from side to side, trying to shake it off. The terrible blind head was moving closer.

If it "kills" me, the demon thought, *then I shall find myself back in Hell.* And what a hassle that would be, not to mention, in all probability, painful. The head flung itself back, the tongue uncoiled—and then the ex-immortal was dragged off Zhu Irzh. He could hear the badger growling. Zhu Irzh lay panting on the ground, and then Chen hauled him to his feet. The maiden, with swift, calm efficiency, was binding the ex-immortal's hands behind its back with its own tongue. The spines seemed not to inconvenience her at all; her hands glowed with a faint, repelling light.

"Thanks," Zhu Irzh said to the maiden.

"You're welcome. I am deeply relieved that we have found him. I did not want to go back without him, though of course the other one, Deveth Sardai, has to take precedence."

Chen frowned. "Why so?"

"I shall give him a sedative," the maiden said as though Chen had not spoken, "and I suppose we shall have to leave him here. My primary self will send someone to fetch him, since the kylins have run away. And now we must head on to the village. I am not sure how long the light will last."

The ex-immortal slumped in her grasp and she arranged him neatly by the roadside. "There we are. Follow me."

Zhu Irzh could think of nothing to say and it seemed that Chen was in a similar state. In a silence both startled and ruminative, they pursued the marching avatar up the hillside.

蛇警探

It became evident that they were approaching Bad Dog Village by the increased amount of filth along the roadside. Gnawed bones littered the dusty earth, along with piles of shit and scraps of material. Zhu Irzh wrinkled his nose. The badger gave an earthy, choking cough.

"Why do you think it's *necessary*, Chen, for souls to pass through here?" Zhu Irzh asked.

"I think it's a test," Chen said. "Like the razor bridge."

"But why should souls be tested?" the demon asked. These theological speculations were new and disturbing. "Haven't they already passed through the test of death? And if they're judged on the events of their lives, then what difference does it make if they pass or fail?"

"Bad Dog Village is a part of that judgement," the goddess' avatar said over her shoulder. "Some souls hang in the balance, and cannot go on to either Heaven or Hell. They must remain here, until a judgement is made."

"What if a judgement isn't made?"

"Then here they stay."

"That doesn't seem very fair," Zhu Irzh said, blinking.

"A remarkable statement, coming from a demon," Chen said without rancor.

"Yes, I know, but—someone should do something about it."

He saw the goddess smile behind her hand, and it annoyed him. What, he wasn't allowed to point out the obvious simply because of his origins? Perhaps it was time to own up to this conscience of his, Zhu Irzh thought. It gave him enough trouble; maybe he should start acting on it…

"There's the village," Chen said, pointing ahead.

It didn't look like much of a place to the demon, but he was becoming accustomed to the impermanent appearance of the Night Harbor. A sudden howling suggested that the inhabitants had become aware of their presence.

"So what's the plan?" Zhu Irzh asked. "We just go in and ask for Deveth? What if they refuse to tell us?"

"They will not refuse me," the maiden said.

The demon took a deep breath. "All right. I'll take your word for it."

"You'd best be elsewhere," Chen said to the badger. "See what you can find."

"I dislike dogs," the badger said, and disappeared into the darkness without further comment.

The dogmen swarmed around them as they came up to the gate, drifting and changing from their dog-form to half-human, and back again. But it was clear that they recognized something of the maiden's nature, for they were curiously respectful: keeping their distance and bobbing up and down in the travesty of a bow. Their respect did not extend to Chen or the demon. Zhu Irzh cuffed away a nose that was becoming over-familiar with his crotch, and shouted to the maiden, "Can't you control them?"

"We will go inside," the maiden said firmly, and swept through the gate with the pack in her wake.

蛇警探

They were sitting in what amounted to state, in a long room filled with an untidy muddle of furniture. This, it had been explained to them, was the pack leader's parlor. The maiden had been taken into another room, leaving Chen and Zhu Irzh to cool their heels with a pot of tea that tasted like wet straw.

"I hope she'll be all right," the demon said.

"I'm sure she can look after herself," Chen replied. "She *is* a goddess, after all."

"Yes, but her body isn't."

"Her body is still that of a Celestial and these creatures know better than to touch one of those. They don't want to bring the wrath of Heaven down onto the Night Harbor, after all. Kuan Yin may not have jurisdiction here, but everyone knows that it's a delicate balance."

At that point, the maiden reappeared in the doorway, assuaging Zhu Irzh's fears.

"They know a little of this woman," she said. "They say that she came through the village and was transformed, but then she left—ran into the mountains and has not been seen since. It seems our journey here has been pointless. We should leave."

"No, wait a moment," Chen said, but the maiden winked at him, an extraordinary effect to Zhu Irzh's mind, given her deific origins.

"Come on," the demon said, rising. "Let's get out of here."

The dogs watched them go with smug self-satisfaction. The pack leader went as far as to express the hope that Zhu Irzh had enjoyed his visit.

"Greatly," the demon lied. He was sorely tempted to add, "Though I'm really more of a cat person," but managed to restrain himself.

As soon as they left the gates of the village and turned the corner of the road that led back to the port, the badger shuffled out of the shadows.

"Well?" Chen said.

"There is a trail."

"Of the dogwoman, of Deveth?"

"Perhaps. It is hard to say. But this you should know," the badger said. "There is another immortal here."

"Yes, the one whom we left on the road," the maiden replied. "The goddess—I—has sent someone to fetch the poor lost soul."

Zhu Irzh repressed a snort as the badger went on. "No, not that one. I know its scent, and your own. This is another."

The maiden became very still. Zhu Irzh, recognizing the goddess' statue mode, waited.

"Another?" the maiden asked, in a small, cold voice. "Are you sure?"

"I am rarely mistaken," the badger said.

"Is it male, or female?"

"It is male, although this was not obvious to me at first. There is someone with him. A human, and not a soul, either. A living person."

"Goddess," Chen said. "You have to tell us what is going on."

"I cannot. At least, not here. You are right, you need to know. But first we have to find these people." She turned to the badger. "Can you lead us to them?"

"I believe so. But I do not think they escaped. They were taken by the dog-men. The scent of them is all around."

"Very well," the maiden said. "Then lead on."

THIRTY-NINE

Robin had no idea where they had been taken. At some point during the previous night, she had been roughly roused from sleep, dragged from the hovel, and bound: a gag placed across her mouth, her wrists secured behind her back and her legs shackled. Then she had been led out into the compound and hoisted onto a cart. Mhara, to her relief and dismay, was already there, similarly constrained. They could look at one another, but not speak: the gag was an effective one. The cart rumbled off, jolting and bouncing over the rough ground. She could not see what might be pulling it, but once she looked to the side of the road and saw Deveth, in her dog-form, trotting along beside. Deveth looked at her and gave a vulpine grin, then vanished from sight. Robin worked steadily at the bonds, but with no result. They were made of thick hemp rope, and they would not budge.

Although it was dark, she could tell that they were climbing. The air, however, did not grow any fresher: it smelled as though they were moving through a cellar, musty and fungal, with an undertone of decay. Her hands felt gritty, covered in dust, and there was a faint wind blowing which covered her face in the dust, too. Soon she found it more comfortable to close her eyes, though she tried to keep them open in the off-chance that she might be able to glimpse their destination or their route. Eventually the cart slowed and she was lifted down.

The dogmen were growling and snapping at one another again: it was a moment before Robin realized that they were actually communicating. They pulled and tugged her into the narrow mouth of a cave, then released a lever. An iron grille rattled down, sealing her and Mhara behind it. Deveth peered through the bars.

"You'll be kept here. Don't worry, they're not leaving you to rot. Someone will bring you food and water tomorrow; until then, the gags stay on. I suggest you try to sleep."

Robin produced a series of strangled protests. Deveth's grin widened.

"That won't do you much good. I don't have a lot of say in this, you know. It wasn't my idea." Somehow, Robin was certain she was lying. She kicked at the bars, but Deveth was already bounding away down the mountainside. Robin watched her go, consumed by a flurry of emotions: rage, despair, frustration. Mhara nudged her. She looked up and his eyes were full of understanding and compassion. She leaned against him, looking out over the dark mountain to the lights of what must be the Night Harbor port. They were dim and fuzzy, like lanterns seen through rain, and very far away. She sank down to sit with her back against the wall and fell into an exhausted sleep.

蛇警探

The bars rattled her awake. Something was reaching in through the grille, a long, bare arm with claws that raked down her shin and brought fire in their wake. Robin screamed through the gag and scrambled away, waking Mhara in the process. She looked out onto a mouth filled with teeth, a narrow, bald head. Mhara and Robin shuffled back as far as they could, but the cave came to an abrupt end. They were trapped, and now the thing was questing about, its blind head raised as if testing the air. It made a small noise of approbation, then took hold of the lever. Mhara pushed himself in front of Robin and an undignified shackled scuffle broke out as each sought to protect the other. The grille shot up, the thing bounded into the cave and lashed out at Mhara. Robin hurled herself at it, caught her foot on a rocky outcrop and fell heavily to the floor. The thing, in turn, fell over her and sprawled across the cave. Then something lightning-quick and growling had entered the fray. Robin, trying to rise, glimpsed a long, narrow head and eyes like scraps of night. It was a badger—but whatever was a badger doing here? Then she heard shouts and a tall snarling form in a black coat seized the bald thing and banged its head repeatedly against the wall. A shorter man was there, then, accompanied by a girl. Together, moving with calm efficiency, they released Robin and Mhara from their bonds and tore away Robin's gag.

"Thank you!" Robin whispered. It was all she could manage, for her throat was raw from lack of water.

"I'm glad we found you in time," the man said. Robin looked into a round, pleasant, unremarkable face.

"You're *human*," she said. The relief was overwhelming; she sagged in his grasp.

"Detective Inspector Chen. I'm with the city's police force. This—" he pointed to the tall person, who had finished his assault on the thing and was now securing its hands with a pair of handcuffs "—is my partner, Detective Zhu Irzh. He isn't human, as you can probably see, but don't worry about that."

"My name is Robin Yuan. And who are you?" Robin asked the girl. She had never seen anyone so delicately beautiful: the girl made Robin, who had always considered herself to be a slight person, feel like an ox in comparison. And what lovely perfume she was wearing: it filled the cave, canceling the odors of decomposition and dust.

"I am a friend," the girl said with a curious firmness. Robin would have pressed the issue, but something about the girl's demeanor stopped her in her tracks. Though the girl looked so young, there was an impression of great age about her. She and Mhara were staring at one another.

"You know each other," Robin said, dismayed and suddenly jealous. Of course Mhara would have had friends in Heaven. And how could she ever think that she could compete with that?

"Yes, I believe we do," Mhara said, but he was not smiling. The girl said, with an odd diffidence, "I have come to bring you back."

"I know."

"Who are you?" Chen's colleague asked and Robin moved a little further away. He was so obviously a demon.

"My name is Mhara."

"You're a Celestial, aren't you? It's as plain as the nose on your face. The badger said he'd picked up a Celestial's scent."

"If it wasn't for the badger, we would never have found you," the girl said. The perfume intensified. "Creature of Earth, I owe you a debt."

"It is my work," the badger said, evidently somewhat offended. "I serve my master."

"What passes for dawn in these parts is not far away," Chen said, glancing toward the port, where the sky was indeed beginning to glow gray. "I suggest we try to make it back down the mountain before dogtown discovers your absence. I don't want to take on the whole village."

There was no disagreement. Zhu Irzh, muttering, hoisted Robin's unconscious assailant over his shoulder and they set off down the mountain, following the badger.

"What happened to you, back there in the village?" Mhara asked Robin quietly, as they made their way down the banks of scree.

"Not much. They kept me prisoner. I had a talk with one of the women. Deveth came to see me." She did not want to worry him with the attempted rape.

"And I also. She taunted me. I suppose it is her right. She said that they would have fed me to her, at the end, while the village watched: her recompense for her own murder. I told her that this would surely send her spirit on to Hell and she merely laughed, said that she would make her way in Hell as she had in the world so far." Mhara looked contemplative.

"But she could not actually have slain you, could she? You're a Celestial."

"My spirit would have lived on in her, had she eaten me. A prisoner, within her." Mhara shivered. "I can think of few worse fates."

"And that…thing." Robin nodded toward the creature slung over the demon's shoulder. "What *is* that?"

"It has the sense of Heaven," Mhara said.

"It doesn't look very Heavenly to me!"

"Nonetheless… I think someone may have sent it after me, Robin."

"To hurt you?"

"To bring me back. And I think it has become another of Jhai's experiments."

"Jhai turned a Celestial being into that monster?"

"It is no worse than what I became," Mhara said. He was not looking at her, there was no sense of blame, and yet the guilt flooded back all over again, hot and fresh. Robin said no more, but fixed her gaze on the distant port and tried not to think about what might be to come.

蛇警探

By the time they reached the outskirts of the port, it was much lighter. To Robin's relief, they had met no more horrors on the journey, but she kept looking over her shoulder all the same. The dogmen must surely have discovered their absence by now. She touched Chen on the shoulder.

"What now? Are you going to take me back to Earth?"

"I am not sure what's happening," Chen admitted. "I have a—suspect to find, but the person in charge is this young lady."

Strangely, Robin was not surprised. "I see." She felt herself grow colder. The girl would want to take Mhara back to Heaven, and probably Robin would be dispatched to Earth, to what remained of her normal life. And at the very least of it, unemployment, without references. "Who's your suspect?" she asked, to distract herself from this unwelcome prospect.

"A murder victim. A woman named Deveth Sardai. I need to question her about her death."

Robin found herself thinking furiously and hard. She had told Chen her name, back there in the cave, and if he had been assigned to the murder case then he would surely know all about her. She could not tell him that she knew very well who had murdered Deveth and risk him arresting Mhara. She was determined not to see Mhara face trial—but perhaps the human authorities wouldn't try him, Celestial being that he was. Yet

Tserai ought to be brought to justice… Guiltily, she became aware that Chen was watching her. His face was expressionless. Mhara nudged her.

"Robin. I will deal with this."

"I can't let you—"

"*Robin*." His hand closed warningly around her arm and Robin fell silent.

TA CH'U:
THE TAMING POWER
OF THE GREAT

FORTY

Zhu Irzh had never thought that he might be happy to see Kuan Yin's boat again, but it was not until they were on board that he finally felt able to relax, despite the irritations of the Heavenly vessel. His shoulders ached from having to lug the transformed Celestial all the way down the mountainside, but now the being had been confined in the lower reaches of the boat. Kuan Yin had departed from her maiden, who was now resting, exhausted, in her own cabin; it must be tiring, Zhu Irzh considered, to be possessed, especially by a goddess. He had the feeling that they were probably high maintenance. The young woman, Robin, was also resting, and her strange Celestial companion had been closeted with Kuan Yin for more than an hour, while Chen and Zhu Irzh were once more served tea by another of the goddess' handmaidens. Zhu Irzh was obliged to admit that the surroundings were nicer, and the quality of the tea higher, than those of Bad Dog Village. He gazed around at the pearly lacquered walls, inlaid with scenes of Heavenly life, with only mild distaste. Chen leaned forward and tapped him on the knee.

"So. Robin Yuan. What does that name mean to you?"

"Sardai's girlfriend?"

"Exactly. Yet she said nothing when I mentioned Deveth's name, and we still have to find Deveth and question her. Now that the goddess' business has been more or less accomplished, we need to think about our own."

"Deveth was killed by something, not necessarily someone. But the investigation didn't clear Robin. She could be implicated. And she's traveling in the company of another immortal. What if he's the killer?"

"Robin works for your girlfriend."

"She's not exactly my—oh, all right. Robin's in it up to her eyes, if you ask me. All we have to do is find out how."

Chen appeared about to speak, but then glanced around him, startled. On the table, the tea bowls rattled a little and then were still. "Hang on. We're moving."

Zhu Irzh followed him on deck, at a run. The ship had indeed upped anchor. The lights of the Night Harbor's port had already fallen behind to a hazy line along the shore and the boat was moving out past a narrow breakwater with a squat lighthouse at its end. Ahead, lay the immense void of the Sea of Night. At that moment, they passed the Harbor arm and into the Sea itself. Zhu Irzh, looking over the side in dismay, caught sight of distant stars, deep below the water.

"If Kuan Yin thinks—" Chen, about to utter blasphemy, fell silent and headed back to the row of cabins with the demon at his heels. He raised a hand to the goddess' door, then let it fall. Zhu Irzh, however, had decided to abandon any attempt at Celestial decorum. He pounded on the door.

"Madam! We're moving!"

There was the sound of footsteps and a moment later, Robin Yuan came up behind them. Her face was startled. "We're sailing!"

"I'd noticed," the demon said.

"Where are we heading? Heaven?"

"I suppose that's the idea." Zhu Irzh was strongly tempted to spit. "But not me. We're going to turn around and head back to the Harbor. Where I'll be getting off." He gave the door to the goddess' cabin another blow, but it remained firmly shut. "Open up!"

Chen plucked at his sleeve. "Zhu Irzh, stop it. You can't talk to her like that. She's a goddess."

"Yes, a goddess who's in the process of kidnapping me. If you let them get away with things, Chen, it never stops. Why do you think Hell got created in the first place? Something has to limit Celestial arrogance."

"Look, theological speculation is all well and good, but we're on the goddess' own boat, with no way off it unless she decides to throw us over the side."

"There might be a lifeboat."

"On a Celestial vessel? Why would they need one? Let's go back to our own cabin. And Miss Yuan, could you come with us? I want to talk to you." Chen had a light in his eye that Zhu Irzh did not see very often, but with which even he was disinclined to argue. He trailed after Chen and then poured more tea once they were back inside the cabin. Pity the goddess did not appear to have anything stronger, but what could you expect of Heaven?

"Now," Chen said, sitting down opposite Robin. "I know you work for Jhai Tserai. I know they've been trying to develop a drug that changes the nature of Celestial beings. I strongly suspect that one of those beings murdered your girlfriend, Deveth Sardai, and that she in turn was not exactly innocent of such machinations herself. You're going to tell me what you know."

And Robin Yuan, pale-faced and twisting her hands in her lap, did so.

"And I haven't told anyone this, either," she concluded, "but Mhara made a prophecy. He saw the end of the city."

"Wow," the demon said, wide-eyed. "Jhai thinks big, doesn't she?"

"And do you know who Tserai's contacts in Hell might be?" Chen said to Robin.

"I have no idea," Robin admitted, clearly frightened.

"And your Mhara. Who is he?"

"I don't know. He's a Celestial being, but I don't know which one. I think he must be a minor scion of some Heavenly house."

"But he is not," a voice said from the doorway. Kuan Yin was standing in the opening, light streaming around her. Everyone stood up. "He is the son of the Jade Emperor of Heaven, and one day he will be one of the most powerful beings in all the worlds that are."

FORTY-ONE

Jhai was pacing up and down, a tiger caged.

"Are you sure?"

"They are even now on their way to the Celestial Shores," the dogwoman said. She was in her purely canine form; as Jhai turned, the dogwoman raised a hind foot and scratched an ear. "I spoke to the girl, your servant."

"She's not my—well, never mind. What did she say?"

"She did not know who your escaped captive is. I am certain of that." The dogwoman snapped at a passing bee zooming in over the hibiscus on Jhai's balcony. "Then we had news that the goddess had left the port, in the company of a human and a demon."

"Yeah. Wonder who *they* could have been."

"The males took the two captives up to a cave, a secure place, and your transformed one went to attack the goddess. But they overcame it and we were deceived: the goddess' party came to the village, and questioned us. Then, we do not know how, they found their way to the cave and released the boy and your servant. All are now aboard the boat and heading across the Sea of Night."

"All right," Jhai said. "Then that's it. Might as well say that the game is up."

"You made me a promise," the dogwoman said.

Jhai nodded. A fleeting moment of spite suggested she should not honor it, but that wasn't the way it worked and besides, she might have use for this creature another day. You just never knew. She went to the desk and, from a drawer, took out a small bag. "Here," she said to the dogwoman. She hung the bag around the thick ruff. "These are the bones of the first founder of your village."

"You have given me my rule," the dogwoman said softly. "I won't forget."

"You did your best."

"I wish you luck," the dogwoman said.

Jhai gave a short, sour laugh. "I'll need it."

From a second bag, she cast a circle of black glittering powder around the dogwoman, who squeezed her eyes tightly closed. A muttered incantation activated the powder, which went up in a blinding flash. When Jhai opened her eyes once more, the dogwoman was gone and the bone bag with her, dispatched back to the Night Harbor and control of Bad Dog Village.

Jhai went out onto the wide balcony and rested her hands on the rail. She could see almost the whole southern half of the city from here: the sparkling line of sea, the islands… It would be hard to give this up, harder still to break it to Opal that they were going to have to bail out. An unhappy conjunction had occurred, like ill stars: Zhu Irzh, Robin, Mhara, Kuan Yin. The worst possible combination, Jhai thought. Heaven would know of her plans: the demon could not withstand the goddess, and besides, Robin had probably decided to do something stupid and pointless, like atoning for her sins. Even if both of them had kept their silence, there was, of course, Mhara himself.

Goddess, thought Jhai, and it was the image of great Kali who rose in her mind, and Durga the tiger-rider. *How was I to know who he was?* When Mhara had first been brought to her circle, summoned by Deveth, Jhai had assumed that he was a minor Celestial being, a runaway youth, rebellious, who wanted to experience the sins of Earth before settling down into an exemplary life in the Celestial plane. But no. It had been the dogs who had told her, though they would not tell her how they knew. The son of the Jade Emperor Himself, the heir to Heaven, who, like Buddha, apparently felt it necessary to experience Earth's pain and suffering at first hand so that he might better assuage it when his father passed on the ruling to him.

And this had been the person whom Jhai had taken captive and experimented upon. Marvelous. She was determined to blame Deveth, but couldn't quite manage it.

Jhai squinted up into the bright sky, anticipating thunderbolts. Heaven usually took a little while to act: they weren't as quick off the mark as Hellkind. But she was surely in their sights and she had to get out of here, along with Opal. There was only one place she could think of to go, and it wasn't Hell. There, she would be punished for her failure, and punished big-time. The Night Harbor was a possibility, but not an appealing one, and anywhere on Earth was definitely out.

That meant somewhere else entirely, and to Jhai, there was only one choice. Where better to hide from Heaven than in someone else's otherworld? There were few histories of extradition between India and China. She would go to Kali, throw herself on the goddess' mercy, and join the Royal Court. Opal would be delighted to see family and friends, she was sure. She could pass it off as a surprise visit for Opal's forthcoming birthday, and tell her the truth later. True, then Jhai would be nothing more than just another *deva,* and probably one whose favors would be in demand, as a new girl, but it was better than an eternity of torment. There was something to be said for going home.

But in order to gain entry to that world, they would have to leave China. Jhai went back inside, left a message on her mother's cellphone, and started packing.

FORTY-TWO

"Of course, she wasn't exactly a spring chicken when she died," Paravang's mother was saying. "But she couldn't help that, it was an *epidemic*. And she's been seeing a few gentlemen in Hell, but no one really suitable though, of course, she'd prefer a living husband. Everyone would, it's such a cachet, so fashionable these days, and when I met her—it was at a local social event, they have these things, you know—"

Paravang thought that it was a good thing that his mother was already dead, because otherwise he would surely have slain her. She had now been resident at his little apartment for a day and the fact that she no longer needed to draw breath was severely evident.

"Mothe—"

"Quite a small woman, not exactly *pretty*, but very—"

"Mother, I need to talk to you about the money!"

This penetrated.

"What money?" asked Mrs Roche.

"The money I've been giving you all these years. The Hell money."

She was staring at him so blankly that Paravang cracked and told her the truth. "Look, the situation is this. Things haven't been going too well here lately. I lost my license—it's only a temporary thing, I'll get it back—and it was completely unfair. Some demon from your neck of the woods who's working for the police department revoked the license. So, naturally, I had to take steps to get it back and I'm afraid that meant calling in the Assassins' Guild—it wasn't like killing a human, of course. All that would have happened would have been that this guy would have gone back to Hell and stayed there. But the assassin bungled it and died and now they want me to pay. It's a lot of money and I can't afford it. So I'm going to need the money back that I sent you."

"But I don't have it," his mother said, blinking. "I've spent it."

"Spent it? On what?"

"Well, you know. This and that. Things for the house."

"Mother, you live in Hell! How much can you possibly need down there?"

"I entertain a great deal."

"Dear God." Paravang sank into a chair and put his hands over his face.

"But there's really no need to worry, dear. After all, your bride will be bringing you a dowry, so…"

"How much?"

"Well, I suggest that under the circumstances you tell her how much you need, and refuse to marry her if she doesn't produce it," his mother said. Her dead face hardened for a moment. "But I imagine she will. She's really quite desperate. And I happen to know that in life, she wasn't badly off—she took the very sensible step of converting all her money into Hell notes when she realized she was ill, and burning it. So when she got to Hell, she had it waiting for her, you see? And she lives very quietly."

"I see."

"I think you should meet her, dear. Talk it over. She's a mature woman and she doesn't have any family, so it would be quite in order."

"When?"

"As soon as possible."

That afternoon, therefore, saw Paravang once more knocking on the butcher's door.

FORTY-THREE

"The Jade Emperor," Robin said, slowly and carefully, "is your father?"

"My father, yes."

"So who is your mother? Wait, you told me. Zasharou Selay."

"Yes, that's right. But I don't see so much of my mother. She lives in the moon."

"In the moon."

"Yes."

"I see."

They were sitting in one of the maiden's cabins. The shore of the Night Harbor was far behind now, and Heaven lay ahead, somewhere across the ocean of night on which they sailed. Robin was having difficulty coming to terms with Mhara's newly revealed status. She could just about cope when she thought he was nothing more than a kind of minor angel, but this... *I'm in love with a god.* The irony was that she had never considered herself to be particularly religious. Mhara had explained to her why he had come to Earth in the first place—he had told the truth about that—and of course it made sense. He would make a wonderful Jade Emperor when the time came, and naturally Robin was delighted that he would soon be safely home, but—

"Mhara, I have to ask this. What will happen to me?"

Mhara smiled. "I was hoping you'd stay. At least for a while. You might not like Heaven, of course. Some people don't. It's serene, but a little dull."

Robin gave a small, choked laugh. "I don't think the problem is going to be me not liking Heaven, Mhara. More like Heaven not liking me."

"Robin, there were extenuating circumstances. And if I have forgiven you, then no one else in Heaven is going to gainsay that."

"Really? And have you?"

"Of course," Mhara said. He leaned closer, so did Robin, and then he kissed

174

her. He tasted clean, of clear water and light. She did not know what might have happened after that, but the kiss was interrupted by a frantic lurch of the boat. Robin and Mhara were thrown apart and Robin landed on the floor. She scrambled to her feet to find the boat listing heavily to one side.

"What is it?" she cried.

"I don't know!"

Mhara grabbed her hand and they made their way on deck, clinging to railings and stairways to keep their balance. Coming out of the main doorway, Robin cannoned into the demon.

"What the hell!" Zhu Irzh shouted.

A glowing form appeared high in the rigging and drifted quietly downward: the goddess Kuan Yin.

"Lady?" Chen asked, panting from exertion to stay on his feet. The badger was with him, its claws scrabbling on the deck.

"There is a disturbance," the goddess remarked as the boat once more righted itself.

"You're telling me," the demon snapped. "I nearly went over the damn side."

"What kind of a disturbance?" Chen asked.

"The foundation of the Sea of Night is shifting," Kuan Yin told him.

Chen stared at her. "Is that possible? I thought that the Sea of Night was—well, *night*. It's not water, even though it sometimes looks like it."

"And behaves like it," Kuan Yin said. "The Sea of Night connects all the worlds, this you know. And as such, it has meridians which travel along it, just as there are meridians of *ch'i* and *sha* beneath the land. This boat must travel along the path of those meridians. Anyone who wants to disturb the passage of the boat, this far out to sea, must also disturb the meridians themselves."

"Who could have the power to do that?" the demon asked, adding, "Oh."

"I see you have divined the truth," the goddess said. "Senditreya herself, Lady of the Lines of the Land. Traitor and enemy."

"She must be doing this from Heaven then," Chen said.

"Unless she has already left," Kuan Yin replied. "She would have been wise to do so. I sent a message to the Jade Emperor as soon as I could, telling Him everything. He intended to summon Heaven's own *kuei*, the Storm Lords, to take her into their charge."

"If she has fled, then she must be desperate," Zhu Irzh said.

"Desperate enough to disrupt the meridians that hold the words together? If she causes enough damage, the worlds could fly apart," Chen exclaimed.

"What happens then?" Robin ventured to ask, but she thought she already knew. Mhara's vision, which she had shared: the city sinking into flood and ruin. Looking into the goddess' ineffable eyes, she saw that Kuan Yin had read her thoughts.

"What can we do?" she asked.

"We sail on," the goddess said.

蛇警探

As if by mutual consent, Robin went with Detective Chen and the demon, as well as the goddess' handmaidens, to the main cabin to ride out the storm. Kuan Yin herself remained at the helm, steering her boat through the thundering waves of night with a palpable air of serenity with which no one was inclined to argue. Mhara stayed with her, lashed to the plunging rail; the goddess seemed to need no such supports. The main cabin had a porthole facing the prow and thus the occupants could see out if they chose. Robin took the seat nearest the porthole and remained there, welded to the view of Mhara and the goddess at the helm.

"If this carries on," Chen said uneasily, "we're going to have to find some way of strapping ourselves in."

"Or a binding spell," the demon said.

"I've no way of knowing whether that would work out here. Magic is different in different worlds, and here we are between them. Anyway, we don't want to get stuck in case the boat goes over."

"You and I have fallen into the Sea of Night before," Zhu Irzh said.

"Yes, and nearly drowned, or whatever is analogous. I'd have died if it hadn't been for Inari." Chen sighed. "She must be wondering what's happened to me."

"The captain knew we were going to the Night Harbor."

"Yes, but he won't send anyone to look for us."

"Ma might."

"Ma? He's terrified of the Night Harbor."

"I think you'll find a change in Sergeant Ma, Chen. He's really been surprisingly helpful in recent weeks. He—"

But Robin, who had been paying little attention to this conversation, interrupted. "I can see something."

Within moments, they were all clustering around her shoulder, looking at the bright line of the horizon.

"It's Heaven!" one of the maidens sighed. "We are almost home." She clasped her friend's hands with joy.

"Thank the goddess for that," Zhu Irzh remarked with some irony. They watched as the line grew stronger and brighter, but then the ship gave another great plunge and sent everyone staggering.

"Hold on!" Chen cried. Robin could see through the porthole that something was rising up from the surface of the Sea of Night. It looked like a huge spined porcupine, with a mass of waving tentacles and a billowing sail that spanned out behind it into a web of light.

"What," Robin heard the demon say, with the kind of calmness that heralds screaming panic, "is that?"

Robin did not know. The thing made her sick to look at it. It was utterly wrong. The light was a visceral red, an intestinal shade, and moments later it came down to cover the boat. The cabin was cast into a crimson gloom and filled with a smell like old fish. One of the maidens began to gag, delicately, in the manner of a cat about to be sick.

"Please don't," Zhu Irzh said, eyeing her. Then everything went black.

"It's dragging us down!" Chen cried.

"But what is it?" That was the demon, the panic more evident than ever. "I didn't think anything could live in the Sea of Night."

"It is something from between the stars," a maiden gasped. "The churning of the Sea of Night has brought it up."

"So if it drags us with it, this boat will end up in space?"

"Yes."

"I have to see what's happening," Zhu Irzh said, and over Chen and Robin's protests, he threw open the door. A red fold of translucent flesh billowed up like a canopy, showing a field of stars. Robin had never seen anything so bright. Next moment, the air was ripped from her lungs as whatever atmospheric shield that had been protecting the ship was torn away. The teacups that had been rolling around on the floor floated upward. So did Zhu Irzh. Robin caught hold of the doorframe, clasped the demon by his ankles, and hauled him back, but her chest felt as though it was about to burst. Just before her vision went completely dark, however, she saw something like a huge hook flash across the star field. The boat shuddered and shook. Robin passed out.

蛇警探

She woke to brightness. Her chest was still sore, but the air felt fresh and clean, with a faint smell of the sea in summer. Robin sat up and found that she was lying on the deck with one of the maidens kneeling by her side. The boat, with a glittering tow-rope attaching it to a much larger craft made of pearl and silver, rested a little distance from the shore. Robin looked out onto a mass of flowering trees and artfully ragged cliffs. In the other direction, only a dark line at the horizon's edge betrayed the existence of the Sea of Night, now far behind.

"Yes," the maiden said, smiling. "This is Heaven, the Celestial Shores. Welcome."

"God, I need a cigarette," Zhu Irzh said, coming out of a cabin.

The maiden looked scandalized. "This is Heaven! You can't smoke here!"

The demon gave her a disgusted glance. "Why doesn't that surprise me?"

FORTY-FOUR

The atmosphere in the room was growing colder by the minute. Paravang stared hopelessly across the table at his bride-to-be, whose expression was warring between complacent and unhappy. Complacent, because she had finally found a husband, and unhappy, because of the amount of the dowry on which Paravang had insisted.

"It is a lot of money," she muttered. Her fleshy face still bore faint traces of the illness that had carried her off: some kind of psoriatic epidemic, or so Paravang understood. Her skin had a curiously mottled appearance, reminiscent of a stormy sky.

"Well, that may be, but I'm afraid I can't get married without it. There's a price on my head, you see."

"Yes, I understand that." The woman, Mahibel Wing, appeared remarkably unfazed by the news that her intended was a target of the Assassins' Guild, which said much for the kind of men she must have been dating in Hell. She sighed. "If that is what you insist upon, then I suppose that is what I will have to pay."

"And the circumstances of the marriage," Paravang said. "As I understand it, the wedding will take place here and you will then return to Hell."

"Yes, to await your arrival in due course. You do understand, do you not, that this contract means that you will not be able to enter Heaven upon the event of your death?"

"I'm aware of that. It's a sacrifice I'm prepared to make." Paravang managed a saccharine smile. He did not add that the chances of entering Heaven were, in any case, somewhat remote: he had not lived a good enough life for that, despite the necessary offerings to Senditreya. You had to believe in the essential goodness of your fellow man and that, for Paravang, had proved to be the sticking point.

178

"In that case," Mahibel said shyly, "we need to set a date."

"As soon as possible would be good," Paravang said, adding, "otherwise I'll be joining you in Hell rather sooner than expected, in which case I'm afraid the wedding will be off."

"Suits me," Mahibel said with a terrifying attempt at being jaunty. "I will return now—I can't stay long here. I'll call you."

"I'll look forward to it," Paravang said, thinking that an attempt at gallantry wouldn't go amiss. She whirled out of the room in a silent column of dust, leaving Paravang to sit at the table and stare at his hands. The summoning contract that the butcher had drawn up for her had obviously been much less extensive than that arranged with his mother, for the latter was still very much present. He could hear her now, humming tunelessly in the next room as she did the vacuuming. Paravang rose from the table, slipped past the door of the lounge and into the bathroom, where he locked himself in. Apart from sleep, it was the only privacy he'd managed to obtain over the last forty-eight hours. Did she never stop talking? Who did she talk to in Hell, or were there battalions of middle-aged, gossiping dead ladies who all entertained one another? It was almost worth making a final effort to get into Heaven, Paravang thought, but somehow he didn't think that things would be much different there.

He stared at his reflection in the mirror, somewhat horrified. He looked so much older…his unshaven cheeks sunken and hollow, his hair stringy. He was certainly a fitting bridegroom for poor Mahibel, if looks were anything to go by. And the coldness she had brought with her was still there, sipping gently at his will to live. Was that the idea, perhaps? Get him into her clutches and then debilitate him so that he ended up in Hell several years too early? Just like a woman, Paravang thought bitterly. It struck him that if this were the case, then he might as well just give up and succumb to the Assassins' Guild. After all, they could only kill him as well, and they'd probably be a lot more efficient about it.

FORTY-FIVE

As he had expected, Zhu Irzh was not getting on well with Heaven. They had now been taken ashore and led up a pretty cliff path through fields of blossoming trees and into a pavilion. Here, someone so august had been waiting that Zhu Irzh had been unable to look at him and was obliged to stumble outside. It was quite some time before the dazzle had faded from his eyes and, when it did, he looked up to see Chen standing beside him. The badger was at his feet.

"You too, eh?" the demon said.

"It didn't affect me as badly, but yes, the sight of the Jade Emperor is a bit much, I agree." The badger grunted, as if in agreement. "How are you feeling now?" Chen added.

"Weak. This place is sapping me. I can't even think about sex."

Chen looked a little pained, but said that he had expected as much.

"After all, you're a creature of Hell. It's only reasonable that you should react badly on the Celestial plane. Badger doesn't like it either."

"I wish to return to Earth," the badger muttered.

"What's happening back in the tent?"

"Not a lot. Joyful reunions between father and son. Robin's gone to sit outside, but I don't think there'll be any serious difficulty there. She seems to feel pretty badly about the whole thing, but she didn't know what she was doing and she did free him, after all. The goddess wants to speak with me later, I don't know what about."

"So where do things go from here, Chen? Does Heaven take over and sort things out?"

"I don't know. I suppose so. But Senditreya's fled, of course."

"Where to?"

"Either Earth or Hell. There aren't many places for a renegade goddess to go. But what's worse is that the meridian disruption is continuing. And it's affecting the city. I really would prefer to go back and make sure that Inari's all right, at least. Time passes oddly in the Night Harbor—she might be back from Hawaii by now."

"Even Earth's better than this," the demon remarked, gloomily kicking at a tuft of pleasantly scented grass.

"But possibly not for long." Chen looked up. The goddess was approaching through the trees.

"Chen. I need to speak to you. To both of you." She glanced at the badger. "And you, creature of Earth."

Zhu Irzh, the badger and Chen followed her into a grove of flowering plum. As they entered the grove, Zhu Irzh glanced up and saw that a kind of night had fallen: there were blazing stars visible through the white blossoms, visible in a burning azure sky. When he stepped back out of the grove, it was day once more. Kuan Yin was regarding him with an impatient tolerance.

"When you've finished, young man…"

"Sorry."

"There is a problem," the goddess said. She sounded curiously hesitant, as if unused to sharing her difficulties with mortals. Let alone Hellkind, Zhu Irzh thought. "Now that the son of the Jade Emperor has returned, the Emperor has announced His intention to sever links with the other worlds."

"What?" Chen was staring at her, aghast. "That would surely mean that not another human soul can enter Heaven."

"I know."

There goes Chen's pension, the demon thought. Well, it would be nice to have Chen down in Hell in due course, and be able to repay some hospitality, though Zhu Irzh admitted that his colleague might not feel the same way. Chen and Inari should both stay at the Irzh mansion: avoiding Chen's horrible in-laws. With a slight effort, Zhu Irzh directed his attention back to the matter at hand.

"The Emperor feels that things have gone on long enough. We have tried to educate the human world, and we have tried to keep Hell at bay, but it is now the Emperor's view that humanity has been given its chance to learn, and has failed. With this latest plot, to suborn Heaven itself, it is His view that we should withdraw. He will be announcing His intention to other Celestial planes, of course: they may feel differently. If one were to become Christian or Hindu, matters might be entirely other."

Chen was watching the goddess closely. "And how do you feel about this? You don't like it, do you?"

"My feelings on the matter are irrelevant," the goddess said, and Zhu Irzh did not think he imagined the note of sadness in her voice. "I must do as the Emperor commands. But before Heaven can withdraw, there is something that remains to be done."

"Finding Senditreya?"

"Indeed. The goddess is too powerful to be allowed to remain on Earth, or in Hell. We saw that on the Sea of Night. The Emperor, moreover, feels that we have a certain responsibility in that respect. He has therefore asked me to send you back to Earth to track her down, and meanwhile He will arrange for the *kuei* to be sent, when she is found. He does not want to send the *kuei* right away; it will be too disruptive for the people. But I think her temple will be destroyed here."

"Good," said Zhu Irzh, before Chen could answer. "When are we going?"

"Now," the goddess said, and snapped her fingers.

"Wait a minute!" Chen said, but it was too late. The trees around them thrashed as if a gale had suddenly blown in. Stars and plum blossoms alike began to fall, whirling downward, and engulfing Chen and the demon in a pale tempest. Zhu Irzh began to cough and his vision dimmed. For a split second, before his eyes filled with bloody tears, he saw the whole of Heaven laid out beneath like a pastel tapestry: its plains, its mountains, its temples and cities. Its complexity and depth overwhelmed him. He staggered against Chen. Then they were over the Sea of Night and his sight went dark.

When it cleared again, they were standing in the courtyard of Kuan Yin's temple, not far from Shaopeng. The badger gave a sneezing snort, which managed to sound almost happy. Zhu Irzh suppressed an inclination to pat the badger on the head, took a lungful of diesel-laden air and reached for his cigarettes.

"It's *great* to be back."

And at that point, the earth cracked under his feet.

FORTY-SIX

Jhai was halfway out of the city when the first quake hit. The limousine in which she and Opal were traveling was flung sideways across the road, slamming into a lamppost. Jai and her mother were hurled forward, but the seatbelts held them in. Jhai detached the belt, wrenched open the door and leaped from the car. She ran around to the driver's side, where a dazed Colonel Ei was also getting out.

"What the hell—!"

A gaping chasm had opened up along the length of the street. It was not very deep, but cars and a tram had half-fallen into it and now rested at a variety of angles, with people scrambling from them.

"It's a quake," Ei shouted unnecessarily.

"I can see that!" Jhai looked behind her. The chasm extended up the road, zigzagging unevenly across it. No chance of driving anywhere now: they would have to continue on foot. And the airport was a good twenty miles outside town. Once they'd got beyond the quake damage, she would have to find a taxi.

"Jhai?" Opal came to stand beside her daughter, her face creased with fright. "What's going on?"

Jhai could not help feeling that all this earth-heaving wrath was somehow directed at her. Was this Heaven's attempt to strike her down? It seemed uncharacteristically unsubtle. If that were the case, then the best thing to do was to take advantage of the confusion around her and make as quick an exit from the city as possible, before anyone noticed she was gone. At the airport, a private plane to Kerala was waiting. If they could only get there—she would not think about the possibility of damage at the airport itself.

"Ei," she said. "Where's the nearest main road? Apart from this one?"

"Shaopeng." Ei pointed. "Up there."

"Come on," Jhai said. "We'll get a taxi."

"Shouldn't we go back to the tower?" Opal quavered. "It's supposed to be earthquake proof, that nice Japanese man told me. And we can visit Kerala another time."

"No, Mother," Jhai said firmly. Perhaps it would have been better to tell Opal the truth after all. "We're getting out of here. Trust me."

Opal gave her a suspicious look. "Is there anything you're not telling me, dear?"

"Of course not." Jhai took her mother by the hand and led her, followed by Ei, up the street of steps that came out into Shaopeng. Here, to her relief, the traffic seemed unimpeded and the road surface was intact. A few cars had been abandoned by the roadside, but otherwise it seemed that people had resolutely decided to ignore the quake. Jhai, looking uneasily up at the sky, stepped out into the street and flagged down a taxi. It took several minutes, but eventually one slowed to a halt and she pushed Opal inside.

"The airport. Quickly!"

FORTY-SEVEN

Paravang had gone to Senditreya's temple that morning to give the priest-broker the good news, and had been unable to find the old man. Indeed, the whole temple seemed to be in complete disarray, with priests and dowsers running to and fro. Eventually Paravang managed to collar a temple clerk and ask what was going on.

"No one knows!" the clerk gasped. "It's been chaos here. The goddess hasn't been answering prayer slips—not even the highest priests have been able to reach her. And the city is falling apart."

"Apart?" Paravang said, nonplussed. "What do you mean, 'apart'?" He hadn't done any actual dowsing or geomantic analysis since the episode at the murder site; he must be out of touch.

"The meridians are contorted. No one knows what's wrong with them. *Ch'i, sha,* it doesn't matter—the place is starting to crack along them as though they were fault lines. I spoke to a priest this morning and he said that it's as though the goddess has been holding the meridians in her hands like a knot, and now she's just let them slip."

"But why?"

"We don't know. There are rumors of a war in Heaven."

"That's not possible."

"Maybe not, but that's the nature of the visions that people have been receiving. And there have been prophecies about the end of the city." The clerk wrung his hands. "The end of the *world.*" Then, summoned by one of the priests, he hastened away.

What nonsense, thought Paravang. He was sure that this was nothing more than hysterical speculation. War in Heaven, indeed. He decided to concentrate on his own concerns and track down the priest-broker. Then, once the Assassins' Guild had been paid off, he could go back home and have a nice rest for a couple of days, his troubles at a temporary end. Who had ever heard of such a thing as a Celestial war?

But at that moment his theological certainties were undermined by a commotion in the courtyard. It came in the form of a thunderous roar, as though a jet engine was landing in the temple precincts. Paravang clapped his hands over his ears, but it was no use. The whole temple structure was beginning to shake and shudder, cracks and slits appearing in the walls. A shower of plaster fell from the ceiling like dandruff and the floor bucked under him, causing the tiles to snap. Paravang gripped a bench for support and when the ground stopped moving, he ran out into the courtyard with some vague notion that it was an earthquake.

It wasn't. It was the goddess.

Senditreya was standing in a chariot drawn by two fire-colored cattle at the center of the courtyard, on a pedestal of rock formed by the cracked earth around her. Paravang caught a glimpse down one of those cracks and reeled: it seemed to go all the way to Hell. Senditreya herself displayed none of the bovine calm with which Paravang had always associated her. The goddess was clearly furious. She carried the full mantle of her awe about her, the kind of atmosphere that could bring mortals involuntarily to their knees, and her dark eyes were snapping with fire. Paravang caught sight of her snarling mouth and flung himself face down on what remained of the ground. This was not a conscious decision, and moments later, he regretted it. Once more the ground shuddered and shook. Paravang felt as though he were riding a great wave of the sea: he was picked up and flung down again. With the breath knocked out of him, he twisted around and saw that the shivering temple had become overlaid with a triplicity of images: the place of worship with which he was so familiar; a gleaming, glittering palace with stars in its rafters; and a terrible dark hollow, echoing with woe. His paralyzed mind finally came up with the solution to this curious effect: he was seeing Senditreya's temple in all three dimensions, Heaven, Earth and Hell. As he watched, stunned, the Heavenly version of the temple grew stronger, its outlines bolder and sharply illuminated. He saw his fellow *feng shui* practitioners, shuffling back against the meager protection afforded by the temple wall, and he managed to pull himself to his feet and join them. But something was moving down out of the starry sky—a vast rushing shape, its robes billowing out around it like sails, its immense face filled with resolution. Its eyes seemed the size of moons. Paravang, having beheld it, could not look away. Lightning zapped around its hair and storm clouds swirled around it like a cape. It was, Paravang's terror informed him, one of the *kuei*, the Storm Lord enforcers of Heaven. As it sped toward them it reached out a hand, talon-tipped.

"No!" Paravang heard the goddess cry. Her shout came close to rupturing his eardrums. "You shall not!"

"Madam, I shall!" the *kuei* replied, in a voice like thunder. The taloned hand came closer, Paravang shut his eyes and then with a sensation of swift descent he was stumbling back into the courtyard of the earthly temple. Looking up, he saw the Storm Lord's hand close over the roof of the temple's Heavenly counterpart and then the Celestial version of the temple was collapsing, folding in upon itself with unnatural swiftness as if the structure holding it together had simply become unpinned. The hand was gone, too. The temple contracted down to a tiny spinning building and then with a starlit flash it was gone. Senditreya had been banished from Heaven.

Standing in her chariot, the goddess raised her head and shrieked. Beneath the racket, Paravang detected a low moaning noise that he was alarmed to identify was coming from himself. Senditreya raised a flail and brought it down across the backs of the cattle. They bellowed in pain and alarm, and sprang forward, carrying the chariot across the gap and toward the road, within feet of Paravang Roche.

"A guide!" Senditreya shouted. "You'll do."

Paravang, too late, tried to scramble away but felt a hot divine hand grasp the back of his neck and haul him bodily into the chariot. The flail whipped over his head like a thunder-crack and the chariot sped off, blasting through the closed gates of the temple and sending them into a thousand splinters. Paravang, his mouth and nose filled with sawdust, tried to jump down, but the goddess still had hold of the nape of his neck. Her hands were huge—she was huge, in fact, at least eight feet high and built like an ox beneath the billowing crimson and indigo robes. Paravang caught sight of her face and wished he hadn't: looking into Senditreya's eyes was like looking into the pit of Hell.

"I need," the goddess said with dreadful calm, "to go to the home of one Jhai Tserai. Where is it?"

And once he had found his voice, Paravang told her. Several times.

FORTY-EIGHT

Robin rested her hands on the rail of the balcony and looked out across the lake. It was, of course, beautiful. A huge, low moon hung over the water, much closer than it seemed on Earth, although it had been explained to her that this was illusion. If she half-closed her eyes, she could almost see the pavilions and temples that were said to lie upon it in this dimension, the Imperial Court of Mhara's mother, the Lady of Mists. The lake itself was equally lovely: starred with fleets of water lilies and drifts of swans, crossed by a sequence of charming little bridges. Now, under the moonlight, it was a world of indigo and silver. Robin gazed across it and longed for the view into her own grimy back alley. Because what good was it being in Heaven, if you couldn't spend your time with the person you loved?

She had certainly been well-treated. She had been granted a set of rooms in a long, low mansion, dressed in silk robes, and given a maidservant, with entrancing good humor and no sign of obsequiousness, who appeared to regard it as an honor to look after her. But she had seen nothing of Mhara for the last three days. She had asked and asked, and received polite, evasive answers, expressed with exquisite regret. Eventually hope gave out and Robin admitted what she had known all along: she was an embarrassment. The son of the Lord of Heaven wouldn't be allowed to have a mere human as his consort. And when she had gone to look for Mhara, she discovered that all her wanderings seemed to bring her back to the lake, as though the land itself was carefully and cautiously turning her around.

So, Robin asked herself miserably, was this it? Was she supposed to stay here for the rest of her life, in the proverbial gilded cage? How long might that life be, since she was now in Heaven and perhaps, therefore, an immortal now herself. It seemed unlikely that anyone ever died here.

Then, below the balcony, something whistled.

Robin paid little attention at first. The lakeside trees were filled with delightful, sweet-singing birds; their song wafted through the fragrant air from morning until balmy night. But something about this was different: sharper, more insistent. Hope suddenly flared up all over again and Robin leaned over, craning so far that she almost fell off the balcony. Mhara stepped out of the shadows.

"It's you," Robin hissed.

"Robin!" Mhara jumped, caught the bottom of the balcony and hoisted himself over it. Robin could see at once that he was different. The dreaming serenity had been honed to a keener edge, voice and movements were decisive.

"We have to leave, Robin." He took her by the shoulders and kissed her quickly.

"Thank God," Robin said before she could stop herself.

"Well, no. My father has nothing to do with it."

"I can't flee in a dress. These skirts —"

"There's no time. Come on." He dropped from the balcony and held out his arms. Robin gritted her teeth and jumped down into them. It was an awkward landing and they both staggered, but then Mhara caught her by the hand and pulled her into the bushes. "This way. As quietly as you can."

Robin brushed through thick branches of hibiscus and oleander, releasing a scent like roses and cinnamon into the air. That was the trouble with Heaven, she thought, it was all too much. But perhaps it wasn't designed for human senses: perhaps spirits, such faint things as they were, needed overload in order to sense anything at all.

The shrubbery ended by the lake. On a narrow strip of shore, two deer were waiting patiently. They were white with silver horns, and bore saddles.

"We're riding these?"

"They're quick, that's the beauty of them. Don't worry, you won't fall off and it knows where to go." He boosted Robin into the saddle.

"There aren't any reins."

"You won't need them. Just hang on."

And indeed, hanging on to the saddle horn took all of Robin's concentration. The deer moved as swiftly as thought, racing along the lake and into the series of low hills that she had been able to see from the windows of the mansion. Groves of flowering trees rushed by, quiet villages in the folds of hills with fat cows in their fields, picturesque outcrops of rock with water at their feet… Idyllic, and Robin felt that it was all too good for her. It didn't bode well for her life after death, if she actually made it back to Earth. She loathed the Night Harbor, couldn't settle in Heaven—that left Hell and she didn't fancy the thought of that, either. But Heaven with Mhara by her side—heaven indeed, and impossible. She gripped the saddle more tightly and the deer flew on.

At last, just as Robin was beginning to grow tired, the deer took her up the side of a small hill. Heaven's sky was starting to lighten now with the roseate gold of dawn and the air felt pleasantly cold and moist, like early autumn. At the top of the hill stood a little temple, and unlike the rest of Heaven, it was almost a ruin. It had been built of a stone that looked like lapis, flecked with starlit sparks, but the roof had fallen in, leaving the temple open to the sky, and as they drew near a flock of golden birds shot up from it, startled by their approach, and vanished into the dawn. A plant like a small, blue vine had covered much of the temple and Robin could smell fermenting fruit.

"Mhara, what is this?"

Mhara dismounted from the back of his deer and smiled at her. "This is my temple."

"*Your* temple? But it's a ruin."

"I never wanted worship, Robin. Other sons of other Jade Emperors have had temples all over the place, all the followers they could wish for. But I hadn't done anything to merit it, you see. If people were going to worship me, then I wanted to be worthy of it, and I haven't done much with my life so far. I am young, by Heaven's terms, but even so... That was partly why I went to Earth, to see what could be done."

"Yet you said this is your temple."

"It's the only one. Someone disobeyed the edict and built a temple to me. In terms of Earth, it lies just outside Singapore Three—or it used to. The suburbs have crept up around it. On Earth, the equivalent to this building is surrounded by apartment blocks. It's a real ruin; I asked them to desist—and the priest left, so there was no one to take care of it. There's not much left. It sits on a piece of waste ground and it's a home to stray cats, mainly. But here, as you can see, it's in the middle of nowhere. No one comes here, I'm sure all the family have forgotten about it. But apart from through the Night Harbor, it's the one place where I can enter Earth: my own portal. It's how I came in the first place. I should have headed back there, but Paugeng's troops turned up and we were forced into Shai."

"Kuan Yin didn't need a temple to send those policemen back," Robin said.

"No, because all of Heaven is her precinct, and that of the other major Lords. But if she manifests on Earth, she can only do so for any great length of time in her own temple, and if she travels to the Night Harbor, for instance, where she has no place of worship, she has to journey there like anyone else. Well," Mhara amended, "not quite like anyone else, but she still needs a vessel." He glanced at the growing light. "They'll soon notice that I'm not in my bed. We have to get going."

He turned and whispered to the deer, who sprang away down the hillside.

Then he and Robin stepped together into the quiet ruin and Mhara spoke a word.

It was like stepping into a moving lift. The world fell away, rushing past Robin's ears. She felt them pop with pressure. The breath left her lungs and she clutched Mhara for support. Moments later, the air of Heaven was replaced with fumes and the smell of cat piss. They were back.

FORTY-NINE

Chen and the demon stood outside Kuan Yin's temple, waiting for Sergeant Ma.

"Well," Chen said, looking at the cracked roof of the temple behind them. The temple had not been too badly damaged, but the priests had closed it off just in case the roof came down, and now the faithful milled unhappily around its walls as if seeking shelter. "I think that answers the question of whether Senditreya's here or not."

"Here and on the rampage," Zhu Irzh remarked. "But if so, why?"

"It might not even be intentional," Chen said. "The very presence of a goddess where no goddess is supposed to be—especially one that has such a close connection to the land itself—could be disruptive."

"So how do we go about tracking her down?" the demon asked. "Just follow the fault lines and the havoc?"

"The most obvious place would be Senditreya's own temple."

"She's not likely to hole up there, is she? It's *too* obvious."

"Perhaps not, but she's likely to have come to Earth there. And Zhu Irzh—wherever she goes, it will be obvious. She's a deity." He stepped out into the road and raised a hand. "Hey, there's Ma!"

The squad car skidded to a halt. Behind the wheel, Ma's face was white with fright and concentration. Chen, the demon and the badger bundled themselves into the car.

"Senditreya's temple, Ma. Quickly!"

"What?" Ma stared at him. "They're saying that's the epicenter. You'll be lucky to get within half a mile of it. Buildings are collapsing all over the place."

"Sorry, Ma, but we don't have a choice." As Ma took the car out into the road, Chen brought him up to date.

192

"Well, at least the lane's clear," Ma said, after a pause. He was right: the traffic was streaming out of the city center.

Zhu Irzh felt a growing hollowness in the pit of his belly. It had nothing to do with hunger: it was a nauseous, heady feeling exacerbated by the uneven motion of the squad car. But he wasn't normally motion sick... Perhaps it was something to do with the number of worlds he had so recently traveled through—some disturbance of the inner ear. How annoying, and how un-dignified: demons shouldn't suffer from anything except the most esoteric and exotic complaints, not just the need to throw up out of a car window.

Beside him, Chen's gaze widened fractionally and the badger gave a low growl. Outside the curved window of the carrier, a fascinated Zhu Irzh saw, Battery Road was beginning to change. He was aware of Chen beside him, staring open-mouthed out of the window. He could feel the structure of the world altering beneath them, the Shaopeng meridian buckling and turning as it began to alter course, pulling its tributaries of *ch'i* with it.

Ma turned the corner of Battery Road and headed up Shaopeng. The disruption going on underneath the city made Zhu Irzh disoriented and lightheaded, with an undertow of nausea that he was trying hard to suppress. He kept his gaze on the fixed point of the seat in front and gritted his teeth. Chen, visibly shaken, was conferring with the badger, but the beast would not speak. Its narrow jaws remained tightly shut. It closed its eyes. Creature of Earth that it was, the demon thought, perhaps it too was feeling unwell.

Beneath the carrier, the meridian, which ran the length of Shaopeng, lurched and twisted. Zhu Irzh's instinct was to lean forward and put his head on his knees, but he was constrained by the seat belt. He shifted uncomfort-ably. Chen looked at him in some alarm.

"Are you all right?"

"Yes... No. The meridian's changing under Shaopeng. It's making me ill."

The nausea was ebbing, mercifully, but his head was pounding. It felt as though someone had rung a bell in his ear. The world was full of sickly color, coming in waves and accompanied by a hot, electric smell. Zhu Irzh concen-trated on his breathing. He felt unpleasantly hot. Ma took the car onto the highway toward Murray Town, and they were moving away from the main meridian. The sickness faded a little more.

"How are you feeling now?" Chen asked, then without waiting for a reply added: "Goddess! Something's happening here as well."

Zhu Irzh strained to look past him. Through the window he could see a line of intense color, incredibly bright, waist-high along the air. Above it, the shabby go-down entrances and shop fronts were unchanged, but below, the structures were obscured by a seething mass of air, like something seen through a blast of heat. The air writhed and billowed, causing a sort of mental recoil. Passers-by had seen it, too, and were pointing and exclaiming. Slowly, the car ground to a halt. Ma gunned the accelerator, but nothing happened. Underneath the carrier, the ground started to shake, a queasy wave of motion traveling up through the frame of the vehicle and shuddering to rest. It came again, and again.

"Out of the car," Chen ordered. Zhu Irzh scrambled clear, but the sickness was intensifying. Humiliated, he retched into the gutter but produced nothing.

"Sorry!"

"Don't worry about it, Zhu Irzh. Can you walk?"

"I think so," the demon replied. He was by no means sure.

Once they stepped into the road, they had an unobstructed view along Shaopeng. The whole city was bathed in unnatural light, and as they watched, it quivered momentarily, as though someone was shaking a picture. Very slowly, the steep angle of the Eregeng Trade House tilted to one side and the building leaned over gracefully. It hung in the air for a moment, suspended, and then as they watched, the stem of the tower strained and cracked to send the upper stories of the Trade House down into the street. There was a crash so loud it was almost beyond sound, and the earth leaped under their feet. A wave of dust rolled up from the fallen building, and as it did so the ground once more began to quiver. A slow crack appeared in the road, began to widen. Ma stared at it in disbelief. Chen was thrown forward onto his knees, and struggled to get up.

There was a thundering sound coming from further up Shaopeng. *What the hell?* thought Zhu Irzh. It sounded like *hooves*. Moments later, a chariot turned the corner and bolted down Shaopeng. It was drawn by two red cattle with enormous golden horns, their sides streaming with flame as they ran. Steam boiled from their mouths and nostrils. Zhu Irzh, leaping out of the way, caught sight of Senditreya standing in the chariot, wielding a flail. She looked completely mad. Her eyes were wide and staring, her mouth fixed into a rictus of hate. There was someone in the chariot with her, a crouching form, but the vehicle was moving too swiftly for Zhu Irzh to get more than a glimpse. As the chariot passed, the ground cracked in its wake. Zhu Irzh hauled a spluttering Chen to his feet.

"Well, looks like we've found her."

FIFTY

Paravang Roche huddled in the chariot, hanging on grimly, his vision obscured by the goddess' flying skirts. The presence of Senditreya in the chariot with him was almost too much to bear—boiling rage, incandescent anger, a cold hate that was somehow worse than either. The goddess' emotions felt planet-sized. Paravang considered throwing himself from the chariot, but they were moving too quickly. He was dimly aware that something major had just occurred, a wave of sound and dust, but he did not know what it might be. Whatever had just happened paled in comparison with the roaring emotions churning around the chariot. And the flames from the cattle's sides occasionally erupted over the edge of the vehicle, causing the singed odor of hair to become added to the mix.

"You!" bellowed the goddess. Paravang cringed, believing at first that she was addressing him. Then he realized that the divine hand was pointing forward, like an arrow of hate. The chariot ground to a halt, the hooves of the cattle skidding on melting tarmac. The flames shot upward, then ceased. Cautiously, Paravang peered over the rim of the chariot.

There was a car in the road—a taxi. Its windows were grimy with dust, but as Paravang stared, the door fell open and someone stumbled out into the street. Jhai Tserai took one look at the outraged, exiled deity, mouthed something that might have been, "Oh shit," and scrambled back into the cab.

"Stop!" Senditreya cried, but the cab was already spinning around and heading away. The goddess cracked the reins with a sound like thunder, and followed. Paravang, clinging on once more, risked a glance behind him and saw that they were being followed by a police car, blue lights flashing. Paravang's initial thought was of how ridiculous this was, and then he caught sight of a familiar face beside the driver. Seneschal Zhu Irzh. Talk about being caught between the devil and the deep blue sea, Paravang thought. He

195

wished he could faint at will, but it wasn't an option.

They chased Jhai's car along the length of Shaopeng, dazed passers-by hurling themselves out of the way. The chariot caught the side of an awning, already listing to one side, and tore it free. A banner now snapped behind the chariot, obscuring Paravang's view of the police car, but he could hear it, the siren wailing like a condemned soul. And then they turned the corner and beneath the snapping banner and the streaming flames Paravang saw that the spire of the Eregeng Trade House was lying across the street.

Jhai's cab ground to a halt seconds before it hit this unnatural barrier. The goddess gave a shriek of triumph that deafened Paravang Roche, but somehow its force lent him the strength to throw himself from the chariot. He landed almost in the arms of Zhu Irzh. Under the circumstances, seeing the demon was almost a relief.

FIFTY-ONE

Robin liked the little temple, in a way that she had never liked Heaven. It was rough, and somewhat squalid, but it was real. She reached out a hand to one of the shadowy cats that prowled its meager precincts and said, "The city's falling apart."

Beside her, Mhara gave an unhappy nod. "Senditreya's gone on the rampage. And because she is goddess of the meridians, of the earth itself, they are responding to her presence."

It was, Robin thought, as though the goddess had a very heavy footfall. Every step she took caused the earth to crack and tremble. A little earlier, Robin had watched in appalled fascination as the tower of the Eregeng Trade House crashed down into the street, sending up a billow of blond dust that still hung over the city, and filtered the sunlight into a prism of filthy color. When Robin had been a child, New York had been attacked, and this reminded her horribly of those scenes. Terrorism from Heaven: Who would ever have thought such a thing?

"Mhara—what can we do?"

"We have to find her. We have to stop her."

And so they left the temple to its attendant cats and made their way down into the city. At first, Robin tried to get a cab. She still had a few coins in her pocket, but then she realized it was hopeless. The city was hopelessly blocked, by earthquake, by people fleeing from it to the hills, by partygoers who, amazingly, were starting to make merry for the Day of the Dead. Robin supposed that they might have nothing else to lose.

As they walked, Robin tried to talk to Mhara, remarking on the passing scenes of devastation, but after the third monosyllabic reply, she became silent.

"I'm sorry," Mhara said after a while. "I've been thinking. And what I think is this: the only one who can stop Senditreya is me. Heaven has thrown her out, washed their hands of the world. Only a god has the power to stop her, and I'm the only god who is here."

"What about Kuan Yin?"

"Kuan Yin defies the current order as much as she can, but she is still bound by Heaven's mandate."

"And you aren't?"

"Oh," Mhara said. "I've gone so far already, it doesn't matter what I do. Nothing can prevent me from becoming Emperor: you inherit, you don't get elected."

"Then we'd better find Senditreya," Robin said with a sinking heart. In this world, Mhara seemed such a frail being: He'd let Jhai Tserai imprison him, so how could he stand up to an enraged and vengeful deity? As far as she understood things, only the *kuei* had the power to do that, within Heaven itself. And they were not in Heaven now. Mhara fell silent, and they walked on.

As they neared the heart of the city, Mhara suddenly stopped. He leaned against a wall, his face ashen, and when Robin asked him what was the matter, he did not reply, but only shook his head. After a few moments, he said, "It's all right. I'll be all right."

"Mhara? What's wrong?"

"I don't know. I felt—" There was something in his face that could almost have been fear. He said, "Let's move on."

After another hour or so, Robin realized that they were heading toward the temple of Kuan Yin. She mentioned this.

"I know. Senditreya will not be far away, Robin. She's in the city at the moment, but I don't know where. She blames Kuan Yin for her present plight."

"That's outrageous. If she hadn't started bargaining with Hell—"

"She is a goddess, Robin, and an old one who no longer enjoys the power she was once used to. And she was also human once, too. She was a girl, a dowser who mapped the meridians of this region and was elevated to godhood. It's different for those who are elevated. Once they taste the power, they never want to go back. Over a long period of time, one's sense of entitlement grows. I've seen it happen. Whereas the ancient gods know when their time has come, and fade with grace from the Wheel. I am certain that Senditreya thinks that she is absolutely in the right, and that the city is hers to control as she sees fit."

"That's madness."

"Of course," Mhara said, and they walked on.

FIFTY-TWO

Zhu Irzh thrust the dowser to one side and dodged around the chariot. The goddess was carving a character into the palm of her hand, releasing a stream of golden-red blood. She raised the hand and sent a thunderbolt flashing toward Jhai's vehicle. The cab caught the bolt broadside and blew up with a great boiling rush of fire, almost knocking the demon off his feet. Zhu Irzh heard himself cry out but even as he did so he caught sight of Jhai Tserai. She was on the other side of the shattered spire of the Trade House, hustling a middle-aged woman to safety. Colonel Ei sent a shower of machine-gun fire in the direction of Senditreya, but the bullets turned to moths, which fluttered, dazed, up into the sunlight.

"Get back!" Ei barked, firing a round at the demon's feet. It was then that Zhu Irzh realized something: Ei thought that he and the goddess were in league. Given her recent dealings with Hell, this was perhaps understandable, but there was no time for explanations. Behind him, the demon could hear Chen starting to chant something. Gods alone knew what Chen was trying to achieve, but whatever it was, Zhu Irzh had confidence in him and he should be allowed to proceed without distractions. Zhu Irzh spun to face the colonel. He kicked upward at the gun, missed, and caught Ei on the forearm. The gun swept upward and fired into the air, and the tremor came again.

Zhu Irzh turned to see Chen sending a firebolt of his own from a bleeding palm. It struck the goddess between the shoulder blades and took her by surprise. With a scream of rage, she pitched forward over the rim of the chariot and simply disappeared, as if melting into the earth itself. Zhu Irzh stared stupidly at the place where she had fallen, but there was no trace of her passing. The earth, however, shuddered beneath his feet as though a train were passing under it.

Ei lost her balance and turned wildly on Chen, but the detective was already running in the direction of Jhai Tserai. The demon followed.

"Stop!" Ei cried. Zhu Irzh heard the burst of the gun, shockingly loud above the creaking buildings, and something hot and fast raked him in the side and ricocheted from a tilting lintel.

"Down the alley," Chen panted.

They bolted down the alleyway, running between the maze of shacks and chop porches, knocking people out of their path. Everyone had disregarded the standard earthquake instructions and rushed out into the roadway. The alley was filled with people, clutching their possessions to them and shouting. To the right, the roof of a shack had caved in and a body lay unmoving beneath the wreckage. Zhu Irzh had a single image of a foot, clad in a slipper, quite still. The air was full of choking dust and a peculiar acrid smell.

"Hell," said Chen, wheezing. "Lost sight of her."

Many people were on their knees, racked with nausea and coughing. Zhu Irzh came face to face with a woman holding a birdcage, her face distorted by fear. Her distress outweighed any reservations she might have had. She clutched the fleeing demon around the waist and buried her face in his shoulder. Fire shot through his bleeding side.

"Where's Jhai?" Zhu Irzh shouted, trying to disengage her. "Where the hell did Senditreya go?" Moments later, it occurred to him that he might have answered his own question. "Let go of me, madam!" At the top of the street, Ei was nowhere to be seen. The tremors were coming more rhythmically now, wave after wave, and it was impossible to stand. Zhu Irzh and his confidant were thrown apart. The demon grabbed Chen by the arm and dragged him through the shaking street. They had gone no more than a few paces when they were thrown against a doorway, and glancing back up the hill Zhu Irzh caught sight of Ei, pursuing as best she could.

"In here," Chen said. He pulled Zhu Irzh through the door and abruptly the noise and confusion outside were cut off as though someone had thrown a switch. Tentatively, Zhu Irzh touched his side. His fingers came back wet and bloody.

"How badly are you hurt?" Chen demanded. "If Ei comes through here, I'll stop her. Tell me what state you're in."

Pulling aside his coat, Zhu Irzh examined his side. The bullet had scored a long shallow gouge in the flesh. He was bleeding all over the place, and it stung, but though he nerved himself to prod the wound, it did not seem deep.

"I think I'm all right. What should I do? Bind it up or something?"

"Anything to stop it bleeding. I'm not going to rip up my shirt, by the way, if that's what you're thinking," the detective added wryly. He vanished into the room and Zhu Irzh, stuffing his own ripped silk shirt against the wound, stumbled after him. He had thought that they were in an ordinary shack, but now he saw that the room went back a long way. It was unlit, and had no windows, and the walls were painted a dark, dull red, which kept out the light. There seemed to be no furniture, apart from a long bar structure along one side of the room and at the end of the room, there was a door. They went through, and found themselves in a long, winding corridor. From this central artery, doors led off along either side. It was quiet and very still. The floor was steady beneath their feet. Softly Zhu Irzh closed the door through which they had come. Taking a few steps down the corridor, he opened one of the doors to the left and stood stock still, looking through. Chen, catching up with him, peered over his shoulder.

The small room was lined with curtains and the only furniture was a divan, rather baroque and covered with fat, velvet cushions. There was no one there, but someone laughed, all the same, and a spike of flame shot forth, singing the demon's hair.

Zhu Irzh and Chen stumbled back. The demon was trying to work out the route that they had taken. He remembered the cluster of buildings around Shaopeng station, the screaming neon face welcoming customers inside. They had come round Shaopeng, up Battery Road and onto Peipei Street, then come down the hill on foot. He remembered the man outside the doorway, doubled over and retching, and saw from Chen's face that the detective had recalled the same thing.

"We're in a demon lounge," Chen said. "Again." A door to Chen's left opened a crack and an eye looked out, small and orange. Chen stopped. The door closed. From somewhere came the sound of running feet. Around the corner came a short, stout woman with an imposing hairdo, clad in a pink kimono. She pointed an outraged finger at Chen.

"You!" she shouted. "Spying on my girls!"

"They seem well able to take care of themselves, madam," the detective replied, with a glance at the demon's burned hair.

"That isn't the point!"

"We came through the back door," Zhu Irzh started to explain. He stepped forward, out of the shadows, and the woman's jaw dropped as she saw him.

"I'm so sorry, I didn't realize we had such august company," she said.

"We were expecting a room," the demon said frostily, rising to the occasion. Chen shot him an appalled glance, then subsided.

"I'm terribly sorry," the woman said again, deflated. Indicating a door on the right, she added, "You can have this one."

Entering, Chen and Zhu Irzh found themselves in a room much like the demon's own on Lower Murray Street, draped in a dark and somber green. There was a similar overstuffed divan, and a cupboard. Chen shut the door behind them.

"What are we going to do?" Zhu Irzh asked.

"You tell me. I think it might be prudent to wait here for a while and then make our way to the precinct. Why isn't this place affected by the quake?" he asked.

"Because it isn't properly on Earth?"

Chen was frowning. There was a flicker of movement in the dim corner of the room, making Zhu Irzh jump, but then he saw that it was only a mirror, half-concealed by the drapes. The room seemed to have become darker. The surface of the mirror was glossy, absorbing light, and it was like looking down a well. Zhu Irzh watched them both in the mirror: the pale, golden-eyed demon and the round-faced detective, side by side. Smoke seemed to drift across the surface of the mirror, though the room was clear, and in the mirror, Zhu Irzh smiled. Chen turned to his friend, and Zhu Irzh looked back at him.

"Zhu Irzh?" Chen whispered. In the mirror, the demon smiled into his eyes. Rising, Zhu Irzh prowled round the head of the divan, though in the mirror, he was still seated. The room was much darker now, all the light leaching away and the only illumination coming from the lamp in the mirror. In the mirror, the demon's eyes were lambent in the reflected light.

"Zhu Irzh?" Chen asked uncertainly. The words made little sense. The air in the stuffy room crackled in anticipation. Very slowly, Chen stood up. Zhu Irzh watched, frowning. He knew this human creature, somehow, but his thoughts were muddled and jumbled. The human edged around the side of the room. Zhu Irzh watched him, interested. Unhurriedly, he straightened up and came round the end of the divan. The human stopped dead. He froze, holding his breath and keeping rigid. The demon found his gaze wandering. He looked vaguely about him. His spine tensed, and he stretched slightly, a movement that rippled up his back to his shoulders. The fingers of one hand flexed. He could hear the prey breathing out, very shallowly. Zhu Irzh's gaze passed over him without recognition. Someone knocked at the door. The prey jerked and Zhu Irzh was across the room and lashing out at him. Wildly, the prey ducked and the demon's claws grazed his cheek. The prey threw himself on the floor and rolled toward the divan. Zhu Irzh hissed and turned on him, but the prey was already drawn up under the couch. The demon straightened up and walked toward the door. He watched the prey from the corner of his eye. The creature had found something underneath the divan: a bundle of material. Zhu Irzh smelled the pungent odor of blood.

The prey pulled the soggy bundle of material free and padded it together. Then, flicking it across the room, he dived for the door, grabbing at the round handle and wrenching it open. Or would have done, if it hadn't been locked. The demon's hands were around the waist of the prey, plucking him from the door and then he was tossed into a corner of the room. He landed sprawling against the edge of the couch. The demon bent down and the prey threw his arm across his eyes.

Zhu Irzh blinked. His vision hazed, but his mind was suddenly quite clear. He looked down at Chen.

"What are you rolling around on the floor for?"

Chen sat up, then rose from the floor and shot backward out of reach. "Because you attacked me, that's why." His voice was shaking.

"What?"

"Zhu Irzh, if you're going to be prone to these episodes, I think when all this is over, we'd better take you down to the cells for your own protection." Chen passed a quivering hand over his face and sat down heavily.

"I *attacked* you?" Zhu Irzh, appalled, realized that he had absolutely no recollection of the last five minutes. There was another knock at the door.

"What is it?" Zhu Irzh shouted irascibly.

"Is everything all right?" a honeyed voice murmured.

"Go away!"

Silence.

"We can't stay here," Chen said. "But the door's locked."

"What, from the outside?"

Discreetly, they rattled the handle, but the door was tight.

"Chen," Zhu Irzh whispered. "What is behind the drapes?"

Cautiously, they investigated, but there was just paneling, nothing more. The mirror was bolted to the wall.

"Very well," Zhu Irzh said. He strode to the door, paused, then kicked it neatly and sharply so that the lock splintered. Chen followed him down the hallway. The demon could hear a distant disturbance: the sound of voices. After a moment, a young woman in an ochre wrap appeared. She had a geisha's artificial smile upon a painted rosebud mouth. Above the smile, her eyes were shiny and black. Her hands were buried in the wide sleeves of the wrap. Zhu Irzh gave her what he hoped was an impassive stare.

"You wish to go? May I show you out?" she asked. She had a little, breathy voice.

"Thank you."

She stood aside and let them go through a narrow doorway. Zhu Irzh brushed against the hem of her wrap as he went through the door, and winced. She seemed extremely hot. As they came out into an atrium she took a lantern down from the wall; a pretty thing decorated with peonies. Demurely, with eyes downcast, she led them through.

"Is this the door to Shaopeng?" Chen asked her.

What's left of it, Zhu Irzh thought.

"It is."

"You go first," Chen said. The demon felt a light, hot hand fall on his shoulder.

"Okay," he said. "I'm going, Chen. No need to push."

"I didn't."

Zhu Irzh looked back; the geisha stood, still smiling prettily, several feet distant. He took a deep breath and stepped through the door. Outside, Shaopeng Street seemed unchanged, but the day had worn on. When they had gone into the lounge, it had been morning. Now, the strip of visible sky was an evening rose and gold, filmed by dust, and the lights were coming on. The street was full of people, some wandering apparently bereft, but the majority was dressed in their best for the celebrations. The demon took a deep breath of humid air. Passers-by looked at him askance and steered around him. Above him swung the neon sign of the demon lounge. Well, thought Zhu Irzh, and then his heart contracted as if he'd been punched. Chen was not with him.

Zhu Irzh went straight back through the door, and collided with Chen, coming out. Beyond the detective's shoulder, he had a brief confused glimpse of somewhere entirely different: a vast plain, with a bright strip of river crossing it and a sky on fire.

Zhu Irzh grabbed Chen's arm and dragged him down the street, pulling him through the door of the nearest bar. It was packed to the gills, but they were lucky: a couple was leaving, a departure accelerated when they caught sight of the demon. Chen and Zhu Irzh were able to slide into a curtained booth. Beneath the edge of the curtain a hand appeared with a tray. Chen scrawled a drinks order on the paper and put it on the tray with the money. The bar was badly lit. Zhu Irzh rubbed his eyes with his hands, again and again. Fingers locked around his wrist.

"Don't. You'll make them sore," Chen said.

"Okay, okay," Zhu Irzh said, surprised at this sudden paternal consideration. The sake arrived, a half-bottle with tea glasses.

"We've run out of proper ones," an unseen person said.

"I don't care," Chen said. He filled the little three-inch glass carefully to its brim and handed it to the demon, who knocked it back.

Chen said, "Well?"

"I'm really sorry," the demon muttered. He looked away, as if seeking an answer. "What I told you was true. One minute I was all right. Then you were on the floor and I was leaning over you. I don't remember a thing."

"Or don't want to," Chen said neutrally. The demon looked at him for a long moment.

"Is that what you think of me?"

"Zhu Irzh, you nearly killed me. I'm wondering if this memory loss isn't a conveniently selective amnesia. It might be paranoid, but I suddenly find myself in a paranoid mood. Someone who didn't know you as well as I think I do could conjecture that it's a useful excuse for doing whatever you please and passing it off as something you can't help. Whatever Senditreya's virus may have to do with it."

"Would it help if I said that I've wondered that myself on the way here?" Deliberately, he poured more of the sake into each glass. "With the dowser—but it's not like me, Chen. I'm fundamentally too lazy to go around attacking people. You know that. It has to be the virus, but—" Zhu Irzh paused for a moment. "What if it's permanent? This is worrying me, Chen. I don't like zoning out like that. And there was no warning. What if I start to change my appearance, like that Celestial?" He gave a fastidious shudder.

"I don't know." Chen was studiedly calm. "Wait here. I'm going to try to call Ma."

While Chen was elsewhere, Zhu Irzh listened to the conversations around him and realized that he had quite forgotten the date, what with all the fuss. It was the Festival of the Dead.

The first night of the festival had apparently got well under way, in spite of the earthquake. Indeed, the morning's tremors might even have added to the holiday atmosphere; everyone, it seemed, had a story to tell, their own narrow escape from death. The news networks were functioning, and the demon listened along with everyone else. Most of the reports centered on the collapse of the Eregeng Trade House: there was an extensive item on the actual damage, which was considerable, muffled in a sandwich of human-interest stories and geomantic speculation. So far, the death toll was running at three hundred and twenty, and rising every hour. The governor was featured, pleading for calm, and ignored at least by the five thousand or so who had already fled the city for the surrounding hills of Wuan Chih. The airport had been set off-limits. There was some scorn in the bar for those who had taken flight. This was, to a certain extent, justified.

A number of those who had gone were members of the Ereday cult, Zhu Irzh learned. They were claiming it as a personal victory for the judgement that would come. They believed Earth to be in its last days, and the doomsday date had crept forward as the years went by and the world continued to orbit in relative peace. It must have been galling to belong to the cult, Zhu Irzh thought, every time the latest prophecy proved false. You would wonder what you paid your tithes for, and he supposed that it accounted for the decline in membership. Perhaps the number of converts would rise now, after the gratifyingly dramatic events of the morning.

The inhabitants of the bar clearly felt flight to be a spineless option. The mood of bravado in the face of considerable odds grew as the news stories progressed. Someone began to sing, loudly and tunelessly. Another twitched the curtain of the booth aside with a jocular remark. He encountered the demon's icy stare and hastily retreated.

Chen slid back into his seat. "No sign of Ma. He's not answering his cellphone. I've no idea where the badger is either."

"Hell, I'd forgotten about the badger." Zhu Irzh had no great love for the creature, but it certainly came in useful on occasion.

"The precinct's in chaos—part of it has collapsed, and the systems are all down. I think we should go," Chen muttered.

"I agree, but where to?"

"There's going to be another quake, according to Captain Sung. He's been in touch with whoever it is who monitors these things. Shaopeng's close to the epicenter. It'll come later tonight."

"Shouldn't we warn people?"

"That's what the dowsers are supposed to do. The governor's office has issued a series of bulletins." Chen glanced around at the throng. "Looks like this lot has decided to ignore them."

"Do we know what happened to Senditreya?"

"I have absolutely no idea whatsoever. I threw a spell at her, but it wouldn't have killed her—I just hoped to slow her down a bit. She might be in exile, which I think means that her powers are waning, but she's still a goddess and that means that she has abilities which are way beyond anything I could do to her. I don't know why she didn't fight back. I suspect she went somewhere to recoup her resources. Chen was silent for a moment. Eventually he said, "We have to do something, Zhu Irzh. I have a charge more or less laid upon me from Kuan Yin, and I have a duty to protect the people of this city."

"Listen to them, Chen. They have the chance to leave the city, go into the hills. Yet they won't. They know that wasn't the major quake, that there's a good chance of more to come. They stay because they are hoping for a reprieve, or they don't believe it will happen, or because they're afraid of leaving their homes to the looters."

"So you don't think giving a warning will do any good?"

"Maybe, but probably not."

"I'm going to get hold of Kuan Yin again," Chen said. "If I can." His face was filled with dismay; he seemed more ill at ease than Zhu Irzh had ever seen him.

"Sure, suits me. Though she didn't give you much of an option when it came to sticking around. I don't see why Heaven should abdicate responsibility now for the mess it's made."

They forced their way to the door, through the wide-eyed revelers, and then they were out onto what remained of Shaopeng. It was close to midnight now, but the street was still crowded. The air was filled with the burst of firecrackers, stars exploding over the shattered stump of the Eregeng Trade House.

The city government, in a rare moment of public spiritedness the day before, had strung lanterns the length of Shaopeng Street. The red globes bobbed in the little breeze and struck sparks from the uppermost downtown rails.

"Look at that," Chen said, momentarily arrested. "Those are going to catch fire before long. This is typical of this government, no thought—"

Zhu Irzh caught Chen's elbow and drew him back under an awning.

"Not the only ones." He pointed. A troop carrier rumbled ponderously into view, causing an outraged frenzy among the traffic. It rolled forward on its eight fat caterpillar wheels, dipping whenever it crossed the downtown tracks and ignoring the guidance lines. People leaned out and shouted as it veered in front of cars without warning. The driver appeared not to care. On the rear-mounted gun attachment, a gaudy fringe of charms twisted and bounced with the movement of the carrier. Someone had hung a beaming demon at the tip of the automatic, with elastic arms attached to lobster claws, which waved gaily as the carrier rolled unevenly along.

"Is he drunk?" Chen wondered. This was a reasonable surmise. People were having to swerve out of the way of the carrier, which was picking up speed. It canted up onto the curb, rocked for a moment and then took the corner with care, vanishing in the direction of Battery Road.

"I think we should go," Zhu Irzh murmured in Chen's ear. A passer-by turned to the detective and demanded, "Did you see that?"

"I think it's an absolute disgrace," Chen said emphatically. There were nods and mutters of agreement.

"Was he looking for Senditreya, do you think? Has the city government been told what's happening in that quarter? Or was he just out on the town?" Zhu Irzh asked.

"God only knows. I spoke to Sung about it, but he said that the governor was refusing to listen to him."

"This is making me nervous. It's too crowded. We should get off the main street."

The back streets were as crowded as Shaopeng, but even under the brilliant fireworks it was still too dark for anyone to see them properly. Chen and the demon picked their way through the revelers, who sang and whirled through the midnight streets. A woman in a leopard mask, her black hair cascading down her back, seized the detective and danced him round. Patiently, Chen took her by the waist and waltzed her into another man's arms. They were not so far from the harbor after all, Zhu Irzh realized. He could see the cranes rising above the buildings, tipped and tilted by the quake like so many birds' necks, and suddenly they were out into Hangsu Square, where there was a cluster of restaurants before the rough part of Ghenret began. The square was heaving with people, many sitting out at tables, and the place was bright with colored lights and lanterns, strung between the eaves. There was a hectic burst of merriment from a group in the crowd. Someone was singing, a throaty, knowing voice.

Chen and Zhu Irzh made their way through the square toward Kuan Yin's temple. Here, the streets were quieter and some of the properties looked deserted. There were fewer revelers, but when they reached the temple, they found that it had been opened again and was full of people. The faithful had come in their hour of need, hoping that the goddess would indeed hear their cries of suffering, and be merciful. As soon as Zhu Irzh stepped through the temple gate, he became aware of the aura of peace that filled the temple. It made him sneeze and itch. Chen, clearly amused, said, "We won't be here long. You can wait outside if you'd prefer."

"Certainly not," the demon replied, his pride stung. "I believe I can cope with an allergy to Heaven, having been permitted to go there so recently."

He followed Chen into the main chamber of the temple and saw that the statue was no longer there. Chen halted, in indecision.

"She's gone."

"She is out in the world," a voice said. "Doing her work."

And Mhara, crown prince of Heaven, stepped from behind the empty plinth.

INTERLUDE

It had been a very long evening. All the chophouses and restaurants along both sides of Shaopeng were still open, filled with people who were celebrating their survival of the festival with an early breakfast or a late supper, assuming they were not too drunk to eat. Those with their heads on the table or sprawled across the floor were a common sight; waiters, continually sweeping, cleaned around them. The pavements and the roadway were littered with firecracker debris: a midnight tram crushed several live crackers that lay across its rails and they shot howling into the gutter. All the lanterns had come adrift and lay in sad, red tatters across the width of the street, and the pavements were covered with broken glass from the tower windows and the remnants of the mirror war. Those of Western ancestry thought uneasily of seven years' bad luck. A drunk was veering down the middle of the road, the light of sake bright in his eyes, echoing snatches of the poet Han Li Tseng, and declaiming them as his own.

"I'm a genius!" he bawled. "A genius at last!"

A small group of office workers, dressed in the vestiges of their party best, surveyed him indulgently. Flowers trailed from their hair, and the women wore waisted corsets and slashed skirts over high-heeled boots. Their elaborate coiffures were rather the worse for wear now, straggling down over their shoulders, and one woman's dress was ripped from hem to shoulder. They laughed behind their hands, politely. One girl was too far gone to stand, and swayed against her companion, knocking him off balance. They were service personnel, the public face of the corporations, greeters and courtesans.

As they passed, the doors of the demon lounges slid open. The partygoers stopped to look, bewildered. Out of the nearest lounge came a dancing figure dressed in a kimono the color of flames. She carried a lantern, which she tossed into the gutter after a glance at the sky. She bestowed a glittering

209

smile on the staring office workers and struck a theatrical attitude with one clawed hand against her oval brow. A long, barbed tongue licked her cupid's bow lips.

"Nearly time now!" she sang. She turned to the little group of revelers and strode swiftly down the steps. Her eyes, the golden green of a lizard's, swiveled from side to side in impossible rotation. She giggled. The man holding the swaying, drunken girl stepped back hastily as she approached, abandoning his companion. The demon caught her before she could fall and shot him a glance of mock reproach.

"How *could* you?" she asked. "The poor little thing!" She bent her head and whispered in the girl's ear. The girl laughed, then moaned and tried to push the insistent face away. The long, painted nails sank through her upper arm. The demon nuzzled at her ear. There was a noise reminiscent of someone drinking something thick through a straw. The girl sagged limply back into the demon's arms and she lowered the body gently to the pavement, arranging it neatly, her head to one side, as if playing with a doll. When the body was laid out, the hands neatly folded across the chest, she turned to the office workers, who still stood in front of her, too confused to run. The tip of the demon's tongue licked something delicately from her pouting lower lip. Beneath her, the girl's face seemed sunken, like a deflated balloon. The creature leaned back her head and gave a ringing cry. She sprang up, and bounded toward the office workers, seizing the girl's companion and waltzing him round.

"Fun!" she roared. Blood trickled from his ears. He tried to free his hands, to beat at his head, but she laughed madly and whirled him away down the street, swinging him like a rag doll. The remaining workers, stunned, took to their heels and scattered in all directions.

FIFTY-THREE

"Mhara?" Chen said. He stepped forward to greet the Jade Emperor's son. Zhu Irzh managed a quick nod of the head: it was beneath his demonic status, he felt, to pay much respect to gods who'd bailed out of Heaven. Not that he could blame the young deity, having seen where he'd come from. He felt a sudden rush of sympathy for Mhara, an equally sudden appreciation of his own upbringing, his work for Vice. *There but for the grace of God go I,* thought Zhu Irzh. Literally.

"You know who I'm looking for," Mhara said.

"A goddess, I'd imagine. But which one?"

Mhara acknowledged this with a smile. "The one who's causing all the trouble."

"Just as well," Zhu Irzh remarked. "Kuan Yin's gone walkabout. But Senditreya isn't here. She vanished."

"Do you know where?"

"I'd imagine to Hell," Zhu Irzh said. "And as long as I'm not in it, too, I hope she stays there."

Mhara's smile faded. "I don't think that's likely. She won't find her Hellkind conspirators very accommodating, now that she's failed in her plans. It's more likely that they'll kick her out to face the music on Earth."

"They won't find it all that easy to dislodge a goddess," Chen remarked. "Even a failing one."

"Veil between the worlds is going to be very thin tonight," Zhu Irzh said. "What with the Day of the Dead and all."

Chen looked at him. "So you're suggesting they'll try to boot her out of Hell then?"

"And they might make a run at the city, too," Mhara said. Zhu Irzh sighed. He hadn't wanted to raise that subject, since it was all too likely and he was, in any case, hardly on the side of the angels. An assault by Hell on the city sounded like fun for everyone. The demon brightened. Mhara was looking at him, and Zhu Irzh had the sudden uncomfortable impression that the sorrowful blue eyes could see right through his golden ones, into the black soul beneath. He covered his discomfort with a cough, and looked away.

"So there's no question that she'll re-manifest," Mhara said. "The only question is where?"

"Depends whether she's still looking for Jhai."

"Jhai will go to ground. She might even have left the city by now," Chen said. "We can't count on finding them together. Jhai will just have to fend for herself."

"Then how are we to find the goddess?" Zhu Irzh asked.

"We're in a temple, aren't we? We've got oracular equipment. Use your imagination."

Robin gaped at Chen. "That's a risky thing to do, undertake a spell on the Day of the Dead. It's already dark out there."

"All the better," Chen said unruffled. "The thinner the veil, the more probable it is that we'll get an accurate reading."

"And if something comes through?" Robin asked.

"It'll probably be someone I know," the demon said airily.

"So you can deal with it then," Mhara said. He turned to Chen. "Do what you must."

INTERLUDE

In Bharulay, a woman named Mrs Soi came wearily from her back door into the yard. She had spent most of the previous evening trying to placate her mother-in-law, her aunts and her husband, none of whom got on and all of whom expected her to do something about it. She was the first to rise that morning: party or no party, the chickens had to be fed. Everyone slept in one room, and she cringed as she came out into the living area. It was awash with cracker crumbs ground into their one good carpet, paper streamers, something that looked like foam, and a stack of miniature bottles stuffed down the side of the chair, presumably by Auntie Pei who seemed to think that her sake habit went unnoticed. Mrs Soi was thirty-three, but on mornings like this she felt every day of sixty.

She had to wrench the back door open and stepped out, blinking, into the chilly darkness before the dawn. Icicles, sharp as teeth, hung from the overflowed gutter and the hens were bundles of feathers, puffed up against the cold. Those that were still alive, anyway. With mounting dismay Mrs Soi counted the skinny bodies that littered the yard, five as far as she could tell. Dogs? she thought, but they had heard nothing last night and she was awake for most of the time. She'd checked on the hens around midnight, and they had been all right. Then she raised her head and saw the cause. It was sitting underneath the japonica tree, the one good thing about this house, which they had hung with rags and paper twists to keep the spirits away. Mrs Soi noted this rather grimly, for beneath the japonica tree sat a young person with a dark golden face, smiling a pointed and beatific grin.

"You killed my hens," Mrs Soi said, strangely devoid of shock. The young person jumped down and spread out his long taloned hands.

"So sorry." He took a fluttering step across the yard; ochre robes swirled about his ankles and she saw that he had a tiger's eyes, the color of the sun.

He smiled charmingly. "And now, you."

Yin Deng Soi had left her husband snoring in the communal bed. She opened her mouth to cry for help, and then her husband's face rose up before her memory: his mouth open, the smell of old beer, one hand groping for her just as she was falling asleep, the constant demands for food, drink, sex, everything that was wearing her out before she even turned forty. She looked into the demon's golden glowing eyes and closed her own.

"Go on, then," she muttered, and she felt him pick her up and soar high above the Bharulay slums, her slippered feet catching for a moment in the branches of the japonica tree, and when she at last dared open her tired eyes, she saw the rim of the sun, yellow as an eye, engulf the horizon's edge.

FIFTY-FOUR

The spell was not, according to Chen, a complicated one. He arranged everyone in a four-quarter pattern: Zhu Irzh in the south, Robin in the west, Mhara in the east and himself in the north.

"A bit Western, isn't it?" the demon remarked disparagingly.

"So? Who says we can't take the occasional idea from other cultures? As long as the underlying magical structure remains intact. Besides, think of it as a disguise. We're less likely to get noticed this way. Anyone watching will think we're just a bunch of students or something."

Zhu Irzh thought that this confidence might be somewhat misplaced, but he went along with it anyway. He watched as Chen once more scored a bloody line across his palm, scattering a few red drops to the four quarters. The blood flared up as it touched the floor, as though Chen's veins were filled with hot coals. Then Chen began to chant, long strings of syllables that were vaguely familiar to the demon as a spell. Chen did not, Zhu Irzh noticed, use his rosary: presumably Chen had had enough of gods, for the moment. And who could blame him? He could feel the tension in the room ratcheting up through the soles of his feet and tingling up his spine.

On the wooden boards of the floor, a pattern began to form, congealing out of blood and air. There was a familiarity about it and, after a moment's puzzlement, Zhu Irzh realized what it was: a map of the city. The meridians glowed beneath it, blood red, and Zhu Irzh found himself wincing as he understood for the first time what a battering the city had taken. There seemed to be focal points, nexi of light, and the demon began to work them out: the foremost of them was the abandoned temple of Shai. Chen's strained voice continued to chant and as Zhu Irzh watched, a face began to manifest above the little configuration of lights. It was not human, and no longer divine. It was the horned head of a great cow, but instead of the flat teeth of cattle its long jaw was full of needles and its eyes were black as the Sea of Night. It snapped at Chen and spat fire. Chen dodged back and the demon felt the spell falter and fall apart. There was a momentary wrenching sensation within him, as though someone had taken hold of his guts and given them a swift, sharp tug. He heard Robin cry out in pain and then the room was dark.

"Well," Chen said. "At least we know where she is."

Zhu Irzh frowned. "But why has she gone to Shai?"

"I could tell you that," a voice said. Someone stumbled out of the shadows, someone bruised and singed. It took the demon a minute to recognize him.

"Dowser Roche!"

Paravang Roche stared at him with hatred. "It's taken an age to find you. I had to call your captain and everything. My feet hurt. You want to know why she's gone to Shai? You want to know what she's doing there?"

"I'd appreciate it if you could tell us," Chen said, ever polite.

"Oh no. There's a price." Paravang Roche was glaring at the demon. "I want my license back."

"You'll have it," Zhu Irzh said quickly. If that was all the man wanted…but then some humans were notoriously lacking in imagination.

The dowser nodded with grim satisfaction. "All right. What guarantee do I have?"

"I'll give you a written guarantee," Chen said. "Will that do? Although I feel bound to point out that you might find it a bit difficult to find work, after all this is over. The Feng Shui Practitioners' Guild isn't going to be terribly popular."

"I'll take my chances," Paravang Roche said. He accepted Chen's scrawled note, set with the bloody imprint of Chen's personal seal, and stowed it away in his pocket. "Very well, then. That bitch has gone to Shai because it was originally her temple." Mhara was watching the dowser, Zhu Irzh saw, with no surprise. He had known, then. But one would expect him to. The dowser went on: "The Practitioners' Guild doesn't advertise it. Why would we? Senditreya's come down in the world over the last couple of hundred years. She was human first, but then she used to be one of the primary goddesses in this region—not just of *feng shui* but of agriculture and herding—but then technology started taking over and people began to migrate to the cities and, slowly, her worship became eroded. Her priests made the decision to move out of Shai to a smaller temple. Then the land got bought up by the franchise committee and the city developed around it. Shai was just a big, empty space."

"I'm surprised no one bought it for redevelopment," Chen said.

The demon saw Robin shiver. "It leads to the Night Harbor."

"Yes, that's part of the problem," Paravang Roche said, looking at Robin for the first time. "When the temple was abandoned, it started to fall into ruin and then it started to leak. Literally—gaps opened up between the worlds. It's my opinion that it was never sealed properly, but perhaps that's not the case. Any one entering it risks becoming lost in the hinterlands of the Night Harbor, even a member of the Practitioners' Guild. The meridians warp as the worlds meet."

"So the goddess has returned to her old temple," Zhu Irzh said. "Do you think she's planning a last stand?"

"I don't know what she's planning," the dowser replied. "She's raving bloody mad."

"Well, she has to be stopped," Chen said. "Her presence here is causing the city itself to leak—you must be more aware of this than any of us."

Paravang Roche nodded. "The meridians have become hopelessly disrupted. All sorts of things are coming up from Hell, through the breaches."

"And that's not all," the demon said. Briefly, he brought the dowser up to speed on the matter of Senditreya's demonic virus.

"She was planning all that?" Paravang Roche said, startled. "I didn't think she had the wit."

"You don't think much of your patron deity, do you?"

"Would you?"

The demon was forced to agree.

"Very well," Chen said. "We're wasting time. Mr Roche, do you know a way into Shai that won't get us hopelessly lost?"

Paravang Roche looked very shifty. "I believe so. I might have glimpsed an old map somewhere…"

"I'm not asking you to spill all the Guild's secrets. Just get us into Shai."

And after a pause, the dowser nodded.

FIFTY-FIVE

She ran swiftly, swerving to avoid the festive people, her feet taking her unerringly down the alleyways of the portside. Later, when she was herself again, Jhai wondered what they had seen: a young woman, half-known from TV interviews and the burgeoning shrines, the famous face panting and distorted by running, dressed conservatively in a crimson jacket and black trousers. Their faces streamed past her, meaning nothing, their mouths opening and closing as though they were underwater, their hair trailing in the wind from the sea, which suddenly seemed so slow, a mere trickle of air.

The currents ran strongly beneath the port. She could feel the Great Meridian, straining to keep to its appointed bed, remaining only because the unlucky *sha* from the Trade House had been inadvertently removed. Jhai did not know this, but she felt it, an inexplicable lightness in the north of the city. But the Great Meridian would not hold for long; already its foundations were loosened and soon, soon it would tear free and take the city with it, opening all the doors to Hell and they would all be washed through on the changed tide. This unspoken understanding lent urgency to her. Dimly, she could sense Zhu Irzh's presence in the city; he was a little blurred around the edges, but still recognizable. She paused for breath, leaning heavily against a doorframe, sought outward for her bearings, and then she was off again.

Hands caught her wrists and twisted.

"Where are you off to, girlie?" a voice said in her ear. Jhai heard the words, but did not understand. The smell of cheap Japanese whisky was bitter on the man's breath. She snapped his hold downward and broke free. "No, no," he mumbled. "You're going to come back here…"

Jhai growled, deep in the back of her throat. Uncomprehending, she saw his face slack above her and she struck up at it. His head flicked to one side, easily moved, and she hit him again. Rage grew in her, tiger-hot and filling her mouth with saliva. She beat at him, and he went down on his knees, and she could reach his eyes then. He screamed as her hand stabbed, and flung up his arms to protect his face. Jhai grasped him under the chin, pulled up, and twisted. There was a sudden limp heaviness in her arms. She set him down, quite gently, and ran, her tail flickering about her ankles as she did so. The moving presence of the demon drew her on, surely, as though to a fixed star, her magnetic north.

FIFTY-SIX

They were standing outside the back regions of Shai. The journey through the city had been distressing, at least for those folk who weren't Zhu Irzh. The demon had been alternately entertained and puzzled: Hellkind were certainly coming through, but not in any ordered way. Typical, Zhu Irzh thought: no strategy, no planning… He supposed that all of that had gone into the intended invasion of Heaven. The city was responding in a variety of ways, chief among them incomprehension, panic and partying. The demon supposed that was as good a reaction as any.

The temple rose above them in a great arc, a dome of darkness. To Zhu Irzh, it looked impenetrable, but Robin was saying to Mhara, "There! That's where we went in." She was pointing in the direction of the canal.

"I happen to know," the dowser said, "that this particular route will take you right into the Night Harbor. We won't go by water. Come with me—I'll show you where to go."

He led them around the building, to a rubble-strewn courtyard. It looked to Zhu Irzh as though part of the side wall of the temple, perhaps one of the buttresses which supported its squat bulk, had collapsed into the courtyard. A series of fissures and holes were apparent in the wall of Shai.

"Look!" Chen said sharply. "Who's that?"

Zhu Irzh turned to see someone crouching by a pile of fallen mortar. The woman was rocking to and fro, arms wrapped around her waist, murmuring something in an erratic rhythm. With a distinct sense of shock, he saw that it was Jhai Tserai. She was wearing a crimson jacket and dark trousers, the same costume in which he had glimpsed her earlier, and she was perfectly made up, but there was an empty wildness behind her dark eyes, and her face was a mask of strain with a peculiar slackness about the mouth. Beneath the hem of the jacket, a long, striped tail twitched to and fro and her eyes were as golden as Zhu Irzh's own. She said something, but it made no sense; the words were slurred and unformed, coming from deep in the throat. Her *devic* self had emerged, probably conjured by weariness and fear and the proximity of Hell. It didn't take more than a quick look to inform the demon that whatever control she might have had over it, was gone. The disrupted day might have meant that she had forgotten the suppressant drugs, but whatever the explanation, she was all tigress now.

"Jhai," the demon said, soft and encouraging. "Jhai, come here."

"Be careful," Chen murmured.

"I plan to." The demon crouched down on his haunches and called to her, an alluring sound, compelling her to rise and stumble forward. He rose and caught her and her arms went around his neck. He felt her link her clawed hands. As she did so, she turned unseeing eyes on Chen and smiled, a peculiar, lipless grimace. Zhu Irzh stroked her spine, murmuring in her ear.

"What's the matter with her?" Robin said uncertainly.

"Shock," the demon said over Jhai's shoulder. "She'll be all right in a moment."

"She doesn't look all right to me. She doesn't look *human.*"

"Well…" Zhu Irzh had to admit that it was pretty obvious. "Perhaps she's been experimenting," he said lamely. This did not cut much ice with at least one member of the party.

"She is a *deva*," Mhara said, out of the darkness.

"Did you know before?" Zhu Irzh asked.

"No. Only in dreams, but I didn't know if they meant anything real. I was drugged, and she hid it well." Mhara spoke neutrally, but Zhu Irzh could sense trouble ahead. Letting go of Jhai, he grasped her wrist.

"Come with me, Jhai," he said, and it was perhaps more his tone of voice than the uncomprehended words that made her follow, docile.

"Inside," Chen said with a wary glance at Jhai Tserai.

Within Shai, it was much colder, a bitter, wintry cold that Zhu Irzh had only ever felt in the Night Harbor, up in the high mountains, and this was the heart of the summer in Singapore Three. Frost rimed the broken floor and the ceiling glittered. Above them, though they were now inside, the stars shone like lamps in a clear sky.

Zhu Irzh looked back. Through the fissure, which seemed much bigger from the inside, he could still see the shattered column of the Trade House and, beyond it, the high structures of banks and the Pellucid Island Opera, with the lights of Tevereya floating beyond. As he watched, the lights died a block at a time, and the city was silent. Surely, a few minutes ago, people had been running through the streets, laughing and shouting and letting off firecrackers and fireworks? From the sky a single flake of snow brushed Zhu Irzh's cheek. It felt like a hot, floating coal. His shoulders hunched in a sudden shiver. Jhai pulled fretfully at his arm.

As soon as she saw that Paravang Roche was leading them toward the iron doors of the inner temple, Jhai whimpered and pulled away. Zhu Irzh was having a hard time reconciling this wreck of a demon with the flippant, ruthless young woman of recent acquaintance. She was agitated now, pawing at his arm and pointing. Zhu Irzh was straining to see into the shadows about the portals of Shai. He was almost sure that someone was there, waiting by the doors, a hovering presence.

As they neared the great double doors, someone rose fluidly from the steps and turned to meet them. It was a tall person, dressed in a swathed dark robe, with prominent eyes and a long braid of hair. The feet, which were bare, were the feet of birds, knuckled and covered with thick rumpled skin. It smiled, displaying a dual row of sharp teeth. The end of a tail switched about its ankles. It took a long look at them, and then bounded up onto the portal roof, where it crouched, rattling its head from side to side. Jhai looked up at the creature and gasped. It let out a peal of laughter, shaking its pointed head. Zhu Irzh grabbed her wrist and pulled her toward the doors.

INTERLUDE

The emergency services had been working throughout the festival, in Bharcharia Anh, to repair the damage done by the earthquake. Gardeners moved silently through the green, moist gardens mending the torn soil, replanting the uprooted thousand-flower, bamboo, maple and cryptomeria, pruning and replacing. Now, the gardens were once again serene, wet with dew in the early morning, a light mist rising from the damp grass, and throughout the gardens the air held the scent of flowers and rain.

Iso Matabe preferred this time of day to all others, save perhaps the early evening, those times which were neither one time nor another, halfway between darkness and daylight, the times when the veil which separated the worlds drew thin and the beloved dead could be glimpsed. Matabe was now in her forties; a grave woman with a melancholy gaze. She was held to be one of the greatest poets of her day, hiding behind the walls of her house, walking in her green garden, a recluse who shunned performance. She could not bear to see anyone ever again, except the mute servant who drifted like a ghost around the house. She had lost too many: her beloved sisters, her mother, her lover Arei, and where once the house had resounded with the soft voices of the women, there was only a ringing quietness. Legends had grown up around her in the last twenty years.

Every four or five years she would submit another work to her publishers; long, intricate works, revealing a tormented soul.

The veil was very thin today. Matabe had seen it from the window, and rather than changing into the dark robe that she favored, had hurried down the stairs in her stiff morning kimono and straight out into the garden. The grass was damp beneath her slippers, and a single bird was singing: the canary that she kept in an ancient bamboo cage on the verandah. The door of the cage was always open, but like its mistress, the bird preferred sanctuary. The long, liquid song ran down the morning air, cold as snow.

"Tayu?" she called uncertainly into the rising mist. Through the veil she could see an identical garden, with a dark house beyond, its eaves glistening with frost. In the garden a woman was walking, dressed in a green kimono, almost her mirror image. A few moments after Matabe had called to her, she looked up: the time lag was slight but noticeable. She smiled.

"Tayu? You can hear me?" The mist was rising now, like smoke about her bare ankles, and she could see the veil itself, a gleaming brightness laid across the air, and then it was suddenly gone, as if someone had snatched it up into the sky. Her sister stood before her in the garden, her face a pale oval against the dappled background of the trees. Matabe, after an astounded moment, ran to her and clasped her cold hands. Tayu's composed face crumpled. When they both looked back, Matabe's home was no longer there. The canary still sang, a drift of change in the air.

FIFTY-SEVEN

The plain was bright with snow, a glare that reflected from the sunless sky and dazzled the eyes. There were, perhaps, mountains in the distance, an indistinct line of high country that floated, mauve and gray and a pale dull red, above the distant snow. Whenever Zhu Irzh looked at it directly, however, it faded, a dream far away, like trying to see a star from the corner of the eye. He thought he had come here with others—there was a flickering memory of passing through a door, like an old movie reel—but now he was quite alone.

The snow was real enough, however, a thick icy crust which broke beneath his boots, gnawing at his ankles. Above, the sky was a light ethereal blue, the color of a bird's egg. A few last fat flakes of snow still drifted down. He had no idea where he might be.

Zhu Irzh looked around him, turning in the snow. There was no one to be seen. He was on the crest of a low ridge, which looked out across the plains. As he stepped up over the ridge, Zhu Irzh saw something stretching out before him to the distant horizon. It was once more the Great Meridian, a path of energy. On either side of the bright path, a fire was burning. The voice of his own intuition spoke inside his mind, and it said: *This is where you must go.* Striding down the ridge, Zhu Irzh headed for the Meridian.

As he walked, he saw that a gate was beginning to raise itself along the Meridian. It started as a swirl in the air, a frosty glitter emerging from the ground and winding the frozen grass into its design. Within minutes the pillars of the gate were complete, hardening into a lacquered darkness the color of old blood. Along the horizon, clouds were building before the wind and the unseen sun faded as though a shadow passed across it. The pillars stretched high into the heavens, and now the lintel of the gate was building itself; each side putting out a tongue of air, which solidified, hardening to become the carved, curling roof.

The gate was fully made now, a finished and perfect structure, glowing against the bright air. Through it the light wavered, as does the air above a source of heat. It reared above him now, and as he gazed at it he saw with dim surprise that Mhara was standing on the other side.

INTERLUDE

The office worker was nearly ready to drop, snatching lungfuls of the inexplicably cold air as he swung around, dizzy in the grip of the demon's powerful arms. Her roaring had deafened him. His ears had stopped bleeding now, but the rivulets of dried blood down each cheek itched. Why he should be aware of so small and irritating a thing at a time like this, he could not have said. The demon had taken him all over the Shaopeng district, waltzing her toy along. He kept trying to avert his head from her stale, hot breath.

He had long since ceased trying to keep upright: it was easier to let go and let her swing him about as she chose. He was fairly certain that his ankle was broken because he had felt the snap, a wet blow to his lower leg, but he could not feel much anymore. Dimly, he remembered that the demon had killed Chara before picking him up and dancing off with him. He hoped devoutly that she would tire of it soon, kill him too and then it would be done with and over. She did not seem to be tiring, however, and now he saw with despair that they were back at the upper end of Shaopeng. As they whirled along the center of the street, the demon's feet striking sparks from the downtown rails, he felt a convulsive movement beneath them. At first he thought that it was the demon, throwing him around; he was too sick and giddy to think much of it, but then it came again and somewhere within his bruised brain the word "earthquake" reverberated. They had said that another quake was coming, some rumor that had been running rife in Shaopeng since the evening. It threw the demon off balance. She stumbled, and as she did so, she let him go, flinging him haphazardly from her.

He landed at the edge of the road, and with a dulled horror watched his hands sink into the surface of the pavement as they clawed frantically for a hold. The tremor had liquefied the road surface and it trembled and quivered beneath him. He dragged himself, half-swimming, across the pavement and pulled himself upright against a teetering awning. Gasping, his hand to his mouth, he glanced across the street and saw the demon poised on a shuddering shelf of roadway. Slowly, elegantly, she pointed one clawed foot forward and then dived, graceful as a swan, into the molten stone sea below her. The road closed silently over the gap caused by her passage. Unable to move, he grasped the pole of the awning like a man drowning and before his eyes the length of Shaopeng once again opened up and cracked from end to end.

FIFTY-EIGHT

Zhu Irzh shook himself. For a moment there, he had forgotten who he was. As ruffled as a cat rubbed up the wrong way, he turned to Mhara. "Where's everyone else?"

"On their way," the prince of Heaven said calmly.

"I don't even remember becoming separated."

"We weren't. It's just that none of us could see the others. But I could sense all of you, and that's when I realized what had happened. Shai is bending in on itself, causing distortions. The damage that the goddess has done to the meridians is creating an echo in her temple."

Zhu Irzh looked around at the frozen plain, the great gate.

"Where *are* we?"

"In Shai..." Mhara looked thoughtful. "When all this is over, it would benefit the Feng Shui Practitioners' Guild to have this place thoroughly investigated. Shai contains much more than it appears."

Zhu Irzh snorted. "If there's a Guild *left*. If they haven't been lynched by an angry mob."

"There'll certainly be an investigation," Chen said, manifesting from apparently empty air. He was joined by Robin and Paravang Roche, who looked as gratifyingly baffled as Zhu Irzh himself, and finally Jhai, who snarled at the others and slunk to the demon's side. He put a wary arm around her.

"Senditreya isn't far away," Mhara said. "She'll sense intruders." He stepped forward. "Detective Chen, this is something I must do. But I'll need your help."

Zhu Irzh thought that Robin was about to say something, but she closed her mouth and looked unhappy instead.

"All right," Chen said, adding with a smile, "I'm not going to argue with the future Jade Emperor."

"We have the ingredients for a spell," Mhara said. "Something simple, and protective, and old. You five represent the elements—the demon here is fire, because he is from Hell. Robin is water, because she's a woman. Paravang the dowser is earth, and you, Detective Chen—because you are a blade of the state—are metal. And Jhai is wood, the uncertain element."

Chen nodded, and the demon thought he understood. "Together, we are the world," Chen said.

"And even a goddess will find it a little hard to challenge the world," Mhara remarked. "But her powers are waning. She's going back to being the human she used to be, although she won't be there yet. To fight her, I need to draw on powers that are latent in me, and I'll need your strength to do that. Form a circle around me."

Zhu Irzh unwound himself from Jhai and took one of her hands. Since the dowser and Robin were clearly balking, Chen stepped forward and took her other hand. Jhai growled at him, and tried to tug away, but her hand remained firmly clasped within Chen's own.

"Jhai, be a good girl," Zhu Irzh said, feeling ineffectual.

"*Grrrr!*" Jhai said, showing teeth, but she let herself be pulled into the circle all the same. Paravang Roche eyed the demon with loathing and came to stand next to Chen. Mhara stood in the middle, eyes closed, and to Zhu Irzh's demonic sight he seemed suddenly insubstantial, shimmering against the frozen waste beyond. The ground rumbled and the great gate rang like a bell.

"She's coming," Mhara said. By now, the ground was shuddering so much that Zhu Irzh had difficulty keeping hold of the hands of Jhai and Robin. He was not sure whether the suddenly uncertain terrain was responsible for Mhara's increasingly diffuse appearance, or whether the prince of Heaven was doing that all on his own.

The gate clanged, sending the circle staggering. Then it opened, to reveal the goddess' chariot. The cattle had changed. They were black and bloated, their sides mottled with bloody crimson bruises, and they stank of rotting meat. Their horns were all fire now, and sulphurous smoke streamed from their gaping mouths. Senditreya had changed, too. She was monstrous, but where the cattle were swollen, Senditreya was gaunt, her comfortable cowlike flesh gone. She was stripped down to a thin layer of skin over bone and her eyes bulged in their sockets. Her dress hung on her in heavy folds; her skeletal hands gripped the reins. She looked like an ancient, desiccated woman which, the demon realized, was exactly what she was. When she saw who was standing before her, she shrieked. Zhu Irzh saw Paravang Roche cower and quail, and could not blame him.

"Don't break the circle!" he heard Chen cry. But the goddess charged. At the very edge of the circle, no more than a few feet from Chen and Jhai, the cattle stopped and tossed their heads. Mhara, by now, was no more than a glowing being of light, radiating outward. The snow beneath Zhu Irzh's boots hissed and melted, he felt warmth on his skin. The goddess reached into the depths of the chariot and produced a whip of fire, which she launched into the circle. Zhu Irzh felt a bolt of heat travel down his arm: he gasped, but kept tight hold of Jhai's hand. Mhara seized the whip by its flaming end and jerked it out of the goddess' hands: it fell sizzling into the snow. The cattle stamped and roared. Mhara sent a thunderbolt out of the circle: Zhu Irzh glimpsed a bloody, glowing hand from the center of the light. It struck Senditreya in the abdomen, and raced down the sides of the chariot. The goddess staggered, but did not succumb. She raised her hand, spoke a word, and a whirling tornado of snow rose up around the circle, seeping into it like a thousand icy needles. The demon heard Robin cry out as the snow lashed her face; her grip on his hand tightened into pain. And then the petals of thousand-flower were falling all around them and Mhara's form glowed more brightly.

The goddess closed her eyes and seemed to shrink within herself. For a fleeting instant, Zhu Irzh thought this signaled her defeat, but he soon realized that Senditreya was only mustering her forces. She reached out a hand and flicked the left-hand cow on its hindquarters. The beast bellowed as if stung by a gadfly and stamped its foot. Immediately, the earth cracked and split. Above Zhu Irzh, the sky itself shuddered: he thought then that it was no more than illusion, and it was the ceiling of Shai itself that was shaking. The cow stamped again, and then a third time, and the ground rippled up like a tsunami. The circle broke. Zhu Irzh was flung sideways, sprawling against Robin. Mhara was hurled to the ground and lay still. The light that had surrounded him faded and was gone. A gaping crack, several feet across, reached from the cow's hoof to just beyond his body.

Senditreya leaped down from the chariot and strode past Zhu Irzh. She picked up the handle of the whip from where it had fallen into the snow and, once more, fire lashed forth. She brought the whip down on Mhara's unconscious form, leaving a long, bloody groove in his side.

"No!" Robin cried. She was on her feet before Zhu Irzh could stop her. She grasped the goddess by a bony arm, but Senditreya flicked her contemptuously away as though Robin were nothing more than a bothersome insect. Robin flew into a snowbank and did not rise again. With a sinking dismay, Zhu Irzh noted that her head lay at an odd angle. There was no sign of Jhai. Chen was again standing, beginning to chant a spell, but his voice was in rags; he had been winded by the fall. The goddess lashed down with the whip once more.

Zhu Irzh knew that he had little chance against a vengeful deity, and when it came to it, whose side was he on, anyway? But then again, Senditreya presumably wasn't very popular with Hell right now, and perhaps some capital could be gained if he were the one to bring her down—but as he was debating the rights and wrongs of the issue, there was a howl of pure fury from behind.

"You fucking cow!" Paravang Roche ran over the snowbank with remarkable speed and launched himself at his goddess. She was too startled to react as he hit her. The dowser's momentum carried them both into the crack, which closed behind them with a reverberating shockwave. Zhu Irzh blinked. Senditreya was gone. The chariot still stood, with two mild-eyed white cattle in its traces. Above them, reached the high vault of Shai. As Zhu Irzh watched, it began to collapse.

蛇警探

Shai seemed to have retreated, and it was so cold, as cold as the void between the stars. It struck through to the demon's bones and beyond, freezing blood and sinew, welding his tongue to the roof of his mouth, his eyes transfixed, the damp warm air in his lungs turned to ice. Then he felt a single note, very sweet and clear, ring through the whole world. Ice that he was, it seemed to shatter him, break him soundlessly apart so that he spun into pieces, fragments of muscle and glassy bone flying in all directions, followed by an unwinding spool of blood. From a distant place, he watched his blood unravel, a dull silver thread bursting into droplets, and he followed it, all the way across the world, higher and higher and then falling like rain. As each drop fell, it impacted on the iron ground and it was as though all the weight of the world descended. Then he was through, seeping beneath the surface of the earth, the presence of pain, dispersal and then the familiar stretched, dreadful sense of the world itself, spinning ponderously on its axis, one face toward the hearth of the sun, the other touched by the dark and the cold, and the city on the edge of the world just coming into day. Instinctively, he gathered his fragmented senses and pulled toward the bright line of the sun, to where the Great Meridian ran in a fluttering path of fire beneath the city, and his tigress was waiting.

FIFTY-NINE

Jhai finally managed to get a hold of herself as the ceiling fell in. She had blurred, uncertain memories of a snowy plain, other people, a mad goddess, but none of it was clear. There was the taste of blood in her mouth and her spine ached at the base. Coughing, she dodged falling masonry, struggling to find the demon and get clear. There was a searing crunch from the doorway as the lintel began to give way. The front of Shai was subsiding, sinking slowly and gracefully in upon itself. She still had no idea how she had come to be here in the first place. Then the floor heaved and Jhai was knocked to her hands and knees. The lintel cracked with a shotgun report, bringing a shower of dust and plaster down upon her head. Jhai could not see; the chalky dust saturated her nose and throat. She coughed and gagged, knowing that she ought to get up and run. She could feel her *devic* nature surging back in defense. It occurred to her to wonder where she would end up when she died. She thought she knew.

As the doorframe fell inward, however, she felt herself seized, wrenched free and thrust out onto the steps. Frantically, she rolled clear. Behind her, the front of Shai fell in. Jhai lay on the shaking steps, gasping in long breaths of the dust-smothered air. Then, as swiftly as it had come, the tremor stopped. She remained there for a minute and then, retching, got to her feet and rubbed the dust from her eyes.

The morning sun was a pale coin above Wuan Chih, rising up through the mist, and somewhere a bird was singing, a nightingale in the uprooted trees along Shaopeng. Jhai took a step toward the ruin. All four walls of Shai had come down, along with the dome. The ground still shuddered with the aftershock. Detective Inspector Chen was standing by her side, his round face pasty with dust, like a pie, as he gaped up at the wreckage.

"Well," Zhu Irzh remarked from her other side. "Happy Day of the Dead, eh?"

INTERLUDE

The Great Meridian had settled uneasily back into its appointed track, but it would be a while before the tremors ceased entirely. Shaopeng Street had been split straight down the center, and the tram rails had been swallowed by the gaping crack. Most of the shops and chophouses were damaged, either reduced to piles of mortar or leaning unsteadily against one another.

Along Step Street, the shacks had collapsed like a row of dominoes and at least one demon lounge was now buried beneath the mass of buildings that had slid down the hill. The wall of Ghenret harbor had been breached and the water level had risen over the sea sluices and flooded back into the Jhenrai canal and over its banks, placing the go-downs and warehouses in several feet of brackish tide.

Shai was a true ruin now.

The outlying suburbs of Orichay and Bharulay had suffered considerably, slipping down the muddy hills on which they had been built. Much of Bharulay—compartment blocks, warehouses and the tram station—had ended up on top of the mining works, sealing the entrance to the hills of Wuan Chih. The rest of the shattered Eregeng Trade House had fallen into the streets beneath, squashing the Second National Bank underneath it.

The roof of the Pellucid Island Opera House had fallen in, and back in Ghenret the foundations of Paugeng had slipped, causing the tower to list. From a distance, it appeared as if the home of the Tserais had put its ear to the ground to listen. Robin's lab was crushed beneath it.

A later estimate put the death toll at nine thousand, and the city was generally considered to have got off lightly. Three thousand or more were missing, among them a well-known and reclusive poet, gone without trace.

SIXTY

When they finally reached Paugeng through the wrecked streets, they found that its great plexiglass wall had been shattered by the quake, letting in the night and the dusty wind. The tower was listing even further, and from the looks of things, it would not be long before it followed so many of the city's taller buildings, and collapsed. No one had got around to putting any warning tape on it: there was just too much destruction. Zhu Irzh thought of the boys in the port, with their icon of Jhai. If they could see their goddess now, he thought… He hoped they were still alive. Soon, the looting would begin, though from what he'd witnessed along Shaopeng, it already had.

"Surprised to find yourself back here?" the demon asked.

"Since you ask, yes." Jhai rose up from where she had been sitting on a block of fallen concrete, trying to reach her mother on the cellphone. She winced. "I feel as though I've run a marathon."

"You have, more or less. And what now, Jhai?"

The heiress paused, then said with an effort, "*I* don't know." Her voice was tart, but she was staring fiercely into the empty air, and then she passed a hand across her watering eyes.

"Jhai?"

"It's only the wind." She swallowed. "I'm all right. My mother is all right. She and Ei got to the airport, she told me." Then she said, "I thought I knew what I was doing, Zhu Irzh. I reached too far."

"Hubris," the demon said cheerfully. "Gets them all in the end. But you're one of the lucky ones. You've got a second chance. A while ago I checked up on extradition treaties between different realms. As a Keralan, you should be exempt from anything the Celestial Realms might level at you. My own Hell is a slightly different matter, and I'm sure the Jade Emperor will try to make sure that you pay some sort of penalty, but these things take a lot of time. For the moment, I think you might even be safe." *But will I?* he thought. Jhai's virus might still be in his system, judging from the episode in the demon lounge. What if he had another attack? It might be a good idea to start talking about a cure.

Jhai was looking at him warily. "You're sure of that, are you?"

"I'm never sure of anything." He reached out and took her hand. "Except one thing. You'll never really belong with humankind. And you'd be a foreigner in Hell. So now you're an exile, like me." His fingers closed around hers.

Jhai scowled. "Zhu Irzh? Are you *proposing?*"

"What, marriage?" the demon said, affronted. "Certainly not. But I think we could get to know one another a bit. Is your bedroom still intact?"

Jhai looked at him for several moments. He could not read her expression. At last she said, "I doubt it. I suppose we could find a hotel."

Grinning, the demon followed her back into what was left of the street.

SIXTY-ONE

The winter sun lay low and crimson through the bare trees. Droplets of water were strung in icy beads along the branches and the feathers of the long grass. The air smelled of snow.

"God, it's cold," Robin said. She flung her arms around herself for warmth. Beside her, Mhara was scenting the air; Robin watched him curiously. The long braid had come undone and the dark hair streamed down his back. He gathered it together, absently, with one hand.

"Not so far now, Robin."

She smiled. "I don't even know where we are. I thought we were in Shai, but—" She looked at him questioningly, but he did not reply. Instead, he took her cold hand and led her through the trees, toward the sun, and she saw that the trees were blossoming. They were not thousand-flower, but the sweet scent was the same, spilling out into the air.

"If I look," Robin said. "Will I find a star?" She smiled at Mhara.

"You might," he agreed. "But what do you really want to do?"

"I want to go home," she told him.

"You're sure, are you?"

"Quite sure. There's nothing for me in Heaven. I want another life, another chance. Other choices."

"You've always had those." He spoke quietly, as if there was something she should have realized, but she did not know what it might be.

"I know," she said. "But I made the wrong ones. It's important, in Taoism, to place oneself in harmony with one's innermost beliefs, isn't it? I haven't really done that in my life. I haven't done anyone any good."

"Who can say?" Stepping behind her, Mhara put his arms around her waist. "Robin," he said into her ear, "it's winter here. Look—the air's full of snow. We should get moving."—and after a moment she put her hands over his.

"We should," she agreed. She could not tell whether it was snowflakes or flower blossoms that drifted through the frosty air.

SIXTY-TWO

A day later, Jhai and her mother were standing outside Paugeng, surveying the impressively improbable angle at which the building now leaned.

"Hell of a lot to do," Jhai remarked, almost cheerfully. Her mother gripped her hand in sympathy.

"Oh, Jhai, I'm so sorry. All your hard work…"

Jhai looked at her. Opal seemed older, somehow; it must be the stress of the last few days, not to mention her daughter's confession, but at least she was still alive. Jhai said, "Well, mother, we've gotten away with it. You know what I mean. And I can start again. Sometimes it helps, having a clean break." She was aware of a curious sense of anticipation, almost eagerness. Perhaps Heaven would come after her, or Hell. She didn't know how things would work out with Zhu Irzh, but perhaps it didn't matter. After all, she reflected, lovers came and went, but the city—well, the city and Paugeng would endure as long as she could help it. There would be a lot of rebuilding to do. And then, when she had finished with the city, there was the rest of the world to consider. She thought that her business interests had been a little narrow up to this point.

With Shai shattered and fallen, a major gate between the worlds was closed. It wasn't the only one. There had been reports all over the city, from people unable to contact their dead relatives anymore. Hell was sealed and silent. But not, Jhai thought, for long. There were other gates, after all. She thrust the thought aside. They'd solve that problem when they came to it.

"A lot to do," Jhai repeated. She met her mother's gaze, and pulled her fur-collared jacket closer against the unseasonable chill.

SIXTY-THREE

"I have to go back to Heaven," Mhara said. They were sitting on the steps of the little, ruined temple, looking out over the city. The dust from the various quakes had resulted in a magnificent sunset: the sky was a blaze of glory across the port.

"I know," Robin said. She reached out and took his hand.

"My father wants me to begin taking things over." Mhara sighed. "I expect that means he wants me to do things exactly as he would do them—continue the process of withdrawing Heaven from the other realms. That's not what I have in mind."

"No," Robin said. "I didn't expect you to."

"And you, Robin." He turned to her and smiled. "What are we going to do with you?"

"If I could be with you, up there," Robin began hesitantly, but she knew that the Jade Emperor was still in charge, and mortal humans just didn't get to be consorts of Celestial princes. "But I don't think I can. And besides, Mhara, it really isn't my kind of place. Maybe when I die…"

Mhara was looking at her strangely. "You haven't realized, have you?"

"Realized what?"

"You're already dead, Robin."

"What are you talking about?" She looked down at her own apparently solid flesh. "It looks real enough to me."

"But it isn't. You died in Shai. Senditreya killed you."

"Why aren't I in the Night Harbor then?"

"Because I'm keeping you tethered here. But you're free to go wherever you want now. Heaven, if you wish."

"But I can *touch* things, pick things up."

"I said you were dead, not that you were a ghost. You just can't die again,

239

Robin. You'll remain in this form, forever, until you should choose to move on."

"But people can see me?" Robin was still grappling with the concept.

"Yes, you're quite visible."

"I need some time," Robin whispered. "Time to think about all this."

"Then you shall have it. I'll come back tomorrow." Slowly, he faded away until there was only a faint shine upon the air.

When he had gone, Robin rose from the steps of the little temple and walked out. She walked past the shattered shops and collapsed awnings of the upper half of Shaopeng, past the dust-covered parks and gardens, all the way to the port. She stayed there for a long time, looking out across the harbor, the emergency shipping dashing to and fro, the helicopters soaring overhead. And gradually, over the course of the day, she knew what she must do, and when night eventually sank over the port, she walked all the way back again to the temple, to tell him.

蛇警探

He came back the next day, as promised. She told him then.

"You're sure?" Mhara said. He was leaning on the ruined framework. Robin had already made a start in cleaning the temple out. The broken bricks had been removed, and she had discovered a kind of hut at the back, equipped with a sink and other facilities, half-covered in vines. Presumably, it had been the home of the previous priest. She felt light and clear and not hungry—better than she had felt for some time. If this was what being dead was like, then she could live with that.

"I think so. I need some space, to think about things. What I've done, how I can make amends. I need some space away from you, and some time with you. So that's what I'll do, Mhara. I'll keep your temple here on Earth, turn it into the sort of place that's worthy of you. I think you've earned your worship now, and with one less goddess on the scene, they'll need all the help they can get. The people round here look as though they can use it. And maybe I could come and see you?"

"Or I could come here," Mhara said.

"We'll work it out," Robin said, as she kissed him a temporary goodbye. After all, it would really be just like any long-distance relationship.

SIXTY-FOUR

Paravang Roche sat back in the armchair and stretched his feet toward the fire. At least it was warm. Dark, though, but he didn't mind that. There were a few things he missed about his little apartment, but not many, and he had to admit that there were compensations. As long as Mahibel wasn't fussing too badly about the forthcoming wedding, they got along well enough and he had to admit that it was pleasant, being looked after like this. Somehow, he'd always expected the food in Hell to be terrible, but the dishes served up every night were surprisingly good, although he couldn't always tell what they were. And the neighborhood bar was full of elderly gentlemen who held a rather similar view of the world to himself. He and his new bride wouldn't have to worry about money, since the goddess' partners in this neck of the woods regarded Paravang as having conducted their vengeance on Senditreya on their behalf and had been generous in consequence. A good thing that the lords of Hell could be both opportunist and lazy. There had been no reliance on living relatives, which was just as well, since Paravang couldn't see his father parting with much cash in the world of the living.

Even his mother's frequent visits were less unwelcome than they might have been. She was obsessing about the marriage ceremony, of course, but that was only to be expected and it would be over soon. Paravang was letting the women get on with it.

Rising to fetch more tea, he glanced out of the window into the yard. Senditreya was grazing placidly on the little patch of grass. As he watched, she raised her black head and looked at him out of a sour crimson eye. Her mouth opened: she emitted a long, mournful bellow. She was, Paravang thought, of much more use as a cow than she had ever been as a deity, though he didn't think much of the milk. Perhaps a more varied diet might help... But as a dowry, she had saved him a fortune.

He turned away from the window and reached in his pocket. Chen's written guarantee was still there. Paravang studied it for a moment, smiled grimly, and then he threw it into the fire.